"This should never have happened to you, Matt."

He felt a sweet sense of expansion in his chest…and a piercing sense of alarm at the same time.

At that moment she lifted her head and looked at him. "I'm so sorry, Matt." He saw the pity in her eyes. The one thing he didn't want. From anyone. But especially not from Leslie.

He pulled his hand out of her grasp and somehow managed to shrug. "It shouldn't happen to anyone, but I'm sure I'll adjust," he said. "Pity doesn't make it any easier."

"Matt, I wasn't—"

"I should go," he said, stepping away from her. "You should go inside, too. There's no point in standing out here in the cold. It's been good to see you again, Les."

He knew that inside the house friends and family were waiting, full of questions and curiosity. There would be whispers in quiet corners and surreptitious looks. He would have to listen to well-meaning but unrealistic predictions about his future.

But how bad could any of that be compared to what he'd just seen in Leslie's eyes?

Dear Reader,

When I first set out to write the HEART OF THE ROCKIES series, I was pretty certain about the stories I wanted to share for Nick, Rafe and Addy. Matt, however, presented a bit of a problem.

As the middle brother, his personality was a mystery to me, and no clear-cut vision of who he really was developed as I started to flesh out his character. He seemed to have no problems, no axes to grind, no points to prove, not a single roadblock standing in his way to happiness. An easygoing charmer, Matt seemed to be the "golden boy" in the D'Angelo family, the one the gods seem to love and look out for, the fellow who never has to work very hard for anything. A woman would love to find a man like that. But the problem is, who wants to read about a man who's that perfect? Not very interesting, if you ask me.

But that's the great thing about being a writer. Characters can morph into anything you need them to be. In short, I decided to rock Matt's world. Because of one small twist of fate on a snowy winter night, he's forced to discover that not everything comes easily in life. That eventually even the luckiest people in the world have to face adversity and find new ways to triumph.

Of course, he doesn't take this journey willingly. Or alone. It takes a woman from his past, Leslie Meadows, to help him see that he's still the same man she fell in love with years ago, and he doesn't have to be *perfect* to be the man for her. Most of all, she helps him see that together they can overcome any trouble that comes their way.

I hope you enjoy Matt and Leslie's story, and that you're finding the D'Angelo family as much fun to read about as I had writing them. I love to hear from readers. Visit me at www.aboutannevans.com or e-mail me at aboutannevans@yahoo.com.

Best wishes,

Ann Evans

Home to Family
Ann Evans

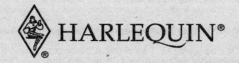

HARLEQUIN®

TORONTO • NEW YORK • LONDON
AMSTERDAM • PARIS • SYDNEY • HAMBURG
STOCKHOLM • ATHENS • TOKYO • MILAN • MADRID
PRAGUE • WARSAW • BUDAPEST • AUCKLAND

ISBN 0-373-71262-6

HOME TO FAMILY

www.eHarlequin.com

Printed in U.S.A.

For fellow critique partner Lori Harris.

Thank you for years of encouragement,
and the occasional, much-needed kick in the pants.

Don't miss any of our special offers. Write to us at the
following address for information on our newest releases.

Harlequin Reader Service
U.S.: 3010 Walden Ave., P.O. Box 1325, Buffalo, NY 14269
Canadian: P.O. Box 609, Fort Erie, Ont. L2A 5X3

PROLOGUE

"I HAVE TO STOP for a coffee," Matt D'Angelo said.

Beside him in the passenger seat, Shayla shook her head. "No, you don't."

"Yes, I do. Just a quick one. If I don't, I'll never make it."

Shayla swung a look in his direction. He could see she was about to object again, so he gave her one of his most winning smiles. They'd been dating only three months, but he knew Shayla was crazy about him, and he wasn't above using that knowledge to his benefit.

As he expected, she gave him a playful, censuring scowl. "You're completely addicted," she told him. "You know that, don't you? And we're already late. Your folks are going to worry."

"Mom and Pop know what the traffic is like this time of year. They won't look for us until after dark."

This was true. It was December twentieth and the usual delays of Christmas travel and snowy weather had put them behind since early this morning. They'd had to de-ice the plane in Chicago before take-off, and by the time the bumpy, overcrowded flight made it into Stapleton in Denver, the swill in Matt's stomach—a cup of weak decaf from an airport kiosk—had long soured. Now the Eisenhower Tunnel along the Interstate-70 corridor would be slow-going, crowded with skiers heading for the slopes and families making their way to holiday reunions with friends and family.

Matt took his hand off the steering wheel and reached across the front seat to rub his fingers along the back of Shayla's neck. "Come on, Shay. How can you be so cruel to someone you're crazy about?"

That got the reaction he expected. She gave him a sharpened look, eyes wide. "You're way too full of yourself. I'm not *that* crazy about you."

He grinned. "Let me stop and get my coffee fix, and when we get to Lightning River tonight I'll show you all the reasons you should be."

"Under your parents' roof?" she said with a small gasp. "I don't think so. For the week we're staying with them, there'll be none of that sort of thing, Matt D'Angelo."

He laughed. "I know a dozen places in the lodge where we can find privacy. I was very inventive when I was a horny teenager."

"Well, you're an adult now. At least you're supposed to be. Abstinence will give us something to look forward to when it's time to go home."

He faked a miserable look. "I'll have a bluuuue…Christmas without youuuu…," he warbled.

She put her hands over her ears. "Stop! You may be a great surgeon, but you're completely tone-deaf." She nudged his arm lightly. "Get your cup of coffee, but then let's get going."

"Yes, ma'am," he said. That had been easier than he'd expected.

He took a turn off the highway that ran through the outskirts of Denver, following a road swept clean by the snow crews. Somewhere along here, there had to be a place they could make a quick stop.

He spotted it in the middle of the block. One of those old dining cars from the railroad days. Duffy's, the modest sign proclaimed. He pulled into the parking lot, found a spot and killed the engine.

As soon as the heater died, Shayla tucked her fingers into the pockets of her coat, already looking displeased.

"Two minutes," Matt promised. "Want anything?"

"No."

He leaned over, fingering a stray lock of Shayla's blond hair behind her ear so that he could skim a kiss across her cool cheek.

She swung a look in his direction. "Are you kissing me because you got your way?" she asked with a skeptically raised eyebrow.

"No," he replied honestly. "I'm kissing you because you're the most beautiful woman I've ever met. I'm a lucky guy, and I know I don't say that often enough."

She looked surprised at the unexpected compliment. He laughed as she practically pushed him out of the car.

A blast of frigid air hit him as he got out, and he hurriedly buttoned his coat against it. The snow had let up, but the wind was as bone-chilling as the worst winters they got in Chicago.

Carefully he made his way up the steps of the diner.

He'd never hear the end of it if he slipped and broke something now. The red light from the neon sign in the window glowed like a spill of blood across the pretty snow mounded on the bushes near the door.

The place was small, a single counter with stools and a few booths along one end. Nobody looked up as he came in, though there were four or five people who had obviously sought shelter against the inhospitable weather.

There was a man seated on the end stool, nearest the door. A young woman with sallow skin but pretty blond hair stood behind the cash register. At the opposite end of the counter, a barrel-chested guy in a spotty apron—Duffy?—nodded curtly at Matt.

In half a dozen strides, Matt reached the counter. "Hi," he said to the waitress. "Can I get a cup of coffee to go? Black, please."

She didn't say a word, just turned around and started to fill the order. Little white bag, napkin, stir stick. Matt blew on his hands to warm them while he waited. The man beside him looked up and gave him a tight smile. Matt nodded.

The service was slow. The blonde turned at last, coffee now hidden away in the bag. Matt could smell it—strong and heavenly, and he could almost feel it warming his insides already.

And then he heard something strange. Bells. Very faint and delicate-sounding. He thought it might be coming from the jukebox at the opposite side of the room—Christmas tunes would be the order of the day—but that couldn't be. The colored arch along the top of the machine was dark, like a dead rainbow.

He realized the sound was coming from the waitress. He caught a name badge over her right breast. Jill. Her hand was clutched on the take-out bag, and it was then Matt noticed that she wore a bracelet. A concession to the Christmas season—small linked jingle bells covered her wrist.

They were shaking. Hard. So was her hand.

In fact, when Matt looked back at her name badge, he could see her heart pumping wildly, moving the plastic back and forth.

"Are you all right?" he asked with a frown.

The girl went white as new snow. Unexpectedly, the man on the stool next to him rose and quickly went around the end of the counter. He hugged Jill to his side, then smiled at Matt.

"Not a problem, man," he said. "Jill's my lady, and we just had a little spat. But everything's okay now. Ain't that right, Jill?"

Jill nodded, trance-like, but nothing in her stiff posture indicated smooth sailing ahead for this couple. *Must have been one heck of a spat,* Matt thought.

And then, in that moment, in one split, God-awful moment of understanding, it hit him. He knew precisely what he was witnessing here, and it wasn't an embarrassingly public lover's quarrel.

The nearly deserted street outside. The unnatural, still silence of the other diners. Jill's barely controlled panic. The tense, wary way in which the man who held her smiled at him.

In that same instant, the older employee at the opposite end of the counter took several steps in their direction. "Turn her loose," he growled, his eyes wild and burning.

The man holding Jill lifted one arm, and Matt saw the gun in his hand for the first time. "Back off, old man," he snapped. "You don't want my kind of trouble."

He pointed the gun at Matt when the employee stopped dead in his tracks. "You. Just stand right there. If you're smart, you won't move."

Matt did as he was told. The robber was short, but he had a bully's jaw and the harsh, fierce eyes of a sewer rat. Matt watched as the man let go of Jill and came around the counter to stand in front of him. With the end of his gun, he motioned toward the counterman. "Finish opening the safe." Jill had begun to cry now, and the robber barked at her, *"Shut the hell up!"* For good measure, he reached across the Formica, yanked her close with a twisting grip on her blouse, and slapped her.

Matt flinched inwardly, but remained still. He knew enough to keep from escalating this any further with a foolish show of bravado. The robber would take the cash and make a run for it. There wasn't any need for anyone to get badly hurt.

Jill bit down on her bloodless lips and went silent.

"Harley!" the sewer rat shouted down the length of the room. "What's taking you so long? Hustle up!"

For the first time Matt realized that a second robber had begun rounding up prizes from the other diners— wallets and rings and anything that looked remotely valuable and portable. He was tall, with long hair that made him look young and oddly innocent.

While Harley worked quickly at the other end of the

diner, the first robber kept his gun trained on Matt. A demented grin snaked across the man's face.

He thumped Matt lightly on the chest with the barrel of his weapon. "Nice coat. Got anything else under there I might like?"

Matt unbuttoned his coat, withdrew his wallet and handed it over.

The man glanced at Jill and made an impatient gesture with his fingers. "Get that ring off."

Unexpectedly, the girl showed a sudden spark of life. "No," she said. "It's my engagement ring."

The guy didn't like that. "I don't care if you inherited it from your dear departed mother. Take it off."

He started to lean over the counter, but Matt took a step in front of him. "You don't have to hurt her," he said, desperate to keep the situation calm and his thoughts coherent. "Go easy. She'll give it up. Won't you, Jill?"

He looked at her, this stupid, stupid girl who seemed willing to go to the mat for a bauble that wouldn't bring one hundred dollars in a pawn shop. "It's not worth getting hurt," he told her, softly.

He felt a swell of relief when she started twisting the ring off her finger. No reason for this to go sour. Unpleasant, yes. A nuisance, really, with the police reports that would have to be filed.

Shayla had been right, damn it. He shouldn't have stopped.

And just as he had that thought, the door to the diner was opening. He turned his head to see Shayla come into the restaurant, her features pinched and cold from too many minutes spent alone in the car.

"Jeez, Matt. How long does it take to get a cup of coffee?" she complained as she came toward him.

"Shayla, wait for me out in the—"

Jill began to wail, a high-pitched, nerve-jangling sound. Matt turned toward her, saw that the robber had turned his gun in her direction, clearly intending to silence the girl once and for all.

"No, don't," Matt said quickly. "Don't…"

"Matt?" he heard Shayla say in sudden, quavering distress.

"Shut up!" the robber yelled at Jill. "Shut up!"

There was sudden movement at the other end of the room and a terrified squeal from one of the diners. Everything happened so fast, almost simultaneously, and yet Matt was vividly aware of every moment, as though they were frozen in place like statues.

The older man reached below the counter, pulling a shotgun from some hidden nook. "You sons of bitches!" he shouted. "You've taken your last nickel out of this place!"

"Harley!" the robber called to his compatriot.

A gunshot exploded.

A woman screamed.

Matt launched himself at the robber closest to him. The man bellowed in surprise, but Matt concentrated on getting control of the gun.

Chaos suddenly. More screams and shouts as gunshots sounded again, so close together that Matt couldn't tell how many or just where they had come from. The robber's gun lay trapped between their bodies now, and as they both grunted and cursed and struggled for control, Matt felt himself shoved hard from behind.

Moments later, when the pain hit, he realized the truth. *Not shoved. Shot.*

And only seconds after that awareness, the gun in his hand went off.

He was free suddenly, the robber sliding bonelessly into a heap at his feet. Matt backed away, aware that he'd just shot another human being.

His legs shook, threatening to buckle. He sank to the floor, his back pressed against the base of the counter, his legs splayed out in front of him. Breathing hard, he just sat there, trying to hold on to consciousness that felt as though it was oozing away. In his ears, his heartbeats sounded like thunder.

He looked down and had the odd, unexpected thought that the coffee he'd ordered had spilled all over the front of his best coat. And then he realized that it wasn't coffee at all, but blood.

His blood.

His head fell back, and he closed his eyes. He couldn't be sure whether he lost consciousness or not, but when he opened them, a woman was kneeling in front of him. He could see his own shock and horror reflected in her features. Vaguely he remembered that she'd been sitting at the far end of the diner when he'd come in.

"Just lie still," she said. "We've called the police and an ambulance."

Matt nodded, feeling the blood stream down the inside of his shirt. "Towel..." he said, his voice no more than a whisper, like dry leaves blowing softly in the wind. "Need to stop the bleeding."

"I'll get one," she told him, jumping up and moving out of his line of vision.

That was when he saw that the diner was insanely cluttered with smashed dishes, glass and blood. When he let his gaze swing to the right, he saw the robber he'd fought with lying near the cash register, his body twisted like a puppet who'd had his strings cut.

He heard someone crying. *Shayla,* he thought. Probably scared to death. He wanted to tell her he would be all right, but frankly, he wasn't sure of anything right now.

He turned his head in the opposite direction. Shayla was lying near the door, a pool of bright blood beneath her. His breath left him in a rush. He bit down hard on nothing, pressing his teeth tight as he looked at her for a long, long moment.

No no no no...Oh God, Shay, get up. Get up.

Her face was partially covered by her long hair, but he could see her eyes. It was the kind of truth Matt would have felt in his bones, even if he hadn't seen dozens of gunshot victims at the hospital. She was dead.

The image of her soaked so deeply into his mind that he knew it would never leave him. Swallowing against sudden nausea, Matt closed his eyes again, lost to everything but regret.

He clenched his fists. Why the hell had he stopped for coffee? Fresh pain owned him then, hot and fierce in his left hand. Frowning, he brought his fingers up in front of him. His hand was a mess. Nothing but blood and bone and torn tissue. He tried to absorb what that kind of damage could mean to his career as a microsurgeon. He tried to care. But he had only one clear thought.

He was alive and Shayla was dead, and all he wanted in those moments was to have it be the other way around.

CHAPTER ONE

One Year Later

WHEN DOC HAYWARD threw his annual Christmas party, always two weeks before the holidays, nearly everyone in Broken Yoke, Colorado, came. It was considered the best of the season, held in one of the last great houses still standing from the days when silver had been king. And since Doc always packed his bags and headed off to California to visit his only daughter immediately afterward, the party presented the perfect opportunity for everyone to wish him Merry Christmas and give him a proper send-off.

Leslie Meadows, the doctor's office nurse and good friend, surveyed the buffet table as she took a sip of white wine. Doc's idea of a Christmas party consisted of watery dip and crackers and a silver Christmas tree that revolved and changed colors. She and Moira Thompson, the clinic's receptionist, had taken on the added responsibility of decorating the old Victorian from top to bottom, as well as handling the caterers. If all the compliments tonight were genuine, the two women could be very proud of themselves. The place looked elegant and festive.

Leslie signaled to one of the circulating waiters to bring in another tray of peeled shrimp. For five minutes she'd been watching Tom Faraday from Faraday's Plumbing Service scarf down handfuls of them like popcorn. It was clear that the diet Doc Hayward had put Tom on wasn't working.

"I thought you were off-duty," a voice said behind her.

She turned to find her date for the evening, Perry Jamison, at her elbow. He looked slightly peeved, and Leslie suspected that he felt neglected.

"Sorry," she said, picking up her wineglass from the table. "Force of habit. I'm used to looking out for Doc, even when we're not in the clinic."

"How about looking out for *me?*" he asked, reaching out to run the back of his hand along her arm.

"I think you're pretty self-sufficient."

"Not when it comes to you, angel."

He gave her a hot, meaningful look that told her exactly what he was thinking. She smiled at him. In addition to being worth a small fortune, Perry was quite a catch. They'd been dating off and on since last spring, and though he lived and worked in Denver, he'd been coming to Broken Yoke with increasing frequency.

He'd made no secret of the fact that he'd cut her out of the herd of eager, young women who'd been after him since his divorce two years ago. Leslie—he'd once jokingly informed her—should consider herself lucky.

She supposed that, in some ways, she did.

She knew that by no stretch of anyone's imagination could she be considered a beauty. Shoulder-length brown hair and hazel eyes didn't create much of a statement, but at thirty she was long past feeling the need to make one. As a nurse she earned a decent living, but she certainly didn't travel in Perry Jamison's social circle. That he'd decided to pursue her was both flattering and unexpected.

"Having fun?" she asked.

He made a noncommittal shrug. "The natives seem friendly enough. What time does the guest of honor get here?"

Leslie gave him a puzzled frown. "Guest of honor?"

"The mysterious Matt D'Angelo. I keep hearing his name, so I figure the guy must be someone special."

"Oh, *Matt.* Yes, I think I did hear that he was coming."

She had to take a quick swallow of wine to stem the flood of color she felt steal up her neck.

You think he's coming? she chided herself. That was a rather bold-faced lie.

She'd known for days that Matt planned to come home for Christmas. His father, Sam, had told her that. And he felt sure his son would make a special effort to say goodbye to Doc, who had been his mentor, the driving force behind Matt becoming a doctor. Hadn't she picked out this dress exactly with his presence in mind, knowing blue was his favorite color?

"So what should I expect?" Perry asked. "Can the guy walk on water, or should I count on nothing more than a little fancy sleight-of-hand? I know Broken Yoke is easily impressed."

She frowned at that slap to her hometown. True, Broken Yoke was small and provincial. It had let her down significantly in her youth, but she'd made her peace with the place. She counted a lot of its citizens as her friends, had made a life here, and now felt almost a protective annoyance toward anyone who maligned it.

But tonight was too pretty, too special to pick a fight with Perry, who measured every town by its ability not to bore him.

She shrugged. "Matt's a town favorite. He was our high-school valedictorian, the captain of more teams than I can remember, teacher's pet, the guy all the boys wanted for a buddy…"

"And all the girls wanted to go to bed with?" Perry supplied.

Leslie couldn't help a smile. "Oh, yeah. Definitely the one every girl in class lusted after. He caught a few of them, too."

"Including you?"

"No. Not me," Leslie said with a thoughtful little pause. "We've been friends for years, but that's all."

She thought about what those words meant. Friends for years. The simplistic description didn't do justice to the relationship she had shared with Matt. How could you accurately describe your feelings for someone who had, quite possibly saved your life?

"Good," Perry said. "I don't like the idea of someone poaching on my turf."

"Thank you. Always nice to feel like hunted game."

She gave him a look of mock severity, though inwardly she felt a stirring of annoyance with him again. His tendency to make assumptions regarding their relationship grated on her nerves and reminded her unpleasantly of her father's possessive treatment of her mother.

He laughed and put his arm around her waist. "How soon can we get out of here? I want to go someplace private. I've yet to give you your Christmas present, you know?"

She hid a frown. There was no way she wanted to leave this party until the D'Angelo family made their appearance. Considering the hell Matt had been through last year, she felt it imperative that she see him again. See with her own eyes that he'd recovered.

"It may be a while," she told Perry, hoping she sounded less irked than she felt. "Now that the clinic's closed for the holidays, I don't want to miss wishing some of our patients Merry Christmas."

Perry looked sulky, but probably knew her well enough by now to guess that she couldn't be talked out of staying. She snatched up a paper plate and began slipping finger foods onto it. Perry liked to eat, and the caterers had done such a wonderful job that everything looked inviting.

There was a slight swell of chatter near the front door as someone new arrived. Leslie watched as the D'Angelo clan entered, dispensing coats and jackets to the hired help and calling out Christmas greetings to friends nearby.

Leslie's heart took a leap. For as long as she could remember she had thought them the handsomest family in the Lightning River area. As a teenager, she'd spent many nights in her narrow single bed wishing she could somehow be magically granted membership to their inner circle. With her mother weeping in her bedroom and her father passed out in the living room from too

much drink, Leslie—through her friendship with Matt—
had seen the D'Angelos as warmer, grander, more fun
than any family she had ever come in contact with.

She was long beyond that kind of fantasizing now,
but she couldn't help thinking that they were still a force
to be reckoned with. With the exception of Rafe, Matt's
younger brother who had left home to seek his own
place in the world years ago, this family could weather
any storm—together.

They'd certainly had to weather one last year with Matt.

Sam, the patriarch of the family, who had suffered a
stroke a few years ago and was still confined to a wheelchair, led the way with his wife, Rose, at his side. Rose's
two Italian sisters, Renata and Sofia followed, looking
almost like twins in straight skirts and bulky Christmas
sweaters. Behind them stood Matt's only sister, Adriana.
She had on a swirling red dress that set off her hair in
dramatic prettiness, and she laughed as Tessa, her niece,
said something in her ear.

Behind them Leslie caught sight of a tall man in the
doorway, a glimpse of shining dark hair. She felt a mo-
mentary constriction in her chest and realized she'd
been holding her breath.

Matt. At last.

A moment later, she saw that it wasn't Matt at all, but
his older brother Nick, his arm around the waist of his
wife, Kari, who looked surprisingly graceful and thin
in spite of her advanced pregnancy.

In the last year, Leslie and Kari had become friends,
and as the baby's due date drew near, Kari had relied
more and more on Leslie for advice, friendship, and oc-

casionally—when her hormones got the best of her—a shoulder to cry on. She had married Nick after a whirlwind courtship last year and was thrilled about the baby, but scared to death.

For a handful of heartbeats after Kari entered the foyer, Leslie waited expectantly for Matt to follow. But suddenly the door swung closed, locking out the cold, night air. Clearly, no one else had come.

"Is that him?" Perry said close to her ear, indicating Nick, who was scanning the room for friendly faces. She caught a whiff of the bourbon he'd been drinking.

"No, that's his older brother."

As though sensing her disappointment, Perry caught her close suddenly and nuzzled her ear. "My sweet angel. Have I told you how beautiful you look tonight?"

Leslie nailed on a soft smile, determined not to let her disappointment show. So Matt had not come after all. Not surprising, really.

The Matt D'Angelo she'd grown up with had always enjoyed being the center of attention—expected it, almost. But with the exception of the quick trip back he'd made last year for Kari and Nick's wedding, he hadn't come home very often. There were bound to be questions, and people here tonight would be filled with curiosity.

Rosa, his mother, had hinted that Matt seemed different now, and though Leslie hadn't had the opportunity to question exactly what that meant, she could imagine how such a tragedy could change a person. How could it not?

The evening wore on. Leslie headed for the kitchen to make sure the catering company brought extra plates to the buffet table. She ran into Doc Hayward and Kari D'Angelo talking in the back hallway.

Doc, who looked younger than his sixty-six years in a bright red sweater that set off his white hair handsomely, motioned her over. "Leslie, you're just who I'm looking for. Do you know if we have any more of that cream at the clinic? The one I prescribed for Kari last week."

"I think so," Leslie told him, then smiled at Kari. "Don't tell me you've gone through an entire tube already."

The woman grimaced. "I've lost it. I don't seem to be able to keep track of anything lately."

"That's really not unusual," Doc said. "You do have a lot on your mind right about now."

"I'm driving Nick crazy. He's posted sticky notes everywhere. I used to kid him about being overly structured, but these days, having his organized mind running interference is the only thing saving me from looking like an idiot."

"You're doing fine," Doc said. He patted Kari's shoulder, and Leslie thought that, with his kind smile and gentle, faded-blue eyes, the old man had a bedside manner that could make any patient feel safe. "Another two months and this will all be behind you."

"It can't come soon enough."

"Any decisions on a name yet?"

"Not yet. And since we don't want to know the baby's sex, the names haven't even been narrowed down to a boy or girl. Everyone in the family has an opinion."

Leslie grinned. "With the D'Angelos, that's no surprise."

"It's just a good thing I love them so much," Kari

said, taking a sip from her glass of ginger ale. "Last week I found a note pinned to the front door of the cabin that said, "Do you like Mercedes?" I spent ten minutes trying to figure out why Aunt Renata wanted *my* opinion about cars before she told me that was her latest suggestion if the baby was a girl."

The three of them laughed.

Perry was suddenly at Leslie's side. He draped a proprietary arm around her shoulder. "What's so amusing?"

They filled him in, but it must have lost something in the translation because he looked as if he didn't really understand. Obviously he didn't see the humor in living in a large Italian clan that could make you feel like the single most beloved person in the world and drive you to distraction all at the same time.

It occurred to Leslie that she didn't know much about what Perry's own family life was like. Or even if he was close to them. Why had she never bothered to ask?

Conversation, light and inconsequential, continued to ebb and flow among the four of them for a few more minutes.

Then Perry said to Kari, "So where's this brother-in-law of yours? The infamous Matt."

Leslie felt her stomach lurch. With that one, bald question, the innocence and fun of the conversation evaporated. Yet a part of her felt no regret. It was an inquiry she'd been dying to make herself.

Kari's smile wavered a bit, but she responded easily enough. "He called from Denver. His plane got in late, so he suggested we come without him." She looked at Doc Hayward. "He'll be sorry he missed you, Doc."

It was Perry who answered with an impolite snort. "I suppose it's easier to hide out for a while than deal with a bunch of nosy questions right off the bat."

Leslie wondered if she was the only one who noticed Kari's posture stiffen. "I'm not sure that's what he's doing," the woman said. "I think he's a lot like Nick and meets any problem head-on."

"Still…" Perry went on. "I can't say that I'd blame him very much if he chose not to come. Who wants to be a freak in the sideshow?"

Leslie frowned and cut a glance at Perry. He had his moments, but he was seldom rude. She knew he'd been drinking steadily through most of the evening—so had she, for that matter—but the comment was uncalled-for. She wondered just how many details of last year's tragedy he'd picked up while circulating among Doc's guests.

"Matt's hardly a freak," she heard herself say. She sounded ridiculously defensive and toned her attitude down a notch. "He's always loved to be around people, and everyone in this house is his friend."

"Doesn't mean they won't be curious as hell," Perry said over the top of his glass. He raised a speculative brow toward Kari. "So what happened exactly? I heard he walked in on a robbery and got shot."

Kari nodded. "A year ago. He was bringing his girlfriend up here to spend the holidays with the family. She was killed, and so were a couple of others at the diner where they stopped. Matt was shot twice. Once in the back, which I understand he's recovered well from. The second came at close range and did considerable damage to his left hand. And since he's a surgeon…"

"It's been a year," Perry remarked. "Surely he's well on the way to recovery by now."

Kari gave Perry a vague, distancing smile. "I'm sure he's doing quite well."

"Life is full of tough breaks," Perry added. "If you can't change things, then you need to stop cursing your bad luck and move on."

Leslie looked at him sharply. He sounded so pompous that she wanted to drive the point of her high-heel into his instep. She felt his fingers tighten imperceptibly along her shoulder. It occurred to her suddenly that he might be jealous of Matt. Ridiculous, of course. There was no reason to be.

Luckily, Kari seemed disinclined to take offense. Forming a smile that did not include her eyes, she said, "Speaking of moving on, will you excuse me? I really ought to say hello to some of the others."

Before anyone could object, she slipped away.

Perry favored Leslie with a questioning glance. "Did I say something wrong?"

Leslie's temper was too provoked to comment right away. Laughing lightly, Doc shook his head at Perry. "Young fellow, I'm not sure you said anything *right*."

Perry's arm still lay across her shoulders like a heavy bar. Slipping out from under it, she said, "I should check on things in the kitchen."

She hated to strand Doc with Perry, but she had to get away from him right now. Why had she invited him to this party? He was bored and behaving as badly as a six-year-old dragged to the opera.

A waiter passed by with a tray of filled wineglasses. She scooped one up and would have made her way into the kitchen, but Althea Bendix, the police chief's wife, pulled her into the front parlor, where a small circle of women were eagerly plotting a surprise baby shower for Kari D'Angelo.

With no children of her own, Leslie found it hard to get excited by talk of games that involved measuring the waist of the expectant mother and trying to guess how many jellybeans could fill a baby bottle. But she liked Kari, she liked these women, and she liked that she was a part of their world, that they considered her one of them.

It hadn't always been that way. As a child, she'd quickly realized that even a place as small as Broken Yoke had a pecking order. Jagged, winding Lightning River bisected the town, and there was definitely a correct, acceptable side of it to call home, and one that some people preferred to pretend didn't exist.

The trailer park Leslie had grown up in—Mobley's Mobile Court—was a run-down eyesore that smelled of misery and failure. Town government considered it a constant source of embarrassment. Her parents, whose fights were loud and legendary, whose mailbox stayed stuffed with late notices printed in increasingly irate colors, had definitely been persona non grata in Broken Yoke. For a long while, Leslie had been sure she was, too.

Until the sixth grade. When Matt D'Angelo had come into her life. Saved her, really. From parents and teachers and the law, and sometimes even herself.

In those days she'd been lonely and disoriented most of the time. The fragile universe she'd managed to create for herself had always been in danger of toppling, but she'd been honestly convinced that no one knew that.

No one knew that quiet, sullen Leslie Meadows considered life to be missing some essential piece she couldn't identify. That happiness seemed to get further and further away from her every day. And that she imagined her heart to be no more than an empty cave where fear and hopelessness dwelt year-round.

No one, that is, except Matt.

One of the women beside her nudged her arm. "Look," she said. "It's starting to snow."

Leslie glanced out the nearest window. The temperature was supposed to drop drastically tonight, and a flurry of light flakes cascaded in the outside lights beyond the wrap-around porch. She listened to the conversation of the other women with half an ear, wishing she could be out there in the darkness, feeling the feathery touch of those snowflakes against her face.

Here, the laughter, the heady, perfumed atmosphere, the warmth generated by so many people made her feel restless and claustrophobic. She thought how clear and sharp the air outside must be right now. Every breath would be almost painful.

Years ago, on a moonlit night just like this one, she and Matt had sat snuggled against one another for warmth, catching snowflakes on their tongues as they watched an impromptu hockey game on Lightning Lake.

He'd been busy with sports all winter. Matt was the

best skier on the school team, and he'd had little time for her as he concentrated on trimming his run times.

She'd missed him so much. How good it felt to have his familiar strength pressed against her, to hear his easy laughter and know that her closest friend had not forgotten her. It was the best feeling in the world, that connection with another human being.

Those hours on the lake had also seen a shift in the dynamic of their friendship. It had wandered into unexpected territory when warmth and closeness had led to a kiss. They'd barely skirted disaster that cold, January night. At the last minute they'd managed to pull back from going any further, laughing nervously with the unspoken knowledge of how close they'd come to ruining everything.

In all the years since then, they'd never spoken of that evening. Happily, the bond between them had remained strong and pure and immutable.

She glanced back out the window as she drained her wineglass. It was snowing a little harder now, soft and silent, and so inviting. Why did anyone stay inside when there was that kind of beauty to be enjoyed only steps away?

She knew that some of Doc's guests would curse the sight of it as they left, complaining as they tugged on coats and scarves and made their slow, cautious way home. Perry would be one of them. He hated the drive back to Denver, even in good weather, and tonight the roads could be troublesome.

But she loved the snow. So did Matt. At least, he always had when they'd been kids.

Where *was* he right now?

Over the murmur of conversation, she heard a hard, harsh bark of amused laughter. It had to be Bob Gunderson, the president of Broken Yoke's only bank. Everyone called Bob "Heimlich" because of his penchant for telling jokes that always ended with a laugh that sounded as though he was trying to expel something from his throat.

She caught sight of Perry standing by the fireplace, nodding as Heimlich finished his story. From the glazed look on Perry's face, she suspected he was wishing himself anyplace else. Poor man. She supposed she ought to rescue him.

Except she didn't want to go back to her place, toast the season, and open up some ridiculously lavish Christmas gift from him that would embarrass her. Perry wasn't perfect, but he wasn't stingy, and he was sure to have gotten her something completely inappropriate given the status of their relationship.

In some ways he was so like Matt. Handsome. Generous. Confident. So energetic sometimes that he took her breath away. And goal-oriented. He lacked Matt's easygoing ways, his charisma, that core of genuine compassion that had made a career in medicine almost a foregone conclusion.

But so what if Perry wasn't Matt D'Angelo? she thought with sudden stubborn rebellion. Why should he have to be?

In spite of a little boorish behavior this evening, he was still one of the most attractive, interesting men she'd ever dated. She should take him home, open a bottle of her best wine and…see what developed.

Leaving would, of course, disappoint half the single women in this room tonight. Just like Matt, Perry attracted attention from females the way honey enticed bees.

Maybe it was a good thing Matt hadn't shown up. Two such potent, available males at one party, and who knew what might happen? Over the years she'd watched so many women try to catch Matt's attention, sometimes with embarrassing results.

Leslie cast one last, long glance around the room. Another few minutes of polite conversation and then she'd wander over to Perry. No point in staying, really. Somewhere along the way, the evening had lost its magic.

Why *hadn't* Matt made a concerted effort to come tonight?

CHAPTER TWO

MATT D'ANGELO had been the only one on the flight from Chicago who *wasn't* upset about their late arrival in Denver.

He'd always considered himself a patient guy, unflappable. That ability to focus and remain calm in the face of confusion and crisis had made him a star during his residency and brought him accolades in the operating room. But this new willingness to suffer delays due to the weather, the airlines, the traffic, and finally, the girl at the car-rental counter with the speed of a baffled snail—this was a pretty sure sign that he really hadn't wanted to make this trip after all.

True, he'd been eager to get away, tired of coming under the microscope of the powers-that-be at the hospital, tired of getting pep talks from his occupational therapist. Most of all, tired of having to reassure wellmeaning friends and associates that he really didn't mind spending Christmas and New Year's Eve alone.

Just tired.

So when his parents had pushed him to come home for a visit, he'd allowed himself to be talked into it.

Now he wished he'd said no. The family, as supportive as they'd always been, would probably smother him with their loving concern. His friends in Broken Yoke would be solicitous, but people who lived in a small town and who'd known you all your life, often assumed they had the perfect right to grill you. They'd be unable to control their curiosity. They'd feel obligated to give advice.

Or worse, they'd offer pity. He knew he'd hate that the most.

In this strange, different year he'd discovered that most people meant well. They wanted to help. But he'd spent months trying to pull a black curtain over that night in the diner. The idea of having to revisit *any* of it, having those memories ambush him in some new and terrible way, made his heart feel as tight as a closed fist.

He wished suddenly that he'd followed his friend Larry's advice—gone to the Bahamas for the holidays, where he could have found a sure cure for the blues under the warm sun.

Instead, he was almost home, watching snow flurries pelt the windshield of his rental car as he took the exit off the interstate.

He passed the familiar, aged sign that welcomed visitors to Broken Yoke. The turn up the mountain road that led to Lightning River Lodge would be just ahead, winding and treacherous in the worst of winter, but still as familiar to Matt as the route he took to the hospital in Chicago every day.

Lightning River ran along the lip of the Arapaho National Forest and widened into a deep, cold, crystal-clear lake. His parents had built the lodge on some of the prettiest land along the Front Range. The views from every window of the resort—mountains, lake and aspen-covered forests—left guests awe-struck, and its proximity to ski slopes, river rapids and quaint, historic towns in the area brought them back time after time.

A few years ago, when his father had first been in-capacitated by his stroke, Matt had considered moving back home. He hadn't really wanted to. His career had been on the fast track as he began to make a name for himself in microsurgery, and he could see endless op-portunities ahead.

For a while, his mother seemed to manage the fam-ily business just fine. Her sisters, Renata and Sofia, had come from Italy to help out. Matt's younger sister Adri-ana had just finished college and was more than will-ing to pitch in until things returned to normal.

But things didn't return to normal. His father's med-ical bills were astronomical. Rainy summer days and lit-tle fresh powder on the slopes to entice skiers made the situation worse. Matt had begun to talk to Doc Hayward about returning home and going into practice with the older physician—something Matt had never, *ever* con-sidered before.

Luckily, his older brother Nick came up with a solu-tion to keep the family business afloat and solve his problems, too.

Nick, an army helicopter pilot who had recently di-vorced, was concerned about having a proper place to raise his daughter Tessa. Matt couldn't help feeling re-lieved when Nick quit the army and came home to take over, building his own cabin only a short distance from the lodge.

The change seemed to have worked. The business was doing well. Nick had added a helicopter tour company, Angel Air, to the amenities they offered guests, and Adriana, an entrepreneur at heart, had finally talked Nick and their father into reopening the old stable where they'd kept horses as kids.

Matt had been glad to leave running the business in Nick's capable hands. And as much as he loved this area, he had never envisioned returning to live here permanently.

Now, he wasn't so sure.

He wove his way through Broken Yoke's downtown, past all the old familiar haunts. He saw that nothing much had changed, although a few more of the buildings looked empty; some were even boarded up.

Glad for a legitimate excuse to stall, he had called the lodge from the airport, telling the family not to wait, to go to Doc's party without him. It was already past ten. Most of Doc Hayward's guests had probably come and gone by now. Maybe even the D'Angelos. Everyone knew that Doc—always a morning person—would have booked an early flight tomorrow.

So if Matt skipped the party entirely, would anyone really notice? Or care?

He felt the muscles along his jaw tighten. *No more avoidance, D'Angelo. Not tonight. You know you want to see Doc before he goes.*

He could catch the tail end of the party. Say a few quick hellos and be gone before most guests even noticed his arrival. He had to. If he didn't get a handle on these subconscious and not-so-subconscious evasion tactics, they would develop their own momentum. And then where would he be?

Doc lived just off Main Street, and when Matt pulled in front of the house he was surprised to see how many cars were still in the drive and along the road. He had to park half a block away and walk back, trudging along the darkened blacktop that glistened wetly in the street lights. Snow, falling like a lacy curtain, obscured his vision and made him tuck his chin into the collar of his coat.

The Christmas lights Doc had put up outside twinkled a festive welcome.

Strange how the sight of those decorations could make his gut go cold.

Matt could still recall how every window in the diner that night had held a lighted candle. He remembered the plastic evergreen that had clung to one corner, blinking a sad welcome. The way his own blood had oozed in a slow spill across the linoleum to soak the cheap Christmas skirt around that tree.

Shayla had worn a sprig of holly pinned to her lapel that night. Even now he could remember the scratch of it against his cheek as he'd bent down to kiss her when he'd left the car.

How long would it be before he'd be able to look at a symbol of Christmas and not think of death?

Feeling his back stiffen as if for battle, he continued up the walk.

The decorations were wasted. There wasn't another soul outside. Too bad. This was the sort of Colorado night Matt loved. Crisp and clear in spite of the snow-fall, so chilly that your breath rose in little clouds around your face. The sky was so deeply midnight blue that it could leave you speechless, and he could barely tell where the mountains ended and the heavens began.

In spite of the lecture he'd just given himself, he approached the front steps slowly, delaying the moment when he'd have to enter the house. Not so brave after all, it seemed.

And then suddenly he realized he'd been wrong. Someone *was* out here in the darkness.

A woman stood with her back to him, nothing more than a black silhouette. Illumination poured from the tall windows in warped, lemon squares of light along the length of the porch. Her body looked as if it had been dipped in gold, as though she'd bathed in it. In spite of the shawl draped around her shoulders, Matt could tell she was tall and slim. Because she seemed intent on watching the goings-on inside the house, he couldn't see her face. She remained absolutely still, a silent observer. He wondered what had snagged her attention. And what had driven her outdoors.

She raked her fingers along the side of her hair. Then she shoved her hand underneath the dark mass of it, scoping upward along her scalp, so that momentarily it lifted off her shoulders. It was a gesture of impatience. Of annoyance. He knew it well. Over the years, that little habit of Leslie's had always given her away whenever they'd squabbled.

It had been like a warning flag. *Back off, D'Angelo,* that movement had said. *You're making me angry.*

He smiled to himself. Of all the people to encounter during this visit, he was ridiculously relieved to have Leslie Meadows be the first. With the exception of a few stolen hours at Nick and Kari's wedding, he hadn't seen her in so long, and he realized just how much he had missed her. Now here he was, running into the moment he'd been dreading, and Les's presence would make it so much easier.

She was so intent on watching whatever was going on inside the house that she didn't hear him come up behind her. He cupped her shoulders, then bent his lips to her ear. "What's so fascinating?' he whispered.

She whirled. The startled look in her eyes turned into exuberant pleasure almost immediately, so that warmth rushed through him.

"Matt!" she said on a little gasp of excitement and gripped his arm. "You're here! You *did* come after all!"

"Of course I came," he said, and when she grabbed him close for a hug, he pushed her dark hair away from her cheek and placed his lips against hers. His kiss was quick, friendly and unplanned. But it was nice—because on a cold night like this her lips were warm.

When he pulled away, he grinned at her. "Merry Christmas, Les."

She angled back a little, and the way she blinked and looked at him said she hadn't expected that kiss, either. But what the hell? After all these months of watching his life take a frightening and unknown course, her welcoming smile was a real treat.

She was, and always had been, the only woman he could be completely comfortable with. The only woman he had ever trusted with his dreams, his confessions and his secrets. More so than his family, his male buddies, or even the shrink the hospital had forced him to talk to after that awful night.

He felt a loosening inside his chest, as though something had given way, and suddenly he was glad he'd come home for the holidays.

In the golden light, Leslie's eyes sparkled and gave her skin a lovely glow. She'd let her hair grow long again. It flattered her face. It seemed impossible that he had known her nearly all his life and had never once realized just how pretty she was.

"I'm so glad to see you," she said. "I've missed you."

"Not half as much as I've missed you. You look terrific."

Difficult to tell in the poor light, but he thought she blushed at that comment. Les had never been comfortable with compliments. He'd always suspected that it came from getting so few of them growing up. Her mother and father had never been demonstrative to their only child. Hell, when it came right down to it, they'd hardly known she existed.

She turned back toward the window. "Everyone will be so glad to see you."

"Hmmm...Can't wait," he offered in a noncommittal tone.

Looking over her shoulder, he peered into Doc's front parlor. Guests stood in little knots of conversation around the room, laughing, talking, sipping wine. He caught no sign of their host, whom he wanted to speak to before the older man headed off to California. Practical, logical, straight-talking Doc Hayward had been the one to guide Matt through every step of med school. He'd know what to make of the mess Matt's life had become.

But passing time with everyone else in there? The thought made Matt's head ache, made his lungs feel as though a band of steel encased them.

"Who's here?" he asked.

"The usual crowd."

"I see Ellis Hughes. And there's Chad Pilcher. What's he looking so sour about?"

"Felicia took him back to court. The judge increased his alimony."

Matt let his gaze drift to another pocket of guests. "Tom Faraday's gained weight."

Leslie nodded. "Doc put him on a strict diet last summer, but so far he's still fighting it."

A statuesque blonde with a figure that had clearly been enhanced by something other than nature passed in front of the window. As first, Matt didn't recognize her. Then he gasped. "Good Lord, is that Stacey Merrick? What did she do to herself? She looks fantastic."

Stacey could be a first-class witch, and he remembered that she and Leslie had never been friends. Not surprisingly, Leslie made a disgusted sound. "She *says* it's because she's found inner peace, but her husband let the cat out of the bag. Dale's complaining that she spent thirty thousand dollars of his hard-earned money getting nipped and tucked."

"Thirty thousand! Damn, I knew I went into the wrong field of medicine." He spotted his brother Nick in a corner alcove and was shocked to see him nuzzling the neck of his wife, whose eyes were closed in pure delight. That kind of behavior from Nick surprised him. "I see my big brother's gotten drunk."

"What makes you say that?" Leslie asked, with a frown in her voice.

"He'd die before indulging in a public display of affection."

Leslie glance back at him, laughing. "He's in love, silly."

Conceding that love made people do crazy things, Matt moved on, catching sight of his sister talking to a tall, handsome fellow he didn't recognize. Most of the men inside wore casual clothes, but this guy had on a suit that hadn't come off any department-store rack. Neither of Matt's parents had mentioned a new man in Adriana's life.

"Who's the blond Romeo talking to Addy? He's better-looking than Stacey Merrick."

"He is, isn't he?"

"Don't tell me he's the new man in her life."

"No." Again, she looked back over her shoulder at him. This time, she smiled broadly. "Actually, he's the new man in *my* life. Perry Jamison."

He couldn't help jerking upright suddenly. In the old days, Leslie had hardly dated, and when he thought of her recently, for some reason he never envisioned her with anyone. He shook his head. "He's not your date."

She scowled at him. "Why? Don't you think I can attract someone that good-looking?"

She sounded a little hurt, and Matt realized he'd made a mistake.

"Of course you can," he said quickly. He lifted a

strand of dark hair off her shoulder, rubbing it between his fingers. It felt like silk. "I just meant he doesn't strike me as your type."

"I don't have a type."

"Sure you do," Matt told her with a smile. "Every woman is drawn to a man for very specific reasons. Whether or not she understands exactly what those reasons are…" He jerked his head toward the window. "So what's he offering?"

"He's attentive and treats me well. Comes from one of the founding families of Colorado—"

"God, a blueblood."

"Good breeding is important."

"If you're a poodle at the Westminster Kennel Club."

She narrowed her eyes at him. "He's confident. Has money. Power—"

"But you're not completely sold on him yet."

"What makes you think that?" she asked sharply, her head tilting to give him a close look.

"Because if you were, you'd be in there by his side instead of out here keeping me company."

He let go of her hair, swinging his gaze back to the parlor. The guy laughed at something Addy said. Matt recognized that sort of false, patronizing good humor, the kind of focused attention that most women seemed to crave. He'd used that trick often enough himself.

"What's the matter?" Leslie asked.

He realized he was frowning, but frankly he was disappointed at Leslie's choice. "You can do better than that pompous ass."

She stared at him, open-mouthed. "You don't even know him."

"I know him all right. And I don't like him."

"Well, I do," she said stubbornly. "And you don't get a vote."

"C'mon, Les. Look at the arrogance in his stance, the superior way he tilts his head, as though Addy's requested an audience with a king. You can just tell that he thinks he's someone special. God's gift to the world."

She made an annoyed sound, though he could tell she wasn't really angry. "Oh, now I get it. You're afraid he'll take that title away from *you*."

"If I was, I promise you, I'm not anymore."

His response stunned him. He didn't like the way those words came out, slightly bitter and angry-sounding. He felt every muscle in his body tense. When Les's smile faded and her posture went rigid, he knew she'd heard it as well.

"Matt—"

"Sorry," he said, hoping to keep her from saying anything he didn't want to hear. "I didn't intend to kill the mood."

Before he could stop her, she lifted his left hand and tilted it toward the light.

Sometimes that hand seemed like a foreign object to him now. A part of him, and yet not. It wasn't misshapen or repulsive, really. Some unattractive scars where the bullet had entered and exited. A network of stitch marks from the last surgery that had excised scar tissue bogging down the tendons. Most of the damage couldn't be seen.

Leslie turned his hand over a couple of times, looking at it closely, like a mother inspecting a messy kid before he sat down at the dinner table. "How bad is it?" she asked in a soft voice. "Really?"

He considered lying. He didn't want to discuss it, not even with Les. But she knew him too well, and because she was a nurse, she'd probably know if he tried to down play it.

Still, he shrugged, trying to sound as if he didn't spend nearly every night wondering how the hell he was going to reinvent a medical career that depended on the most subtle dexterity of *both* his hands.

"The flexor tendons are still totally screwed," he told her on a ragged breath, in a voice he hardly recognized. "There's triggering in both the middle and forefinger so that there's a sixty percent loss of flexibility."

She looked up at him. "Cortisone injections?"

"Back in the beginning."

"Therapy?"

He gave her a grim smile. "I've had some progress since the immobilization cast came off. The ring finger used to be completely locked so I had to straighten it by force, but that's getting better." He shook his head. "It could have been much worse, I suppose, but you know as well as I do what the ramifications will be if I can't get significant mobility back."

Les shook her head at him. "I wish you'd have let me come to Chicago to help you. Doc would have given me the extra time off, and I know I could have made a difference."

That was the last thing he had wanted—Les or his family seeing him at his worst. "I had the whole hospital helping me," he told her. "There's nothing you could have done for me that wasn't already being done."

"I'm not talking about just the physical help," she said. "I know how to make you do what's best for you. How to keep you on the straight and narrow when all you want to do is slack off."

He knew that was true. Les had always been the practical one, the one who never let him get away with anything. But the thought of her witnessing his weakness, his struggle…. In their relationship, he was the one who had always been strong.

"It wasn't a good time," he admitted. "I wasn't someone anyone liked to be around, and I would never subject you to the person I was during all those months of recuperation."

It wasn't just the poor lighting. She looked stunned. He realized that, before this moment, she hadn't had a clue how serious this injury was for a man who'd been touted in a medical magazine last winter as one of country's rising stars of microsurgery. No reason why she should have known, he supposed. God knows, he hadn't shared much of this with his parents, who already had enough to worry about with running the lodge.

Lost in the private misery of his own thoughts, he wasn't prepared for Les's reaction.

Cradling his hand in hers, she bent her head, touching her lips to the center of his palm. Spellbound, he could do nothing more than watch her, every nerve in his body tingling. In all the years of their unique history together, they'd never shared this kind of deliberately intimate moment before. Not once. Not even on that cold January night so long ago.

He felt a sweet sense of expansion in his chest, and a piercing alarm, all at once. He might even have reached out with his good hand to stroke her hair.

But in that moment, she lifted her head and looked at him. "I'm so sorry, Matt," she said in a whisper filled with sadness. "This should never have happened to you. Not this."

Pity was in her eyes. The one thing he did not want to see. From anyone. Especially not from Les.

He felt his pulse strong in his throat, as though he had swallowed a clock and it had lodged there. He pulled his hand out of her grasp, and somehow managed to shrug. "It shouldn't happen to anyone, but I'm sure I'll adjust," he said. "Pity doesn't make it any more palatable."

She looked confused. "Matt, I wasn't—"

"I should go in," he said, stepping away from her. "There's no point in standing out here in the cold. You should go in, too. It's been good to see you again, Les."

Inside the house were friends and family, full of questions and curiosity. They would touch those locked places in his mind. There would be whispers in quiet corners and surreptitious looks. They would stumble through well-meaning, but completely unrealistic predictions about his career. But how bad could it be compared to what he'd just witnessed in Les's eyes?

Leslie made a move toward him. "Matt…" she began in an aggrieved voice, but by then he had already swung away from her and was headed for the front door.

CHAPTER THREE

THE NEXT MORNING Leslie stopped by the darkened clinic to pick up another tube of cream for Kari D'Angelo. Delivering the medicated ointment to her friend offered the best excuse to see Matt again.

The day was cold, with a faint dusting of new snow on all the buildings, so that even the oldest of them gleamed fresh and sparkling. The air was filled with the scent of wood smoke and pine. A brilliant blue sky made Broken Yoke look postcard pretty this morning, Leslie decided.

But she knew the town was barely holding its own. Last year they'd lost one of the motels down by the interstate. This year, the doors had closed on two restaurants, a flower shop and Myerson Cleaners, which had been in business for nearly sixty years. The week-long festival Broken Yoke had held this past summer—Mayor Wickham's brainchild to bring tourists into town—had been an embarrassment and a costly flop. Merchants were still stopping the mayor on the street to complain about the money they'd lost.

The recent economic difficulties hadn't extended to the clinic. With Doc Hayward one of only two full-time physicians in the immediate area, the waiting room stayed busy. During certain times of the year—flu season, for example—Leslie put in so many hours that sometimes her own cat didn't recognize her when she came home.

Leslie realized that her attention had wandered, and she jerked it back to the road. She had always been a terrible driver. It was common knowledge in town that she couldn't parallel park, that her turns were too sharp and her stops too abrupt. Even Matt, patient and filled with the masculine certainty that he could teach any one to drive, had almost given up on her when she'd flunked her test a second time.

It wasn't until she turned off the car's engine in the parking lot of Lightning River Lodge that she finally took the time to sit and gather her thoughts.

The lodge was one of her favorite places, grand without being pretentious, warm and welcoming to anyone who crossed its threshold. Compared to the yellowed linoleum floor and fake wood-paneled walls of the trailer she'd called home as a child, it was like stepping into a dreamscape. Massive log beams. Huge windows. Cozy corners where you could sink into furniture that folded around your body like a glove.

She supposed there were fancier resorts along the craggy, majestic mountaintops that made up Colorado's Front Range, but Leslie couldn't think of any that offered what Lightning River Lodge was famous for— the hospitality of its hosts, the D'Angelo clan.

A gracious reception wasn't just reserved for paying guests, either. Leslie had been visiting here for years, and the family had always welcomed her into their midst. A thought slid into her mind with frightening clarity. The D'Angelos had come to mean more to her than her own family.

Why then, this hesitancy?

She remembered that fleeting vision of Matt's face last night in the porch light, the abrupt end to their conversation. It had started out so well—just like the old days—with laughter and sarcasm and the warm camaraderie that came from being with a person you knew as well as yourself.

But when talk had turned to Matt's damaged hand, he had done something he'd never done before. Not with her.

He had shut down. Pushed her away.

That reaction had been a completely new experience. Over the years they'd naturally had a few disagreements, but there had always been open and honest warfare between them, never that wary, distancing chill.

She knew the cause of it, of course. She should have chosen her words more carefully, should have schooled her features before responding to the sight of his injury. Matt, who had always been so gifted, so confident and bold, had never been pitied in his life. But in just a moment, with a few words she had instantly regretted, pity was exactly what she had offered him.

He had left the party before she could make it right between them, but this morning she would explain somehow. He'd understand. He had to. A real rift between them didn't bear thinking about.

She got out of the car quickly, tucking her serviceable old coat around her for warmth and keeping her hands shoved into the deep pockets. She went up the long drive, her breath blowing warm little puffs against her cheeks. It had to be a good ten degrees colder at this elevation.

The air was as still and hushed as a church chapel. Beyond the hiking trails along the ridge and through the evergreen trees, Leslie caught sight of Lightning Lake. It was small and had been frozen solid for a couple of weeks now. On a beautiful, clear day like today, the surface sparkled in the sunlight, as though the ice were embedded with diamond dust.

She had a special fondness for that lake. It was there, years ago, that she'd had her first real conversation with Matt.

Although they'd been in the same sixth-grade class that year, she'd never actually spoken to Matt D'Angelo before. He was everything she was not—popular with the other kids, a favorite of the teachers. He'd already begun to display a natural talent for sports and a killer charm. His life was headed on an upward course, and Leslie suspected he knew it.

The boys he hung out with were cocky, arrogant creeps. The girls were giggly future cheerleaders already in love with their own images. None of them were Leslie's friends. No one in Matt's circle would have ever sat at the same lunchroom table with someone who lived in Mobley's Mobile Court.

She told herself that their shallow attitudes suited her just fine. In spite of mediocre grades, she wasn't stupid. Living with two volatile parents had taught her a lot about survival. Since summer that year, trouble at home had been particularly stressful. Her father's temper was in full force due to his inability to hold a job for very long. She'd been busy developing an I-don't-care approach toward the world in general from the day school started.

In February the PTA held a fundraiser, and the D'Angelos offered their property for a winter carnival—sleigh rides, cross-country skiing on the trails, ice-skating on Lightning Lake. Everyone said the D'Angelos knew how to host a celebration, and it should be fun as well as profitable.

Leslie had no intention of going.

But the day before the fundraiser she found herself suddenly volunteering to help out. Her parents were in the middle of a three-day argument, and with the weekend ahead and tempers escalating, the last place Leslie wanted to be was home, playing referee and maybe getting in the line of fire herself. Besides, she had a secret longing to see just what was so darned special about Lightning River Lodge, a place she'd been hearing about all her life.

By midmorning her feet felt frozen and her cheeks stung. The job of selling hot chocolate at a booth by the lake bored her. Only pride kept her from marching off and leaving Mrs. Elliott, the history teacher, to run the concession alone.

Every kid she despised seemed to be on the lake that day. She watched as they sailed laughingly around the ice. The boys wove in and out of the crowd with long, wild strokes—imagining themselves professional hockey players, no doubt. The girls spun in short skating skirts, a rainbow dazzle.

She'd seen Matt D'Angelo whiz by the stand several times. He made skating look effortless. His arms never flailed; he never lost his balance. He could stop so quickly that ice particles sprayed out from his skate blades.

Show *off*, she thought, but she couldn't take her eyes off him.

Mrs. Elliott had gone up to the lodge for a few minutes, and Leslie had just poured herself some steaming chocolate when Matt skated up to the stand. Since his family had furnished the cocoa, she thought he might expect a freebie, but he didn't hesitate to plunk down fifty cents.

Without a word she passed him a cup. He wrapped both hands around the plastic and took a cautious sip.

His cheeks were blotchy red, his dark hair disheveled, but there was a undeniable aura of potent energy about him; something in his eyes radiated confidence. In spite of herself, Leslie felt a warm tingle begin in her stomach. They spent several long seconds studying one another in such an odd silence that she picked up her own fresh cup and took a large swallow.

She had to stifle a gasp of pain. The heat from the cocoa seared the taste buds right off her tongue.

One of Matt D'Angelo's brows lifted. "Didn't that hurt?"

"No," she lied, trying to suck cold air through her slightly parted lips.

"You sure?"

"It doesn't," she claimed, mortified. "Okay?"

His mouth quirked. "Guess it's true what Danny says about you."

The mention of his friend Danny LeBrock made her spine stiffen. She hated him. He insisted on trying to torment her with every dumb variation of her name he could think of—Help-Les. Friend-Les. Wit-Les. Lately he'd been partial to Hope-Les. She stared at Matt rigidly, unable to contain her curiosity. "What does Danny say about me?"

"That you're the toughest girl he's ever met."

"He's an idiot. I'll bet he doesn't even know very many girls. What girl would talk to him?"

Over the rim of his cup, Matt's eyes sparkled in a look she'd seen him use on the other girls and several teachers. "Yeah, that's probably true. Danny can be a loser sometimes." He took another sip of chocolate, and she pretended to do the same.

"Can you taste anything yet?" he asked knowingly.

She nodded, though that wasn't really true.

"Mom makes the best hot chocolate. She says the recipe is over a hundred years old and came all the way from Italy. From her mother's family."

She had to admit, Matt's parents seemed like nice people. Mrs. D'Angelo had brought Leslie gloves to wear when she saw that she had forgotten her own. Without muttering a complaint, Mr. D'Angelo trudged down the trail time and again to keep them supplied with hot chocolate from the resort's kitchen. They were so unlike her own folks, she wasn't sure they were real.

Leslie gave him a look of mild interest, refusing to seem too impressed even though the chocolate was completely unlike the watery, instant brew she was used to. The rich mixture had filled her insides like a hot bath.

Someone called Matt's name, and he looked over his shoulder. One of the girls he hung out with gestured for him to come back to the ice. He turned to Leslie. "Do you want to skate? We're going to start up a game of whipcracker if we can get enough people."

Her heart gave a little kick like a can-can dancer. As much as she wanted to say yes, she couldn't. Her flailing trip across the ice would be as inept as a two-year-old child's. Worse, maybe.

She fumbled around for inspiration, but came up empty. "I didn't bring skates," she said at last. "I came to work, not have fun."

She sounded irritable, when she'd meant to sound practical. Matt didn't seem to mind. He gave a little inside chuckle that threatened to draw her into the warm circle of his personality. "Take it easy. I'm just asking if you want to skate a few minutes, not rob a bank. I can snag a pair from the lodge if you want. We always keep extras for guests."

"Look, I'm not interested."

"Why not? I'll bet Mrs. Elliott will watch the stand by herself for a while. She's pretty cool for a teacher."

Panic turned the chocolate in her stomach to an icy waterfall. She'd been hungry for friendship this year, but she wasn't prepared for this overture. Not from someone like Matt D'Angelo, who probably had to beat friends off with a stick.

She gave him a challenging look. "Why are you talking to me?"

He looked genuinely puzzled. "What do you mean?"

"I'm not like your friends." She jerked her head toward the ice, where several of his buddies were clowning around, waiting for him. "They won't like it if you make them be nice to me."

"I don't *make* my friends do anything," he said with a scowl. "And they don't tell me who I can talk to." He tilted his head at her. "Why are you so mad? Do you really want to fight over playing a couple of stupid games on the ice?"

Anger killed all sense of caution within her. "*I can't skate, okay? I never learned.*"

She expected him to laugh, but he didn't. "Is that all?" he asked. "Shoot, I can teach you in two minutes. Lucky for you, I'm the best skater on the lake today."

Someone had to keep him from being so arrogantly sure of himself. "You're not very modest," she told him.

"Why should I be? It's the truth."

"I don't want to learn to skate," she said precisely.

"Sure you do."

"No, I don't. I want you to go away and leave me alone."

She waited to be rewarded with anger from him now. How many times had he been told to get lost? Not many, she'd bet. But in the next moment, she caught sight of real catastrophe on the way. Danny LeBrock had skated off the ice and was crab-walking toward them.

He came up beside Matt and gave her his usual evil grin. "Hey there, Brain-Les." His eyes raked over her mismatched clothes. "Nice outfit. Did you steal that sweater off a scarecrow?"

Most of the time Leslie ignored Danny's taunts, vowing never to let him get to her, but the conversation with Matt had given her a wild, flaring discontent that left her unable to heed anything resembling rational behavior.

She lifted her chin. "Could I ask you a question, Danny?"

Danny looked suspicious. "What?"

"Is it true what everyone says? That your family tree is really just one stick and your father is also your uncle?"

It took him a moment to understand the insult. She caught sight of amusement in Matt's eyes and the slightly off-centered lift of his mouth.

Danny paled and then his features tightened to cold-blooded scrutiny. Even at that young age, Leslie knew she'd made an enemy for life.

He shook his head. "I sure can't figure out how you're too dumb to make good grades when you have such a smart mouth."

"Considering that your belt buckle probably weighs more than your brains, I'm surprised you can figure out much of anything."

Ruddy blotches added more color to Danny's cheeks as disbelief swept over him like a tide. He looked for help from Matt. "Who does she think she is?"

"Someone who doesn't like to be insulted, I guess," Matt said. "Let it go, Danny. Don't spoil a nice day by being a total jerk."

Danny made a move to come around the counter toward her. "Do you know what I should do?"

Matt halted him by taking a small step into his path. "What?" he asked. "Shut up and go back to the ice?"

After chewing the sides of his mouth for a moment, Danny blew a disgusted breath. The tightness in Leslie's chest began to ease as he backed away. "We're getting up a hockey game on the far end of the lake," he said to Matt in a sullen tone. "*If* you can tear yourself away."

They watched him filter into the crowd of skaters, then Matt turned back to face her. "My father says a still tongue makes a wise head," he told her. "You ought to be more careful about the battles you pick."

"Seems to me you ought to pick better friends."

He laughed and tossed his empty cup in the wastebasket. "Most of the time I *don't* pick them. They pick me." With a few graceful steps, he was on the ice again, skating backwards as he called out to her, "Let me know if you and Danny ever decide to duke it out. I'll hold your coat."

Turning, he disappeared into the crowd of skaters. Leslie didn't see him again that day.

On Monday morning Danny LeBrock showed up at school with a butterfly bandage plastered across his swollen nose and a black eye. One of the girls who specialized in classroom gossip told Leslie that Matt D'Angelo had accidentally flattened Danny during the hockey game on the lake. Nobody seemed to know the exact circumstances, but Danny sure didn't seem chummy with Matt that day.

Leslie made a point to catch up with him between classes. She didn't waste time with vague hints as she came up beside his locker. "I hear you whacked Danny LeBrock. Nearly broke his nose."

He stopped twirling the combination lock and looked at her. "Yeah. His face picked a fight with my elbow during the hockey game Saturday. My elbow won."

"Did you do it on purpose?"

"No. Why would I do that?"

"You mean, besides the fact that he's a nasty little creep who probably has a 666 birthmark someplace on his skull?"

"That's not very nice," he said with a laugh. He shook his head and went back to fiddling with his lock. "No wonder you have a hard time making friends."

"I don't. I'm just picky. Unlike *some* people."

His eyes swung sharply back to her. "Danny isn't my friend."

"Since Saturday?"

"Since forever. I can't help who tries to hang around with me. My mother says I'm charismatic. That means—"

"I know what it means," she said. "I hope your mother also tells you that a little modesty is a good thing in a person."

"You know, you're a riot, Meadows. You ought to have your own television show."

He looked annoyed now, and her heart banged up in her throat, but her battered dignity wouldn't allow her to back down.

"I don't need anyone to fight my battles for me," she told him.

"No. You don't," he said in the mildest tone she'd ever heard. But in the next moment, her insides swam with an odd sense of loss when he slammed his hand upward to shut his lock. Giving her a final sullen look, he turned away and left her standing in the hallway.

She was quite sure that that would be the last conversation she'd ever have with Matt. She avoided him for weeks, and he certainly seemed oblivious to her presence. But in the spring, her life suddenly went from bad to worse.

Her father lost his job in construction. After drowning his misfortune at a bar, Quentin Meadows decided that the best way to handle unemployment was to slash his ex-foreman's tires and smash the windshield of his truck. He spent two nights in jail.

Leslie endured those forty-eight hours as though she'd been sentenced as well. She listened to her mother cry, tried to convince her to eat something, and wished she had the nerve to run away.

By then she should have been used to the self-destructive events that seemed to pepper her life as a member of the Meadows family. And this one wasn't too bad, really. Although everyone knew about it, none of the kids mentioned the incident when she came back to school. Not even Danny LeBrock, who had stopped calling her names and was now focusing all his attention on some other poor victim.

Leslie had forgotten about her English teacher and worst nemesis, Mrs. Bickley.

The woman hated her for the lack of thought she put into her homework, for daydreaming in class, but mostly—Leslie was sure—for being poor. Rumor had it that Bickley had come from the wrong side of Lightning River herself and despised any reminder of that past, especially from a slacker like Leslie Meadows.

The last-period bell had rung when Mrs. Bickley caught the attention of every kid. "Just one moment, class," she said, sounding as though she'd just remembered something. "Leslie, I meant to speak to you."

Leslie didn't say a word as she stood beside her desk and waited. It was her first day back, and she was determined to keep a low profile. All around her she could feel the other kid's stares, their eagerness to go. The girls blew impatient breaths. Behind her Danny LeBrock smothered an oath. Beside her Matt slowly stuffed homework papers into his notebook.

Mrs. Bickley gave her a sweet smile. Leslie should have known right then that trouble was coming. "Can you come to school early tomorrow morning?" she asked. "I'd like you to make up the test you missed yesterday."

"Sure," Leslie said. "What time?"

"Seven o'clock?" the woman replied, pretending to hunt for her scheduling book.

That was another bad sign. Bickley was a neat freak who knew where everything on her desk was.

After a moment, the teacher frowned. "Yes. Can you make it that early? I mean, your father isn't still…going through his current difficulties, is he?"

There was a snort of laughter from the back of the room and a few tittering whispers. Blood pounded loudly in Leslie's ears. That swipe had to be deliberate. It had to be.

"You mean, is my Dad still in jail?" she asked in a voice that hardly shook at all. "No, he's out. I don't know what terrible trouble he's got planned next, so I'll get Mom to bring me."

Bickley gave Leslie one of her mechanical smiles that never reached her eyes. "That will be fine, then. I'll be waiting for you at seven. Class dismissed."

Leslie nodded and stumbled awkwardly out of the room. She didn't stop for anything or anyone. She didn't take the bus home that day. She ran past the school's track-and-field hut, through the open meadows that were just starting to pop with spring wildflowers, down the back alleys of Broken Yoke where trash cans overflowed. She followed Lightning River all the way to the turnoff for the interstate, and only stopped running when the stitch in her side doubled her over.

By the time she went home it was almost dark. She was drenched in sweat, breathing so heavily that she felt dizzy. Her parents weren't home, but that didn't surprise her. She fell on the old plaid sofa that smelled of beer and cheap perfume and wondered just how fast your heart had to beat before it killed you.

The next day she felt better. The horrid feelings that had curdled her insides yesterday were locked down so tight there was no way they could get out again. She was completely calm. She got to school early.

The door to Mrs. Bickley's class was already open, but the English teacher wasn't there.

Leslie went over to the woman's desk and pulled on the top drawer, relieved to find it unlocked. She'd half expected to have to pry it open. Inside were all the supplies Mrs. Bickley treasured, everything tucked away in tidy little compartments.

She fished the jar she'd brought out of her backpack, unscrewed the lid, and dumped a quart of raw honey into the drawer.

She didn't expect to get away with it. She didn't really care. She was almost in a stupor, watching the honey spread in a slow, golden river over everything in its path.

When the classroom door opened and closed, she knew it would be Bickley. Drawing a deep breath, she straightened, fully prepared for a shriek of horror and a swift march down to the principal's office. The wrath of God was about to descend on her pretty quick.

But when she lifted her eyes, it wasn't Mrs. Bickley she saw coming toward her. It was Matt D'Angelo.

He didn't say a word, and neither did she. She watched him inspect the damage. His features didn't give much away. Maybe his mouth tightened a little.

Finally, he looked back at her. "I thought you were just fooling everyone with your grades, that you were really pretty smart. But you're actually dumber than a box of bent nails."

Those were practically the first words he'd said to her since February. She crossed her arms and gave him a sullen look. "I wasn't expecting an audience."

"Doesn't matter if anyone sees you or not. Bickley's gonna know you did this. Everybody will."

Leslie shrugged. "I don't care."

"No reason why you should, I guess. Not after what that bitch said in front of everyone yesterday."

She blinked. She'd never heard Matt say anything remotely nasty before. Maybe she wasn't the only one who would end up in hell someday.

He went quiet again, staring down at the mess in the drawer. He shook his head as though he couldn't believe what he was seeing.

"How did you know I was in here?" she asked.

"I watched you from Coach Mitterman's office. I'm his gopher this semester. I figured you weren't coming in early just to make points with Bickley, so I thought I'd check it out."

"I'm glad you didn't get here in time to stop me," she said in a determined voice. "You couldn't. And I'm not going to run away and pretend I don't know anything."

He snorted. "No. You wouldn't want someone to keep you from getting a three-day suspension. If not more."

"I don't care if they expel me from school for good. It will just be what everyone thinks I deserve anyway. No one expects anyone in the Meadows family ever to amount to anything. Including you."

He frowned, looking annoyed. "I've never said that."

"You don't have to."

He stared at her, hard, while she continued to throw him mutinous looks.

"You know what your problem is, Leslie?" he said at last. "You're so busy trying to make sure no one thinks you care about anything that you don't know how to act normal. You have a chip on your shoulder as big as Mount Rushmore. You never say please or thank you or…" He gave a rough laugh, as though disgusted with himself. "Oh, forget it. Bickley's gonna come in here any minute and have a cow. You'll probably make matters worse by spitting in her eye, and then she'll flatten you but good. That's probably what you need anyway."

Surprisingly, his apparent dislike for her hurt more than anything Danny LeBrock had ever said. Tears stung the back of her eyes, but she refused to let them come. "Then you'd better get out of here. I wouldn't want you to see what happens if she tries to lay a finger on me."

He sighed heavily and shook his head. "There's no saving you. Danny was wrong. You're not Hope-Les. You're Clue-Les."

She bristled. "At least I'm not so full of myself that I have to duck my big head to get it through the doorway."

He gave her that smile that made the girls giggle nervously. "Smart aleck."

"Over-achiever."

"Idiot."

They subsided into a strange silence then, and in that moment the classroom door opened again. This time it was Mrs. Bickley. She approached them both with a frown between her overly plucked eyebrows.

It didn't take her long to see the damage. The honey sent up a sickening sweet odor that began to turn Leslie's stomach a little. When it came right down to it, she wasn't sure just how she'd handle the woman's reaction.

Mrs. Bickley, as pale as her crisp, white blouse, ignored Matt completely and snapped her gaze over to Leslie. She knew perfectly well who the guilty party was. "How could you do such a hateful thing?" she asked through the middle of her teeth.

"Actually, she didn't," Matt spoke up from behind her. "I did."

Even after all these years it was still so clear to Leslie—the shock on Mrs. Bickley's face, her refusal to believe Matt capable of such a trick. He stuck to his story, that he had done it because she had given him a B on the last test when he'd been sure his essay had deserved an A. Leslie had come into the classroom after he'd poured the honey, he told the astonished teacher. When Leslie opened her mouth to protest, he gave her such a threatening look that she clammed up again, so shocked she couldn't have spoken anyway.

What could Principal Smith do in the face of such a calm, unshakable confession? Matt was suspended for three days.

No one had ever gone out on a limb like that for Leslie. All her fights had been fought alone, and she was shaken by Matt's gesture, then suspicious. Why had he done it?

Finally, she recognized it for what it was.

On the third day of his suspension, Leslie hitched a ride up to Lightning River Lodge. Mr. D'Angelo was in the lobby, stoking the huge fireplace with pieces of wood as big as the television set at home. She asked to see Matt, and when he scowled and told her Matt wasn't allowed to see anyone, she begged. He told her she could have five minutes.

She found him around the back of the lodge, chopping wood. There was so much of it piled around him that he looked like he'd been doing that chore for a week. When he saw her, he stopped and waited for her to reach him, wiping sweat from his brow with the sleeve of his shirt.

He didn't look mad, though she wouldn't have blamed him if he had. All the words she'd rehearsed up the mountain road deserted her. Panic began a slow crawl up her spine because she knew she wasn't going to get this right.

He frowned. "Now what have you done?"

She shook her head, unable to speak.

He pointed to her face. "Then what's with the plumbing problem?"

She realized that her cheeks were wet with tears. Humiliating. Such a stupid reaction. She wished she could turn around and run down the mountain, because she realized that Matt D'Angelo had offered her something she didn't think existed. With his gesture of friendship, he had changed her whole life.

She remembered the short lecture he'd given her in Mrs. Bickley's classroom. Plunging in before she lost her courage, she said, "You were right. I do have a chip on my shoulder. But you're wrong about one thing. I do know how to say thank you, because I'm saying it now. Thank you."

He stared at her for a long moment, while her heart missed beats. Then his deep, generous smile was all the reward she could have asked for.

From that moment on, they were friends.

CHAPTER FOUR

THE REALIZATION that her feet were freezing brought Leslie back to the present. She checked her watch. She'd been standing—lost in those early memories—on the snowy trail that led down to Lightning Lake for twenty minutes. She turned and trekked back up the path, recognizing this small side trip to the lake as a subconscious delaying tactic.

Why should she delay entering the lodge? The Matt D'Angelo she knew had never been the type to hold a grudge. If he was upset about last night, he'd say so, and they'd talk it out.

But that's your real fear, isn't it? What if he's not the Matt D'Angelo you know anymore?

The sort of thing he'd been through last year could change even the strongest person.

She drew a deep breath. With renewed determination she turned away from those uncertainties. They'd been friends too long to let something like this spoil everything.

Halfway up the trail, Leslie encountered Tessa D'Angelo.

Last year Nick's daughter, full of adolescent high spirits and hormonal confusion, had inflicted a great deal of worry on the family, but she seemed to have settled down considerably since her father had married Kari. She was normally cheerful and upbeat, but this morning she wasn't smiling.

"Good morning," Leslie said as the teenager approached.

"Nothing good about it," Tessa replied.

"What's wrong?"

"If you're smart, you'll turn around and head back down the mountain right now before it's too late."

"Why?"

Tessa jerked her head toward the lodge entrance. "World War Three is about to break out in there between Nonno Sam and Mr. Waxman."

Leslie gave her a surprised look. Sam D'Angelo had been friends with Leo Waxman, the town electrician, for years. Both men served on the town council together, and she knew that Sam and his wife, Rose, were godparents to Leo's son. "But they're like brothers."

"Yeah, well, that was before a chipmunk somehow got in the back door and Mr. Waxman's German shepherd chased it all over the place and destroyed everything in its path. It looks like someone took a chainsaw to the lobby."

Leslie noticed that Tessa gingerly cradled a dish towel in her arms, and suddenly the material moved. "Is that it?" Leslie asked.

As though the chipmunk wanted to acknowledge her interest, it squeaked softly.

"Yep. Poor thing is scared to death, but it will chill out once I let it go down by the lake. I just wish it hadn't climbed up the Christmas tree."

"Not the big one in the lobby?" Leslie said, almost in a whisper.

"That's the one."

Leslie's eyes widened. After all these years she knew the D'Angelo family Christmas traditions very well. Sam D'Angelo's hunt for the perfect blue spruce—one for the lobby and one for the family's private quarters—was treated like a mission handed to him by God. And Rose spent hours decorating them, insisting that every ornament be hung just right, that every light be held erect with a pipe cleaner so that it stood like a candle.

"The tree fell over," Tessa continued. "Dad and Uncle Matt are trying to get it to stand again, but I think it's a goner." She placed a gentle hand on top of the towel, as though offering comfort to the little creature inside. "Really, if you were a chipmunk being chased by a big dog, wouldn't you head up the nearest tree to escape? And it's not like it *planned* to come into the lodge. It was probably looking for somewhere out of the cold."

"Let's just hope it's the only chipmunk with that idea."

"Don't even think it," Tessa said, starting off down the path again. "Good luck. Don't say I didn't warn you."

The chaos Tessa had described met Leslie when she entered the lobby. The Christmas tree, which topped out at twelve feet so it wouldn't be dwarfed by the high, beamed ceiling, was awkwardly being held upright by Nick. Leo Waxman hung on to the collar of his excited dog, who barked repeatedly at nothing in particular. Kari and Rose D'Angelo were picking up fallen ornaments. Broken tree limbs dangled, raining needles everywhere. Decorations swung back and forth on the tree as though trapped in a gentle wind.

Leslie caught sight of Matt on the floor, half-hidden by the limbs. He was on his stomach, trying to replant the tree in its stand and evidently meeting with little success. The massive spruce tipped every time Nick loosened his hold.

"Can't you make that beast be quiet?" Sam D'Angelo growled at Leo from his wheelchair. He held a cardboard box on his lap, filled with broken ornaments.

"He's excited," Leo explained, stroking his dog's head to no avail. "When that damned thing came charging at me, he thought I was being attacked. He's trained to protect me."

"From a rodent no bigger than your fist?" Sam exclaimed in disgust. "That dog is blind as well as stupid."

"Brutus isn't to blame if—"

"Leo!" Rose spoke up. "Take the dog outside. Sam, sit there and be silent. Shouting at one another doesn't help." As Leo hurried out the front door with Brutus, Matt's mother caught sight of Leslie and nodded. "Hello, Leslie. As you can see, we've lost a little of the Christmas spirit this morning."

"I heard. Anything I can do to help?"

"Can you grab one end of this?" Kari said from the side of a huge leather couch that sat in front of the fireplace. "I think some ornaments rolled under it."

Hearing her request, Nick stopped fiddling with the tree and stuck his head around the spreading limbs to shake his head at his wife. "No, you don't. You're not lifting the couch. With or without someone's help." He threw an irritable glance toward the floor, where Matt was groaning now under the effort of trying to wedge the tree back in the stand. "Come on, Matt. What's taking so long? Trade places with me if you can't manage it."

"Damn it. Just give me a minute," Matt called up at him.

That impatient cross exchange made Leslie realize that the brothers were out of sorts with one another. Did Nick think he could make a faster job of it? Was a lack of dexterity and strength in Matt's left hand making him feel as though he wasn't up to the task? Or was it all just the frustration of the situation?

Rose picked up a delicate-looking silver sleigh ornament and saw that one of the runners dangled. She made a little sound of distress. "This was given to me when I was a little girl," she said. "By my grandmother."

"It's all right, Rosie," Sam said. "We'll fix it good as new."

Matt emerged from under the tree, his hair tousled, brushing needles from his flannel shirt. He opened his good hand to reveal a few pieces of metal resting on his palm. "Two of the screws snapped. Do we still keep extra hardware in the back shed?"

"My tool box should be on top of the big red cabinet," Nick said. "Try there if you can't find anything in the storage bins."

Matt nodded and headed in the direction of the dining room. Leslie grabbed a broom and began sweeping up stray bits of glass and needles while Kari managed the dustpan. Sam started working on a length of garland that rested in his lap, restringing the beads as though they were pearls to be fashioned into a necklace.

A couple of guests came down the stairs, viewed the damage and made an abrupt, uncertain halt.

With a breezy laugh, as if this kind of catastrophe happened every day, Brandon O'Dell, the front-office manager, ushered them through the wreckage toward the front door. "Don't worry," he told them. "We won't put you to work helping to clean up."

Brandon was an old army buddy of Nick's, an ex-helicopter pilot who had been working at the lodge for six months. A recovering alcoholic, he seemed to be making a home for himself here, and Leslie knew that he'd recently begun to take a particular interest in Moira, the clinic's receptionist.

With his free hand, Nick pulled a broken limb out of the tree. The removal left a gaping hole, and Rose gasped as though she'd been wounded. "We can fix it," he said quickly.

Sam made an angry sound low in his throat. "I'm going to sue Leo—*and* his dog—for destruction of property."

"I'll check on Matt," Leslie said, eager to escape.

She went through the dining room, then through the double swinging doors of the kitchen, the place she had always thought of as the geographic and social center of D'Angelo family life. Rose's sister Renata nodded at her, but was too busy managing the last of the guest breakfast orders to stop.

"How bad is it?" the older woman asked, jerking her head toward the lobby as she set a plate of scrambled eggs on one of the waitress's trays.

"A mess," Leslie said.

"Dogs inside the house," Renata said with a disgusted shake of her head. "Trouble just waiting to happen."

"At least it wasn't chasing a mouse. Just imagine how that would have looked."

Renata gasped, clearly envisioning what the sight of a mouse running from the kitchen would have done to the guests' appetites. "*Madonn!* True disaster!"

Matt's aunt began muttering in Italian as Leslie headed out the back door. The tool shed was actually a good-sized room attached to the back of the lodge where Sam had indulged his wood-working hobby before his stroke. Now it was nothing more than a place for miscellaneous clutter.

The door stood open, and Matt hadn't bothered to turn on a light. He hadn't been home in a year, but he probably knew where his organized father kept every screw and nail. Leslie came silently to the doorway.

The morning sun seeped through the blinds, striping the shabby gloom in mellow bands of light. Matt was standing in front of the shoulder-high tool chest.

Just standing there.

His attention seemed fixed on a jumbled mass of items that littered the top of the chest. In a moment she realized they were some of his old trophies, a few of the ones he'd won over a lifetime of athletic achievements. Track and field, skiing, hockey—Matt had excelled at anything he attempted. We'll have to add on another room to hold them all, Sam had once joked.

She saw now that there were several on top of the chest, dull and dusty, the result of some spring cleaning that had probably taken place years ago. Matt, competitive and skilled, had always been more interested in playing the game, whatever it was, than whatever prize came with it. He wouldn't care that a few of them had ended up here.

She was caught, however, by the tightness of his profile. He lifted his hand to run one finger slowly over his name etched in the metal plate, and she could guess his thoughts. The boy who had won those awards had turned into an equally talented, blessed adult. He had never failed, never been beaten by circumstance. But this past year his soul had been lacerated.

She knew the exact moment he sensed her presence. Without turning to look her way, he stiffened. His finger continued to move slowly down the plaque, as though he were caught in memories of past glory.

When he spoke, she could hardly hear the words. "Do you ever feel lost, Les?"

That question seemed to fall out of him like a burden he was delivering. She thought of all the years of her early childhood, when she truly *had* felt lost and disoriented. And she thought of how those feelings had evaporated in the sweet warmth of her friendship with Matt.

"I used to," she said softly. "I haven't for a long time."

He looked at her then. Was it a trick of the poor light that made the lines on either side of his mouth look deeper than they were? "No, you're beyond that now, aren't you? No insecurity or doubt."

The energy seemed to have bled out of him, and he looked so solemn, so unnaturally solemn, that she shivered. "Things will come right again, Matt. You'll see."

"Will they?" He lifted his damaged hand, frowning

down at his splayed fingers as though he'd never seen them before. "Sometimes the simplest task seems beyond me."

"Matt—"

He jerked his head up. "Don't feel the need to say anything. Pity terrifies me almost as much as the idea that my days as a surgeon may be over."

"I don't…" She broke off, sighing heavily. "This is ridiculous. I've never known us to have such difficulty communicating."

He gave her a small smile. "You've always been so honest. That's one of the things I value most about our friendship."

Her senses flooded with warmth. He had always had the ability to make her feel special, to make her heart feel as though something had reached in and touched it. "I have to talk to you about last night," she said. "I know I sounded… It came out all wrong."

His gaze stayed fixed on her for a long moment. Then a small frown overtook his features, and a few quiet strides brought him right in front of her. She stood waiting, blinking once very slowly, and then again when his hands settled gently on her shoulders.

"Don't, Les," he said in a voice that sounded as gray as his face looked. "I'm the one who should apologize— for making you feel the need to offer one. For making you feel uncomfortable." He lifted his left hand. "You live with this night and day, and pretty soon it's the only reality you know. You forget what it feels like to be any different. But I can't let it change who I am, or let it affect how I treat the people I care about. Will you forgive me?"

It was so quiet, so still. Matt didn't seem to be breathing; she knew she wasn't. Something barely defined lay between them in those moments. Her heart thumped in her throat, making her feel so uncomfortable that she gave a short little laugh and shook her head in a desperate attempt to break the spell.

"Of course I forgive you," she said dryly. "After all these years, do you really think you could damage our friendship that easily?" She went around him, heading for the tool chest. "Now let's find something for that tree. Nick will be all over you if you don't come up with something soon."

He didn't try to stop her, and the awkwardness of those moments slipped away.

A COUPLE OF DAYS later, Leslie opened up the clinic, cranked up the heat to take the chill off, and began laying drop cloths in the waiting-room alcove. Since coming to work for Doc Hayward, she'd always used the weeks of his Christmas vacation to complete much-needed projects she didn't have time for during the rest of the year.

This year she planned to create a children's play area to keep kids entertained and out of harm's way while they waited. Armed with a dozen cans of paint, a book of designs and the firm belief that the most rudimentary artwork wasn't beyond her limited talent, she took a deep breath and charged ahead.

Moira Thompson had promised to come in later, saying she would welcome the diversion. The receptionist had recently broken up with Danny LeBrock, who had not matured one bit since middle school. A blown knee had ended his hopes for a professional football career long ago, and he'd come home to work in his father's insurance company.

Bitter and filled with resentment, Danny was known to have a quick temper and, given their past history, Leslie avoided him whenever possible.

If Moira showed up, Leslie suspected Brandon O'Dell wouldn't be far behind. She knew he had feelings for the young woman, though he had yet to act on them. When Leslie had asked him why he didn't, he admitted that he had already ruined one good relationship with a woman because of his alcoholism, and only Nick's job offer had kept him from ruining his life as well. He wasn't ready. He needed time.

By nine-thirty Leslie had come to the conclusion that she might have overestimated her artistic ability. To highlight the silver-mining history of Broken Yoke and Colorado's pioneer days, she'd planned a detailed mural of covered wagons, men on horseback, miners panning the river and Western storefronts.

But when she backed away and surveyed her work, she realized that the scale of everything was off, her people looked like little more than stick figures, and her horses…well, four legs and a tail did not make them Black Beauty. Hands on hips, she scowled and wondered just how tough an art critic a child would be.

She heard the key turn in the clinic's front door. "Leslie?" Moira called.

"I'm here," she answered from the alcove. Footsteps came across the cloth protecting the carpet, but she didn't bother to turn around. She couldn't take her eyes off the pathetic river scene she'd drawn on one wall.

"Oh," she heard Moira say. "You've already started painting."

"Don't laugh. Just tell me, do you think this miner looks like he's panning for silver, or on his knees praying for divine guidance?"

"Les, honey," a male voice said with a short laugh. "I'm sorry, but I think he looks like he's relieving himself in the river."

She swung around. Moira stood there with Matt right behind her. Leslie must have looked as surprised as she felt because Moira smiled at her and explained, "I ran into help coming in."

Matt unwound a wool scarf from his neck and shrugged out of his winter coat. He wore a dark-chocolate turtleneck sweater the same color as his eyes. "Heard you talking the other day and figured you could use some help." From the back pocket of his jeans, he pulled out a large paintbrush, holding it up in his good hand. "I brought my own equipment. But I can see it might be all wrong for this job."

She studied his face. In the bright, overhead lighting he looked tired, and for the first time she saw tiny lines carved in his features—lines he was too young to have. But he seemed more at ease this morning, lighter in spirit, so she let the worry go for now. Frankly, no matter what his mood was, she would always be glad to see him.

Moira pointed toward a row of figures Leslie had sketched near the baseboard. "I like the dance-hall girls."

"Those are Indians."

"Oh. Well, they're very pretty."

Leslie took the paintbrush from Matt's hand and replaced it with a smaller one. "Pick a color, Picasso," she said. "You've got major work to do."

MATT LEANED BACK from the wall, eyeballing the line of Conestoga wagons he'd painted. He didn't want to brag, but his horses *were* better. So were his cowboys. As for his Indians...well, they sure didn't look like dance-hall girls.

While Moira had been in the examining rooms restocking the cabinets, he and Les had worked in silence for nearly an hour. He glanced over to his right, where she sat making a pitiful attempt to create a pioneer town out of the cluster of rectangles and squares he'd sketched for her earlier. So far the buildings looked like dull, brown building blocks.

The tip of her tongue was caught between her teeth, and a frown furrowed her brow. He didn't have the heart to tell her that her efforts were fairly pathetic. Les was a terrific woman, but she was no artist.

He was relieved that their friendship was back on track. As much as he loved his family, spending the holidays with them wouldn't have had nearly the same appeal if Les hadn't been part of the equation. In a way, she *was* family.

She turned her head to look at him suddenly. "I know what you're thinking," she said, then pointed toward the wall with the tip of her paintbrush. "It doesn't look like a rootin' tootin' pioneer town. It's more like a setting for a Stephen King novel."

"It's a work in progress," he hedged.

He'd given her his best poker face, but as usual, she saw through it. She grimaced at him, letting her chin settle on her palm. "An elephant holding a brush in its trunk can paint better than I can."

She sighed heavily, got up and went over to the soda machine that stood in the far corner. In a few moments she came back with a soft drink for each of them.

They sat side by side on the drop cloth, watching the paint dry and sipping their drinks. It was a companionable silence. Like the old days, he thought. Like coming into sunshine after a bitter winter.

"How does it feel to be home again?" Les asked after a while.

"Not as claustrophobic as I feared. But the women in the family have definitely decided I'm hopeless and need to be taken in hand. Whether I'm willing or not."

"They just want to help."

"The aunts talk so much about fattening me up that I feel like a doomed turkey at Thanksgiving. Mom thinks my physical therapy regimen should mirror Pop's, even though I told her our needs are nothing alike. I hardly know Nick's wife yet, and already she's offered to show me yoga techniques that relieve stress."

Leslie made a choking sound around a mouthful of soda. "Somehow I can't see you…" She broke off and ducked her head. Matt was sure she was hiding a smile as she imagined him in some strange yoga position.

He expelled a little snort of displeasure. "And Addy—God, she's driving me crazy."

"In what way?"

"Every time I turn around she's lecturing me about vitamins or herbal remedies. I keep finding brochures on my bed, which is about as subtle as Addy ever gets."

Leslie grinned. "Your sister's always been health-conscious. Nothing wrong with hearing her out."

"Oh, I do plenty of listening," he complained. "She's lost the power of persuasion, but not the power of speech."

"They love you, Matt."

"I know. But I'd prefer not to be everyone's pet project."

She swung her head quickly to pull her hair over one shoulder. Under the harsh, unflattering light, it had a healthy, mink-brown shine that was prettier than anything that could be artificially created in a salon.

Leslie curled her feet under her, rocking back. "I think it would be wonderful to know so many people care about you. When we were growing up, I always envied you having a big family." Her gaze flicked in his direction. "Burdens just never seem quite as heavy when they're shared."

He thought of all the moments they had shared in the past, times when they had plunged into each other's lives. "Speaking of burdens…"

"Matt," she said in a warning tone. She raked her hand along her hair, then scooped it off her shoulders, that movement of annoyance that always told him when he'd overstepped.

"I know," he said, and held up one hand to forestall her reprimand. "It's the paint fumes getting to me. Delete that, and let me start over." He tried to look sincere. "How is your father?"

She shrugged, willing to be mollified. "He has good days and bad. Luckily, the bad days don't last. I think he longs for company now that Mom is gone. And since he knows I won't stay if he's been drinking, he tries to do better."

Matt gritted his teeth, not trusting himself to speak right away. This wasn't what he wanted to hear. He hated that old man. Hated what he had done to his family. Hated what he had done to Les. As far as Matt was concerned, Quentin Meadows could live on the next continent and it wouldn't be far enough away to suit him.

"How often do you see him?"

"Not as often as I should."

"But probably more than he deserves," Matt muttered.

In a quick, exasperated movement, she tossed down the paint rag she'd been using. "He's my father, Matt. I can't just turn my back on him, no matter what he's done."

"He could have killed you, Les."

She looked away, staring at her soda can as though it were a seer's crystal. This was an old argument between them, still raw and painful, one of the few that was destined never to be resolved.

"Because of you, he didn't," she said, in a hard, steady tone. "And he wasn't himself. You know he wasn't. You're a doctor. You're supposed to have compassion for people." She turned toward him suddenly. "Why can't you have compassion for *him*?"

He knew why, and nothing she said would ever change that. He didn't think he'd ever forget that hot and sticky summer day years ago when he'd gone to pick up Les at the trailer park.

He'd walked right into trouble—a Meadows family fight that had gotten out of control. Les's mother had been weeping and white, cowering in a corner. Her drunken bastard of a husband was in the back bedroom, going after sixteen-year-old Les with a belt for some perceived grievance. The real ugliness that Les had lived with for so long had revealed itself to Matt that day, in that single instant as he had rushed into the room.

Only a week before, he had convinced Les not to run away from home. Things had been edgy in the Meadows household, he'd acknowledged, but they'd get better now that her father had found another job. Her grades had improved dramatically; a college scholarship was within reach. She couldn't blow everything she'd worked so hard for in the last few years just because she'd had yet another fight with her father. Matt wouldn't let her.

But in all that sensible rationale, he had never once imagined a home life like this. Difficult, yes. Unfortunate. But not like this. Never like this.

Everyone had known that Quentin Meadows was a heavy drinker. He'd been injured on one of his construction jobs and had spent a year flat on his back. Drinking had killed his pain, Les had told Matt, but it hadn't killed Quentin's bitterness over the fact that he could seldom hold a job for long and was barely providing the minimum necessities for his family. At one time, Matt might even have felt a little sorry for the man. But all that had disappeared on the day he'd walked into that back bedroom.

Shocked by the violence of his own feelings, Matt

had plowed in, yanked Quentin Meadows off his daughter and knocked him down with one punch. The man was too drunk to get up, so furious that he had turned a rich purple.

Matt himself had been seeing several other colors, including red. With the blood still pounding in his ears, he'd stood over Les' father and told him in a quiet, scorching voice what he would do if the son of a bitch ever, *ever* touched her again.

"You can't forgive him, can you?" Les's voice cut across his memories.

"No."

Slowly Matt began cleaning his paintbrush. He was enjoying this time with her too much to spoil it. Besides, she'd never be persuaded to abandon her father.

"You going to spend Christmas Day with us this year?" he asked. "Or with him?"

Because Les's mother had passed away around Christmas time, her father claimed that he couldn't stand the holidays. Usually, after spending a small amount of time in Quentin's company on Christmas morning, Les came up to the lodge to eat dinner with the family.

"Actually, Dad and I will have to exchange Christmas presents early this year. He's going to spend the holiday at Aunt Tanya's house in Salt Lake."

Matt's eyebrows rose. As well as he could remember, Quentin Meadow's sister wasn't all that fond of him either. "I thought they didn't…get along that well."

Her hopeful smile almost broke his heart. "I've been working hard this past year to get them to mend fences."

"So how did you accomplish that miracle? I remember your Aunt Tanya. She wasn't exactly afraid to give him hell."

"True," Les acknowledged. "But she bought a house last summer that needs a lot of work. *A lot.* And when Dad's feeling pretty good and not drinking, he can be a handy guy to have around. So this way he gets to spend Christmas with family and feel like he's making a contribution as well. It's the perfect solution."

"When does he go?"

"I put him on a bus to Salt Lake next week."

"Good," Matt couldn't resist saying. "Maybe he'll decide he wants to live there permanently."

"Matt…"

"I know," he said, giving her a small smile. "This is usually where we change the subject, isn't it?"

She was quick to nod agreement.

The moody awkwardness that any conversation about her father invariably led to began to dissolve. He busied himself mixing yellow and red paint to make orange. "I spotted a new doctor's office on the way into town. What's the scoop with this Doctor Kline?"

Leslie settled back on her heels. With her hands occupied, she had to use the edge of her sleeve to swipe hair out of her eyes. "He opened his office last spring," she told him. "Young. Not a lot of experience, of course, so he's a little hesitant with patients. Doc thinks we need to give him a chance, send a few people his way. In spite of some people leaving over the years, Broken Yoke is big enough for two doctors."

"Trust Doc to help the competition."

She nudged the strand of wayward hair again. It sifted back immediately. She blew a breath outward to chase it away. "They have an arrangement. I'm supposed to call his office rather than send anyone all the way down to Idaho Springs." She made a disgusted sound, turning her face toward him. "Damn it! Move this hair, will you? It's making my nose itch."

Still on his knees, Matt maneuvered in front of her. She stared straight ahead as he caught the dark filaments. He felt the warmth of her breath against his palm, the heat of her high cheekbones with their sweet curve to the jaw as his fingers swept the strands carefully behind one of her ears.

She had such a fine face, delicate-featured and yet full of character and strength. He'd dated women far more spectacular, but their cold, plastic pretension couldn't hold a candle to Les's natural beauty. He caught himself smiling at her with tender affection.

Suddenly aware that he was staring, he heard her ask, "What's the matter?"

"Nothing. I was just thinking that you've turned into an attractive woman."

She eyed him suspiciously. "Flattery won't get you out of fixing my storefronts with that magic brush of yours."

"I wasn't trying to get out of anything. I was being sincere."

She blinked, and a long, ragged breath slid from her throat. "Oh."

He watched a warm tide of color spread over her cheeks. There was a look on her face he'd seldom seen before: uncertainty. He'd thrown her off stride, left her momentarily speechless.

But he wouldn't take back a single word. He'd made mistakes in his life, ruinous ones. But this wasn't one of them. This was the truth. And if last year had taught him anything, it was that life was too short to leave the important things unsaid.

He wanted to tell her that someday she'd make some lucky fellow a terrific wife. She was smart and resourceful and caring. Had a good sense of humor, too. One could see it in the sparkle of her eyes and in the teasing lift of her lips, in a mouth that almost defied description. That mouth. That very kissable mouth...

When he realized where his thoughts were taking him, he was a little stunned. In all the long, comfortable years of their friendship, they'd unexpectedly trespassed into dangerous territory only once...with very poor results.

Seeing the discomfort on her face, he rescued her— and maybe himself, too—by giving her a cocky smile. "Don't panic. I'm not practicing the art of seduction."

"Then what *are* you practicing?" she asked, giving him a long look.

"I was just thinking that—"

A blast of frigid air swirled into the clinic as the front door opened.

As though she'd been caught doing something she shouldn't have, Leslie jerked away from Matt. He looked over his shoulder and saw that a man had entered the waiting room, so bundled against the cold that his features were indistinguishable.

Les seemed to recognize him, though. She jumped

up and went toward him with a look of absolute delight on her face. "Perry!"

A little too much enthusiasm in her welcome, Matt thought. Stanley hadn't greeted Doctor Livingstone with this much pleasure.

Who the hell is this? he thought. He didn't know this guy. And then Matt remembered the Christmas party at Doc's the other night and suddenly he knew exactly who the man was.

Ah, yes. The boyfriend.

CHAPTER FIVE

PERRY JAMISON'S gloves were the first things Matt noticed about the man. Expensive Italian leather with little scoops cut out across the knuckles. They were way too fancy for this neck of the woods, and, for no reason he could name, that annoyed Matt.

What annoyed him even more was how pleased Les seemed to see Perry. So pleased, in fact, that a little flare of something heated Matt's insides. It felt almost like jealousy—but of course, it couldn't be.

"Hello, angel," Perry said, planting a quick kiss against her mouth. "How's it going? Are you ready to concede defeat and let me hire someone to paint a nice mural for the kiddies?"

She pushed him away playfully. "Absolutely not. Matt and I are so good at this we're thinking of opening up a little business on the side. Come see."

She led him over to the alcove. Matt rose. He wasn't about to keep painting from a sitting position and let Jamison literally talk down to him. He turned toward the two of them as they approached, managing a tight smile.

He had a suspicion that any encounter with this guy

would tax the good manners his mother had instilled in him. His brief conversation at Doc's party had left him with a brutally clear impression—Perry Jamison was rich, influential and a first-class jerk.

And no way in hell could he be Les's idea of Happily Ever After.

Les smiled up at Perry. "You remember Matt D'Angelo from the other night, don't you?"

The man stuck out his hand. "Of course. Nice to see you again." He sounded sincere. And when he looked past Matt to the painting on the wall, his brows rose appreciatively. "Very nice," he said. "I'm impressed."

It would have been a lot easier to dislike the man if that remark had been at all condescending. The picture wasn't Louvre material, for Pete's sake, and a little ribbing was to be expected.

"It's really Matt who's pulled it off," Les said. "I've discovered that I can't even manage a good doodle."

"Of course not," Perry replied. "Doodles are a sign of self-indulgent, unfocused minds. That's definitely not you."

Les was way too enchanted by this man. Her smile poured over him like sunshine. Matt stared at her, wondering when she'd become such an expert at the intricacies of flirting.

"Still," she went on. "I wouldn't mind having *some* artistic ability. I'm reduced to filling in the sky and cleaning brushes."

"You have other talents," he said softly.

Matt watched them, taking an increasing dislike to Jamison even though the man hadn't really done anything to warrant it. Had to be Les's appalling reaction that made him feel this sour.

"So…" Matt had to clear his throat; it felt rusty all of a sudden. "What brings you to town, Jamison?"

"Please. Call me Perry." The man swung his attention right back to Les. "I came to see if you'd like to go to lunch. We could drive over to the Wisteria Inn and have your favorite chicken salad."

Matt shook his head, suddenly feeling perverse. "Her favorite is ham and Swiss on wheat toast."

"Good grief, Matt," Les said with an incredulous laugh as she rolled her eyes at him. "Not since I was *twelve*."

There seemed little reason to continue this conversation. Matt turned and began applying a coat of white paint along the tops of the mountains. Instant snowy peaks. Only the paint beneath wasn't dry, and it bled a little. *Too bad,* he thought. He wasn't being paid to be Monet.

"So what do you say?" Perry asked her.

"I suppose we could take a break."

"Wonderful! Would you care to come along, Matt?"

"Moira's here, too," Les added. "Trying to make some sense of Doc's files. She'd probably like to stop for a while. Aren't you hungry, Matt? We could make it a foursome."

He glanced back over his shoulder, determined not to express any form of emotion one way or the other. "I had a big breakfast. Why don't the three of you go without me?"

Les's lips parted as though she might object, but before she could say anything, Perry pulled her close. "Perhaps later we could talk? Just the two of us?"

"About what?"

"About the two of us spending more time together," he said. The words sounded like a gentle caress. "It's been too long since you've come down to Denver for a real visit."

Not nearly long enough, buddy, Matt wanted to say. But he kept silent, kept painting. Exercising patience and restraint.

It occurred to him suddenly that he and Les were not the people they had once been. She was in his world, but not in his pocket any longer. No matter how well-intentioned, he didn't have the right to tell her how to live her life, and clearly, she no longer wanted him to.

He let his breath move out with slow care, waiting. In spite of his best efforts to eavesdrop, he couldn't catch Les's response to the idea of a visit to Denver. Perry, however, didn't seem to mind an audience. Maybe he thought he needed to let Matt know he'd staked a claim on Les.

"Then let's have dinner tonight," Matt heard him suggest.

"I can't. I'm going to my father's place tonight so we can exchange Christmas presents."

"I'm not crazy about that idea," Perry said, clearly displeased. The tone matched Matt's feelings exactly. It was damned annoying to discover he and Jamison could have common ground after all.

"I wasn't asking permission, Perry," Les said, and Matt heard a note of pique seep into her voice.

"Have you ever met her father?"

Matt realized Jamison was speaking to him. He glanced over his shoulder again. "Many times."

"I find him a little…rough around the edges."

Oh, you're in for it now, Matt thought. Les would make mincemeat out of this guy. He had to resist the temptation to lay down his brush and take a seat in the waiting room, just to enjoy the fireworks. Perry Jamison was a dead man.

"I've already had this discussion with Matt today," Les said in precise little words. "While I appreciate your concern, I'm not sure why either of you feel you can lecture me about my relationship with my father."

Any overt support of Quentin Meadows would be immediately suspect, but Matt felt compelled to take her side, if only to keep from playing on the same team as Perry Jamison. "Les is extremely loyal," he told the man. "Always has been."

Perry frowned. "I simply don't think it's wise—"

Les held up a hand. "Stop. In this case, it doesn't matter what you think. And criticizing him won't get me down to Denver for a visit, Perry."

He was immediately contrite. "Sorry, angel. Let me make it up to you over lunch."

It disappointed Matt no end to see that Perry's "angel" seemed perfectly willing to let him off the hook. She gave him a forgiving smile, then looked at Matt. "Are you sure you don't mind if I go?"

"Not at all," he said quickly. "I'll finish up here and get out of your way." He'd meant those words to come out unconcerned, disinterested, but damned if that last bit hadn't sounded lightly spiced with sarcasm.

Les must have heard it, too. "You're not in my way," she said. "When I get back—"

"Actually, I promised Pop I'd spend time with him this afternoon." He faked a look at his watch. He'd be damned if he'd sit here waiting for her like a poodle dropped off at the vet. "So maybe I'll finish up these mountains and head out. I can always come back another day."

He spoke without looking at her, concentrating on recapping the cans of paint without spilling. He hadn't used his injured hand much all morning and it had stiffened up a little, making it awkward to manage the lids. He could sense both Les and Perry watching him.

"All right," Les agreed, sounding a little hesitant. "We don't have to do it all today." She bent to grab a pot of paint. "Let me help—"

"I've got it, Les," Matt said quickly. The words came out sharper than he intended. He didn't know why he sounded so angry. He wasn't mad at her.

He was torn between wanting her to get the heck out of the clinic and trot off with Perfect Perry, and hoping that she'd tell the guy she didn't have time to indulge in high-priced chicken salad at the Wisteria Inn after all. He didn't know what was wrong with him. He just knew that the easy camaraderie he and Les had shared all morning had been knocked all to pieces.

He finally looked at her. Her forehead was gathered in harsh lines. He might have enjoyed seeing that sudden concern if he hadn't been cursed with a conscience. What was he thinking? Did he really have any right to make her feel guilty about going to lunch with this guy?

He summoned up a smile. "If you're going to beat the lunch crowd at the Wisteria, you'd better get started."

"He's right," Perry said, giving Les the grin of a chess player who had seen his way to a checkmate. She nodded.

Perry pulled her coat and gloves off the pegs near the door. In another moment he had helped her bundle up against the cold. He led her away, and she didn't look back. Just before they went outside, he tucked her against his side. The hard, masculine authority of his arm encircled her waist, and Les allowed it.

The message Perry Jamison sent to anyone watching couldn't have been clearer.

Mine.

SAM D'ANGELO gave his wife Rosa his best smile, even though she was planted in front of the stationary bike in the lodge's small workout room, glaring at him.

"Enough, Samuel!" she said for the third time.

He didn't stop pedaling. In fact, he didn't slow down one bit. He had a keen eye on the bike's digital readout and knew how far he'd pedaled and how long, down to the second. His legs were quivering with exhaustion. Sweat dripped down the sides of his face. But he wasn't about to stop.

"This is ridiculous," Rosa muttered.

"You think that now, but you won't when I'm finally able to carry you up the stairs and make love to you in the honeymoon suite."

"If making love is what you're after, then come to the bedroom now. We don't need the honeymoon suite."

Sam shook his head. "I'm getting up those stairs, Rosa," he gasped out. "By summer I'm getting up them, or I'm going to die trying."

"It's the 'die trying' part that frightens me," Rosa said. She laid her fingers over his on the handlebar. "Will you please stop?"

Matt walked into the room just then. Sam's son had promised to play cards with him before dinner, but that was out now. He knew his limitations well. When he finished this workout, the only moves Sam wanted to make would be to the family den to take a nap.

Matt frowned. "What's going on?"

Rosa turned toward their son. "Will you talk some sense into your father? He's gone long past his usual therapy session today. I've tried to get him to stop, but I'd have better luck trying to open an oyster without a knife." Then, as though making the decision that sterner measures were called for, Rosa swung away from the two men. "I'm calling Doctor Wendell," she threatened, and headed out the door.

"Go ahead and rat me out," Sam called after her. "Up those stairs by summer, Rosa! You hear me?"

Matt drew a deep breath and crossed his arms. "Want to tell me what this is all about?"

Sam pointed toward his wheelchair, which sat within easy reach of the stationary bicycle. "Certain things happened today to convince me that I'm not getting out of this chair fast enough. So I'm changing my therapy routine. Going from thirty minutes three days a week, to an hour, five days a week." He waved his hand impatiently toward his son. "Now get out of my way. I'm trying to catch Lance Armstrong in the Tour de France."

"What things happened today?"

"Nick told me he wants to put in an elevator."

"What's wrong with that?"

Sam narrowed his eyes at Matt. "I know why he wants to spend that kind of money. So do you."

"No, I don't."

"I know you and Nick talk about me. Don't pretend ignorance."

Matt laughed. "Sorry. In this case, I *am* ignorant."

"These are not the answers I want from you."

"Then stop asking the wrong questions. Talk to Nick."

"Don't get cheeky with me, Matthew. It's never too late to cut you out of my will."

When Matt just smiled, Sam stopped pedaling and settled back. He was ready to get off—the bicycle seat was as comfortable as sitting on a bent coat hanger—but he wasn't willing to make the transfer to his wheelchair while his legs were quivering so badly.

"Nick says it's time to upgrade," Sam explained around a harshly drawn breath. "His argument is that no guest wants to trudge up to a third-floor room, that George is getting too old to haul bags up all those flights. But I know darned well it's because of me. He knows I hate not being able to get upstairs anymore. Being cut off from part of my own business."

"So you're upset because he's trying to make it *easier* for you?"

"Foolish waste of good money," Sam complained. "He doesn't think I'm ever going to get out of this chair, that's what." He wagged one finger at his son. "But let me tell you, *he is sorely mistaken.*"

"Pop…"

"If we're putting in any new equipment, it's going to be this."

From his shirt pocket Sam withdrew the flyer he'd printed off the internet and handed it to his son. Matt scanned it quickly.

His brows rose. "An underwater treadmill for the pool?"

"Low impact. Gait training and balance. I'm taking my therapy to the next level. Your mother thinks I'm going to overdo. Women are such timid creatures. Always playing it safe."

"Mom is hardly timid, and she has a point. You need to take things slowly. If you have another stroke or a heart attack—"

This was not what Sam wanted to hear. He pointed toward Matt's hand, the one that son-of-a-bitch robber had shot. "Are you taking things slowly with that?"

"No."

"So then, why should I? You know what I've been turned into around this place? A lighthouse in the middle of the desert—brilliant, but useless. But I'm changing that, as of today."

His son walked over to the stack of towels they kept handy for the guests, pulled one off, then held it out so Sam could wipe the perspiration from his face. Then he leaned against the sidebars of the nearby treadmill.

"Sometimes you don't get to decide those things, Pop," he said slowly. "Sometimes you have to accept your limitations."

"*Ridicolo!* Are *you* accepting? Are *you* quitting microsurgery?"

Matt stared down at the carpet for a long moment, then looked back up. "No. Not unless I'm left with no choice."

"Good. I'd hate to think that fancy college education was wasted."

Since his son had come home for the holidays, Sam had seen just how much that shooting at the diner had changed him.

Of all his children, Matt had been the golden child, the easygoing charmer. He plunged into everything with a ready smile and the confidence of ten men. Taking risks had been as natural as drawing breath for him, because he almost never failed. But now he sometimes seemed paralyzed by physical and emotional exhaustion. It made Sam wince to see it.

He gave Matt a sharp, challenging look. "Why should either of us give in to some cruel fate that dictates we are less than we once were? We can move a mountain if we continue to carry away small stones one at a time. You understand what I'm saying to you, son?"

"All right," Matt said with a slow shake of his head. "But can I talk to Doctor Wendell first? See how he feels about increasing your therapy? You're scaring Mom. You don't want to do that, do you?"

"No."

"Then let me make an appointment for the three of us—you, me, and Mom. We'll talk to the doctor, see if he thinks you're ready for a little more aggressive therapy routine."

"Or I'll get another doctor."

"I suspect Wendell will be glad to write the referral."

Sam nodded sharply. "*Bene.* Now help me get off this thing."

Matt brought the wheelchair close, then reached out to assist Sam off the bike. Even this little bit of help embarrassed Sam. He hated the way his legs shook under him. But he was determined that it wouldn't be like this much longer. Summer, he'd told Rosa. And he meant it.

As soon as he was settled, he said, "I thought you'd be at the clinic all day. With Leslie."

"I was. Until her boyfriend came in and whisked her off to lunch."

"You mean that Jamison fellow? He's pleasant enough, I suppose, but for some reason I don't like him. Watching him with her is like seeing a Stradivarius handed to a gorilla."

"Les doesn't seem to mind. In fact, she seems enthralled. Perry's a successful businessman—"

"Being a man of success is not the same as being a man of value. She'll tire of him soon enough. Besides, she's interested in someone else. She just doesn't know it yet."

Matt looked up, frowning. "Who?"

"Brandon O'Dell."

"O'Dell!"

"He's got his eye on her," Sam said, shifting in his seat. His son's very vocal reaction interested him. "Doc told me Brandon has found a lot of excuses to show up at the clinic. Either he's the clumsiest fool on the planet, or he's trying to get up the nerve to ask her out."

"When did Les become so damned popular?" Matt

asked without raising his head. "When I was living here she hardly dated."

"Well, you haven't lived here in a long time."

His son glanced up at him suddenly. "Did you know her favorite lunch is chicken salad?"

"Why would I know that?"

"Never mind. It's not important."

It was only a moment, but Sam noticed the hardening round his son's mouth, the vertical line between the eyes. A ferocious relief swept through Sam and he laughed. "Blessed *Madonn!* You're jealous!"

"No, I'm not!" Matt almost growled. Then in a voice that shifted into flat control, he said, "I'm just…concerned for her. That's all. I'm her best friend, and I want her to be happy."

"I don't think I understand," Sam said. "Leslie can't be happy liking chicken salad?"

He felt suddenly lighter. Only it wasn't the workout producing this euphoric feeling. It was knowing that, in spite of everything that had happened to his son last year, Matt was ready to begin living again. Taking an interest in something besides the potential damage to his hand and career. This was a wonderful sign. Wait until he told Rosa.

Matt backed away. He spent a few moments gathering hand weights that someone had left scattered on the floor, then straddled the bench press. Finally, he shook his head, as though embarrassed to have mentioned Leslie in the first place. "I don't know…when we were together today, it really felt like the old days. And yet, it wasn't the same. She's different somehow."

"*You're* different. So is she. She's definitely *not* the same person you used to know. She's come into her own over the last few years. She has a good life now, a meaningful one, and someday she'll find the right man to share it with."

That comment got the reaction Sam hoped for. Across the distance that separated them, he could feel his son bristling. He mustn't rush the flowering, Sam told himself. The seed had been planted. He must back off and allow it room to grow.

"I saw her father today," Sam said after a short silence. "I tell you, Quentin Meadows makes me believe in reincarnation. Nobody can become such an *idiota* in just one lifetime."

As much as everyone in the D'Angelo family adored Leslie, they despised her father. Matt would have preferred that she wash her hands of him entirely, and Sam shared that sentiment.

He had grown up living next door to Celeste, Leslie's mother, and had watched his childhood friend beaten down into a frightened, pale imitation of herself over twenty miserable years of marriage. A fatal bout with cancer had seemed like a blessed relief to Celeste, and Sam didn't have a single doubt that she'd deserved that release.

Leslie had a blind spot when it came to that man. The same soft, caring compassion that made her good with patients made it impossible for her to give up on Quentin. But some people couldn't be saved. And Sam, burdened with secrets that Celeste had entrusted to him at the end of her life, had often been tempted to tell Leslie just why she shouldn't bother.

He became aware that Matt was speaking to him. "What?"

"You saw Quentin Meadows today?"

Sam nodded. "That's the other thing that got me riled. We had a few words, none of them pretty. I wanted to come out of this chair and plant my fist in his face. Meadows has never liked me, you know? Always thought I had a thing for his wife—which was his own warped imagination working overtime. He also hated the fact that Leslie spent so much time up here with us instead of home waiting on him hand and foot like her mother."

"Where did you see him?"

"Here, of course. That damned fool Waxman hired him. Meadows still does odd jobs to make money, so next thing you know he was up here busting down the walls for the new pantry your mother wants put in. I sat and watched him. Not exactly mind-boggling work, just hard. But you should have seen the result."

"Not to your liking?"

"Ha! He damned near took out the supports with a sledgehammer. If I hadn't stopped him, Leo would owe us a new kitchen in addition to the tree that dog of his destroyed. Watching Meadows is what made me rethink my therapy schedule. In the old days I never paid anyone to do that kind of job for us. Did it myself. And a darned sight better, too."

Matt grinned. "I suppose you told him that?"

"Of course I did. I said we had words, didn't I? Only I don't know why I bothered."

"The man's a stubborn ass. He'd never listen."

"He *couldn't* listen! Had too much liquor in him to hear a word I said."

An odd expression overtook Matt's features. "Meadows was drunk?"

"I can't honestly say he was drunk, but I smelled booze on him, no doubt about that."

Matt had come off the bench now. The look in his eyes was so severe that Sam felt as though a cold draft had just shimmied down the back of his neck.

"When was this?" Matt asked sharply. "What time?"

"About two this afternoon," Sam told him. "I'm going to call Leo tonight and tell him not to send Meadows again. I'd rather cut that wall down with your mother's cuticle scissors than see him back on this property. He's— Where are you going?"

Sam might as well have been talking to himself. Matt was already out the door.

CHAPTER SIX

Matt hadn't been to Mobley's Mobile Court in years, but as he and Les pulled into the development, he didn't think it seemed to have changed much. Same forgotten landscape. Same trailers that had never been taken off their wheels, dying slowly of a cancerous rust. Same air of neglect and desperation.

Up at the lodge, the snow made everything look magical and new. But here, it seemed reluctant to relinquish its hold and was only a melting, dirty slush that probably hid a multitude of neighborhood sins.

His gut tightened. Les had lived here until she'd turned eighteen. How could anyone feel safe and happy in this environment, where nobody cared about your life because it was clear they'd given up caring about their own?

He slid a glance to the passenger seat, where Les sat staring out her window as they made their way through the deserted streets in the pewter twilight. He could feel the tension radiating from her in waves. The irritation. He knew she was still angry with him, but frankly he didn't care. He was here now, and that was all that mattered.

She carried her head high, a little thrown back. Her

hair was a loose, effortless upsweep, exposing her neck so that she looked elegant and beautifully remote. There had been long spaces of silence between their words.

After that conversation with his father, Matt's heart had been knocking in his chest like a fist trying to find an escape. Knowing Quentin Meadows could be dangerous when he was drunk, Matt had gone straight to Les's house and insisted on accompanying her to her father's place.

She'd balked, of course. But he'd put his rusty college debating skills to good use and finally convinced her. That didn't mean she had to like it. And clearly, she didn't.

He saw her pull her coat closer around her. "Do you want me to turn up the heat?" he asked.

"Does it make any difference what I want?" she said.

"You know, if your father really *is* fine, your bad mood isn't likely to make him feel very comfortable."

She gave an incredulous breath of laughter, as though trying to see a joke that wasn't there. "I wasn't *in* a bad mood until you showed up at my door determined to play Caped Crusader."

"I never played Caped Crusader. Green Hornet, maybe."

"Don't think you can charm your way into my good graces. I'm mad at you."

"Would it help if I apologized?"

"No. It would help if you dropped me off at Dad's door and then went home. I'll ask him to take me back to my house."

He shook his head. "Sorry. No can do."

"I don't care what your father said," Les protested. "He was wrong. Dad's not going to be drunk. He's looking forward to this visit, and he wouldn't jeopardize it."

"I hope you're right. I really do. But just in case he's not, I want to be there."

"He's not crazy about you either, you know? Watching you sit in the corner like some…some chaperone out of an Austen novel is just going to make him angry."

"Tell you what," Matt said. "If we get in there and your father hasn't been drinking—and I mean if he's *stone cold sober*—I'll come back out to the car and wait. That's the only deal I'm willing to make."

She swung her gaze back to the road. Her lips were still drawn in a tight, pale line, but Matt sensed that she didn't *want* to be angry with him. They were, after all, the best of friends, and friends always looked out for one another. They'd been doing it for years, and this time was no different.

"Come on, Les," Matt coaxed. "Do you really think I *want* to be there? I just need to make sure nothing…unexpected happens. For all our sakes."

She was silent as he maneuvered around a patch of black ice that gleamed in the car's headlights. Another few turns and they'd be there.

Finally, he heard her sigh. "All right," she said at last. "I suppose you mean well. It's your delivery that stinks."

Some of the tension in the dark interior of the car dissolved. She was still too quiet, though. Maybe he could make better headway if he changed the subject, got her to thinking about something else.

"How was lunch with Perry?" he asked, since that was something he wanted to know anyway.

One eyebrow flared upward in displeasure, and he knew he'd picked the wrong topic, the wrong approach. She gave him a pained look. "Lunch was…perfect. And that's all I'm going to say on that subject."

He frowned at her. "You used to tell me everything."

"No," she denied with a mysterious smile. "I didn't."

What was that supposed to mean? They'd never kept secrets from one another. But before he could give it any more thought, they were in front of the Meadows' home.

Matt came around the car to help Les out since the edge of the property was treacherous with snow and ice. Taking his arm, she walked gingerly up the driveway, clutching a nicely wrapped Christmas package close against her body. Through the thickness of her coat he thought he felt a tremor run through her. Whether it was from the sharp chill of the night or a sudden bout of nervousness, he couldn't tell.

He inhaled deeply. The air was sharp in the lining of his nostrils, like peppermint. "Nice evening," he said, trying to break the tension.

Evidently polite conversation was off-limits. She didn't even nod. "While you're in there," she said, "you have to promise me—no arguments, no sarcasm, no making faces behind his back. This is our last chance to be together before Christmas, and I don't want you spoiling it."

Now *he* was annoyed. "Damn, Les. You *do* remember that I'm a grown man and not a five-year-old, don't you?"

"Yes, but *do you?*"

He swore softly under his breath again.

"Matt…"

"I promise," he said.

The old trailer had been bullied by weather and neglect over the years. Matt stood beside Les on the front deck, under the jaundiced eye of the porch light, and wondered why Quentin Meadows hadn't made any effort to make the place more respectable. With back problems that tended to come and go, he hadn't held a regular construction job in years, but he could have put some of those old talents to work, couldn't he, when he was going through a good spell? Maybe he'd lost interest after Les had moved out and his wife had died.

Then the door was swinging open, and he was face-to-face with a man he hadn't seen in nearly ten years. A man he'd once punched and threatened in his own home. Les was right; this could be an extremely uncomfortable evening.

"Merry Christmas, Dad!" Les said in what Matt considered an overly bright voice. She encompassed her father in a hug, and they were suddenly shutting out the cold air and stepping into the excessive warmth of the trailer.

Matt stood to one side, sizing up Les's father quickly. He was shorter and thinner than Matt remembered, but he seemed in reasonably good shape at the moment. He was deeply tanned—all those jobs outdoors had taken their toll on his skin. He wore an old but clean shirt and a tie fashionable enough to be Les's influence. His face was beaten by time and too much drink, but he still had a full head of hair. He'd wetted it down to keep it in place, and Matt could see the tiny rows a comb had made as he'd raked it through.

There was no scent of liquor on him, and Matt felt his insides uncurl a little in relief. In that moment he realized just how much he would have dreaded an ugly scenario.

Les touched the sleeve of Matt's coat, smiling at her father. "You remember Matt D'Angelo, don't you, Dad?"

The man's gaze turned on him, but surprisingly, after one hard look and a tightening of his jaw, his features settled into an opaque gray shield of polite withdrawal. He nodded. "I remember you."

But definitely not in a good way, Matt thought. He held out his hand, and the man took it, though there was nothing warm about that quick exchange. It was an uncomfortable truce, but evidently Meadows had decided that, for Les' sake he'd be on his best behavior.

"I was worried about all the ice on the road, and Matt offered to bring me," Les explained. "You know what a terrible driver I am."

Seeming to accept that excuse for Matt's presence, Quentin Meadows made no comment. Instead, he indicated they should take off their coats and hang them on the coat tree near the door. Then he ushered them further into the living room. Matt knew Les would want him to wait in the car, but he wanted to see Meadows in action first, just to be sure. He chose a swivel rocker near the television while Les sat on the couch next to her father.

Quentin went to get them sodas from the kitchen. Matt glanced around the room. Though he and Les had never spent much time here for obvious reasons, he didn't think its bland, functional look had changed much from the old days, though he thought there were a few touches here and there to make it brighter—probably Les's efforts.

There wasn't a single Christmas decoration anywhere, except on top of the television where a small artificial tree sat blinking madly. Beneath it lay one gift.

"I like the music," Les called to her father. A scratchy version of "White Christmas" floated across the room from a worn-looking stereo that looked like a relic from the sixties. "Is that Mom's old tape?"

Meadows returned and passed around sodas. "I dug it out of the closet," he replied as he settled beside his daughter. "Thought you might like it."

"I do," she said, and took a sip from her drink.

Matt remained silent while they talked of inconsequential things. It was stilted, impersonal conversation, almost painful to witness. Both father and daughter seemed awkward and ill-at-ease with one another.

He thought about the way talk flowed around the kitchen table up at the lodge, the easy laughter, gentle teasing and spontaneity he'd been surrounded by all his life. The way a person could be gone for a long time and come back into the D'Angelo family circle as though he'd only stepped out of the room for a moment.

He didn't want to be here. Quentin Meadows was clearly in control tonight. There was no need to stay, to watch and listen to a conversation that had a rehearsed quality, like some bad play.

Matt drained the last of his soda and stood. "I can see

you both have a lot to talk about," he said. "I'll wait out in the car."

Les nodded quickly, but unexpectedly, Quentin Meadows put out a hand to stop him. "It's cold out there. Sit down. We'll only be a few more minutes. No reason for you to miss Leslie's surprise when she sees what I've given her for Christmas this year."

Obviously the man wanted an audience when Les unwrapped his gift to her. Sending a apologetic look in Les's direction, Matt sat back down.

She picked up the package she'd set on the couch and placed it on her father's lap. Matt watched the older man rip into the paper with hands that were nicked and scarred from years of physical labor.

In spite of the fact he looked physically fit, there was something sad about Quentin Meadows. As though all the life had been gnawed out of him. For the first time ever, Matt felt a tiny sliver of something other than hatred dig into his feelings for the man.

Meadows pulled a down jacket from the tissue and held it against his body.

"I hope you like it," Les said with a nervous little breath. "I want you to throw away your old one. It's not nearly warm enough, and if you're going to be working outside for Aunt Tanya, you'll need it."

"This will last me forever," the man said. Then he tipped forward to give Les a kiss on the cheek.

"Have you already packed? If not, I could come over tomorrow and help you decide what to take."

He looked at her as though she'd lost her mind. Matt would have bet Quentin's idea of packing was to throw a few things in a paper sack. Les had told him that he'd never been much for planning ahead.

The man shook his head. "I know what to take. I've taken trips before, you know."

Les looked embarrassed. "Of course I know you can handle it. I just thought I'd offer. Are you looking forward to it?"

"I guess. Hope Tanya's kids don't drive me up a wall."

Matt knew that Quentin had never liked kids. Remembering how insane Christmas morning could be in the D'Angelo household with children around, Matt thought it should be an interesting day for the guy.

As though eager to change the subject, Les held out her hands expectantly. "Okay. So where's my gift?"

Setting the jacket aside, Quentin rose quickly to go to the Christmas tree on top of the television. Les gave Matt a look that practically shouted, "See, I told you he was fine," and he gave her an acknowledging smile to say yes, it appeared he'd been completely wrong. Although not one bit more enjoyable to be around, Quentin Meadows didn't seem to be drunk. Then he was handing her the small gift Matt had noticed earlier.

"I still wish you hadn't done this, Dad," Les said to him, though anyone could see she was ridiculously thrilled. Two bright spots of color lay against her cheeks. "I told you, you need to save your money." She had the paper off the box now and had lifted the lid. She rustled through the tissue. Then her hands stilled.

Matt couldn't see what the box held, but he could tell

by the look on Les's face that she hadn't been expecting it. Her lips parted in surprise. She blinked, as though her vision needed adjustment.

"Oh, Dad," she said in a soft whisper. "You really shouldn't have gone to such expense…"

"You see?" her father said proudly. "I remembered. I'll bet you didn't think I would, but I did."

"I see that."

"Do you like it?"

"Of course I do."

Whatever was in that box, it hurt her. Matt saw it hurt her.

She pulled the item out of the tissue and held it up. "Look, Matt. It's perfume… my favorite scent."

His stomach vaulted as the hope that somehow Meadows had managed to please his daughter settled into cold, black fury. *You damned son of a bitch.*

The gift was indeed perfume—glinting like some exotic, golden poison in its artfully designed bottle.

It might as well have *been* poison. Les was allergic to perfume and always had been.

Evidently, her father had not remembered that fact.

Matt held Les's gaze, wanting to go to her, wanting to walk across the room and shake that old bastard until his teeth rattled. But the look she gave him defeated his anger as nothing else could. Her face had gone very fixed and still, and he could see it flickering in her eyes, that desperate plea for him not to make a scene, to pretend that nothing was wrong.

"It's very nice," he said at last.

Meadows looked happy, and Les looked relieved.

Matt continued to sit there and watch all the sad, injured love in Les flow into meaningless thanks and self-conscious hugs and more quick pecks on the cheek. He couldn't wait to get out of this hot room, this tight, unbearable atmosphere.

When Les finally rose, sweeping the torn ribbon and Christmas paper into the trash bin, he could barely contain his eagerness. She said goodbye to her father with heartrending dignity as Matt pulled on his coat and then helped her on with hers. Meadows, obviously feeling that the evening had gone well, gave him a final smile before seeing them out the door.

Les didn't say anything all the way down the drive. Matt caught her hand in his. She hadn't bothered with her gloves, and her fingers were like ice. He doubted that it was the cold.

They pulled away, and he drove slowly back the way they had come. She didn't say a word from her side of the car. Matt watched the trees and darkened houses float by like boats and thought his heart would break. He could see her thoughts as clearly as if an artist were sketching them.

"Are you all right?" he asked at last, knowing she could not possibly be.

She nodded.

"Les?"

"I'm fine, Matt. Don't make a big deal out of it."

He didn't say anything more. He kept his eyes on the road, thinking that those few words were as icy and impenetrable as the frozen surface of Lightning Lake on the coldest night in winter.

LESLIE HAD THOUGHT that any foolish dream of growing closer to her father had shriveled inside her years ago. She stared numbly out the passenger window as snowflakes spiraled like giddy stars against the glass, waiting for despair to give way to blessed, blank indifference.

It didn't.

She had counted too much on this evening. Hoped too hard. But it wasn't going to work. Tomorrow, and all the tomorrows after that, her relationship with him would be the same imitation, shoddy proposition it had been every day of her life.

Matt pulled into her driveway. The house was dark. She should have left a light on. She'd bought the place a few years ago after she'd finally paid off her student loans. Matt had taken vacation time from the hospital in Chicago to help her move in, building bookcases and stripping wallpaper with her in the kitchen.

Her father had never visited this house, no matter how many times she'd invited him. Not once.

A thick, heavy sense of futility threatened to settle on her heart, but she refused to allow it. She mustn't over-dramatize this. He'd meant well. What did she expect from him, really?

"I'll talk to you soon," she said as she gripped the door handle.

The light from the dashboard reached upward to Matt's hand as it came down on her sleeve. "Les, wait. Stay here. Talk to me."

She swung back to him. "About what?" she asked,

incredulity escaping in a short laugh. She lifted the Christmas present off her lap. "This…this waste of good money was my mother's favorite perfume, not mine. Do you want to tell me how right you've always been about my father? About how he's just a broken-down old fool or that his brain is so pickled that he doesn't even remember that his daughter can't wear perfume? Is that what you want to tell me?"

"No."

She realized that she sounded angry with him when she had not meant to. His calm reply made her feel ashamed and more miserable. She couldn't be mad at Matt.

"I'm sorry. I'm taking it out on you, and that's not what I intended."

"I know that."

The streetlamp on the curb sent light into the car, throwing his features in sharp, midnight shadows. She saw nothing in his face but warm sympathy. "I lived eighteen years in that place," she told him. "How could he have so completely forgotten who I am?"

Matt cut the car's engine and turned in his seat. "He's not a young man," he said. "He got confused. Or maybe he just didn't think it through."

"Don't make excuses for him."

"Remember when I bought Mom that gold bracelet one year for her birthday, and you had to remind me that she only likes to wear silver? I *forgot*, Les. You know guys don't pay attention." He grimaced and reached across the seat to rub the back of one hand along her coat sleeve. "Yes, it hurt your feelings, but he was obviously *trying* to please you."

She gave him an intense look. "Why are you defending him? You don't care about him."

"No," he admitted. "But you do."

"I just wanted…"

She broke off, furious with herself now because she couldn't seem to get a handle on the hot grief that suddenly tore through her insides. She turned her face away, unable to meet his eyes for long.

Matt's hand came against her cheek, stroking lightly. "What, Les? What do you want? Tell me."

Mistrusting her voice, she couldn't speak for countless moments. Then she said, "I just want what other people have. What *you* have…with your family." In spite of her best efforts, there was a betraying wobble in her voice that she hated. She took a deeper breath. "I want my father to know who I am, to care about me the way a real father cares. I've longed for it all my life. This year I've tried so hard to get him back on his feet. Improve our relationship." She turned toward him. "Is that such an impossible hope?"

"No."

"I thought I was making headway, but I'm just fooling myself. Mom always said that Dad never wanted kids, that he's always been a loner at heart. It's no different now. He tolerates my visits. He takes my money when I insist. But he'll never *really* want me in his life. So what do I think I'm accomplishing? Why won't I ever accept that I can't change the past?"

"No, you can't change the past," he said in a quiet, serious way that seemed so unlike the Matt she'd always known. "Believe me, I know that for a fact. But you can continue to work on the future."

She shook her head. "I'm not sure I want to anymore."

"You're just upset right now, but you can't change who you are. You've never been the kind of person to cut your losses and run."

The gentle understanding in his voice made fresh hurt well up inside her. She lowered her head into her hands. "I'm too tired," she said softly.

Her throat clogged with tears—the last of her battered dignity giving way. She hated that, too, because even in the presence of someone as close to her as Matt, she seldom cried. She was horrified when she heard one jagged spasm of sound escape her.

Matt reached across the distance that separated them and pulled her against his chest. "Don't be such a brave fool," he soothed. "Sometimes tears are the only way to get past a hurt and start again."

She stared up at him through a prism of tears. "I never cry."

He hugged her closer, laying his cheek against her hair. "I know. Just rest a minute, then."

As if some control switch in her had broken, she started to cry harder. It was humiliating, but she couldn't stop. "I'm sorry," was all she could find to say. "I'm sorry."

He lifted her chin with his fingers. His eyes were troubled, filled with starlight and such tenderness that her heart melted.

"Please, Les. Don't let him do this to you," he said softly, as though her tears hurt him. "Don't let him break your heart into pieces too small for me to fix."

He held her face in his hands, and his thumbs gently

coasted along her cheeks, wiping away the tears. For a moment, she couldn't seem to move. She felt filled with a strange lassitude.

"Oh, Matt," she said at last on a shaky breath. "Don't you know there are some things that even *you* can't fix?"

A shadowy smile touched his lips. "We'll see. I'm the guy who always wins. Remember?"

She nodded, then burrowed against him, trying to hide in his embrace. Nestled against Matt's warm strength, his hand rubbing with slow, comforting strokes, she thought how good it felt to be in his arms this way, like being in a blissful coma. No one understood her like Matt. No one.

Eventually she stopped leaking tears like an idiotic child. She and Matt grew quiet and still. With the engine off, the car started to lose its heat quickly, but their heavy coats kept the cold at bay. She didn't want to leave this dark cave. She closed her eyes, thinking how easy it would be to fall asleep like this. The easiest thing in the world, cuddled next to Matt in peace and protection.

Just a little longer, she thought. *Just one minute more.*

His fingers came against her temple, smoothing a lock of her hair away, then stroking there, like the touch of warm velvet. She made a soft little sound of pleasure and felt the answering rumble of amusement in his chest, the pounding of his own strong heartbeat beneath her ear.

She felt the whisper of his breath against her scalp, the lightest pressure of his lips against her hair. Something stirred inside her, warm and lovely. His lips were at her cheek, more intense this time, more deliberate. *Nice,* she thought. *So nice. Don't stop...*

He didn't. His lips had moved to at the corner of her mouth now, sending little tingles into her. Her breath died in her throat as her sensitive nerve centers registered swift alarm. Her eyes flew wide.

At first she was too surprised to move or speak. She knew the difference between offering comfort and offering caresses. Somehow in the last few moments the easy intimacy between the two of them had reshaped into something else entirely. Possibilities that they must never entertain if their friendship was to survive.

She made a move to sit up. Matt held her still. "Les…" Her name came out a whisper. "It's all right."

No, it wasn't. She couldn't do this. They must *never* do this. It would be disastrous, like that night on the lake years ago.

She pushed against his chest and, thankfully, he let her go. She gave him one quick glance, afraid to really look at him. Afraid to see the impulse, the wanting that might be mirrored in her own eyes. The lamplight highlighted the upward curve of his small smile, making it seem genuinely wicked.

"I don't know what I was thinking," she said. "We'll freeze out here."

She belted her coat tighter, glad to have something to do with her hands, something to keep her attention focused anywhere but Matt's face. She dug into her pocket for her gloves, then took an excessively long time pulling them on.

Beside her Matt was silent, but she could feel his eyes on her. What was he thinking? Feeling? She couldn't imagine.

She let out a slow breath to steady herself, then turned to face him. He'd swiveled in his seat a little, and now she caught only the vaguest outline of his features.

She saw that he was going to say something, however, so she rushed to speak first. "Thank you for making me feel better about tonight. Your friendship is very precious, and I would never want to lose it."

He was silent for an uncomfortably long moment. Then he said in a quiet voice, "You'll always have it, Les."

CHAPTER SEVEN

AS FAR AS Matt was concerned, the chicken salad was nothing special.

How ironic that he should now be seated in the Wisteria Inn, pushing an artfully presented lump of too much style and not enough substance around a lunch plate. Had it really been only the day before yesterday that he'd listened to Les and Perry make plans to come here?

Although the Wisteria Inn tried to look as though it had been around since the days when silver had shaped the area, the place had been built less than ten years ago. Matt hated the fake historic feel to it, this artificially cozy atmosphere. There was too much lace, too much bric-a-brac. He'd never seen so many flowers jumbled on wallpaper before.

They'd spent a successful morning up at the local Christmas tree farm cutting down a replacement blue spruce for the damaged one in the lobby; it had just never looked right after what was now referred to as "the chipmunk fiasco." The new one was sure to please their father. Kari had suggested someplace different for lunch, the Wisteria—a recommendation from Leslie.

So here they all were. Stuck in Queen Victoria's parlor.

Seated beside him on a lavender banquette, his niece Tessa nudged his arm. "What's wrong with your chicken salad?"

Matt looked up. Nick, Kari and Addy were all watching him, too. "Who said anything was wrong with it?"

"You're poking around like you have to dissect it for biology class."

He set his fork down on the white-covered tablecloth that was anchored with a ridiculous amount of silver. "Everything tastes like flowers."

The women laughed, but Nick's eyes met his and his eyebrow rose, a clear indication that he was concerned and curious.

Matt turned his attention out the window, pretending an interest in a snow-covered garden where quaint paths led nowhere. He shouldn't have let his dissatisfaction show. Sharing a bedroom in their youth, he and his older brother had always been close, and Nick seldom missed a thing.

Luckily Addy took over the conversation, her voice full of enthusiasm. "How would all of you like to go pony-skiing tomorrow? I want to see how Sheba reacts to being around a lot of people."

As a licensed helicopter pilot, Addy had been helping her brother fly guests on tours, an activity Lightning River Lodge had been offering since Nick had come home to manage the family business. But everyone knew that her first love had always been horses, and last summer, she'd finally talked Nick and their father into reopening the stables. Sheba was her latest acquisition, a bay mare with a sweet face and soft mouth.

"What's pony-skiing?" Kari asked.

"Something you won't be able to experience until next year," Nick said. He covered her hand with his. His glance dropped to her rounded stomach where the next addition to the D'Angelo clan presumably lay sleeping.

Kari gave Nick an endearing smile, full of secret meaning. Matt understood what had turned his tough-as-nails brother into such a hopeless romantic. These two had been married over a year now, and they still acted like newlyweds.

"We used to pony-ski when we were kids," Addy explained. "You throw a wagon hitch on a horse, clamp on a pair of skis, hang on to the reins and get towed over the snow."

"Becky and I tried it when we went to Breckenridge last winter," Tessa tossed in. "It's like sledding, only ten times cooler."

"And ten times more dangerous when you get a nag that won't lead," Nick said. He sent a sharpened look to his daughter across the table. "You didn't tell me you and Becky had gone pony-skiing."

Tessa ducked her head and developed a sudden interest in the last of her French fries.

"I think it sounds like fun, "Kari spoke up, sending a grin toward Nick. "Teach me next year, and we'll see who makes it across the meadow first."

As though eager to keep her father's attention focused elsewhere, Tessa said to Matt, "How about you, Uncle Matt? Want to partner up with me tomorrow?"

He noticed that Nick and Addy were silent, watching him. He knew what they were thinking. Controlling hundreds of pounds of horseflesh required dexterity on the reins, strong hands. As a teenager he'd been a whiz at it, even better than their brother Rafe, who'd been the daredevil in the family, but now...

"It's a date," he said, unwilling to consider any other response. "Stick with me, and I'll make you feel like you're hitched to Pegasus."

He listened with half an ear while Addy decided they should all meet tomorrow afternoon at Wolf Creek Meadow. Soon she had whipped out a pad and pen to create a list of friends who might like to join them.

Matt only drifted back into the conversation when he heard Kari ask, "What about Leslie? Can she pony-ski?"

"She and Matt were always a good team," Addy said. She looked at Matt. "Shall I invite her?"

"She's pretty busy with the clinic right now."

"She can't work *all* the time."

"When she's not there, she's with the new guy in her life."

"Great! We'll invite him, too. That should give us a chance to get to know him better."

Matt took a swallow from his water glass to hide his annoyance. He didn't want to get to know Jamison any better. He didn't want him anywhere *near* Wolf Creek Meadow if Les showed up tomorrow.

No, that wasn't true. He'd love to see Jamison pulled behind a galloping horse. Face down, preferably.

"Sure. Fine," he said. Their waitress had been hovering around their table, and to keep any more of his rotten attitude from spilling out, he caught her eye. "Could we get our check, please?"

Addy went back to her list while Tessa and Kari made suggestions. Nick gave Matt an odd, questioning look, which he refused to acknowledge.

He hadn't talked to Les since that night in her driveway. She hadn't made an effort to contact him, either.

At first he'd been a little relieved. He hadn't had a relationship with a woman since Shayla. Hadn't wanted one, really. The guilt he still felt over her death had been with him so long he'd begun to think that the only thing sleep was good for was nightmares. And until his hand was one hundred percent, until his career got back on track...

But that was the terrible thing about desire. It insisted on surfacing when you least expected it, without permission. Putting physical distance between himself and Les hadn't done the slightest bit of good. Neither had all the lectures he'd given himself since the other night.

Truthfully, if Les had been any other woman, he wouldn't have hesitated to flirt with her. He was used to having a certain effect on women. For him, taking risks in a relationship had always been as natural as drawing breath.

But this was *Les*. Practical, logical Les, who never threw off the bonds of caution and common sense. The boundaries of their friendship had been clearly drawn for years. And now, all he could think about were ways to cross them.

He jumped when his cell phone rang. In this sickeningly sweet setting, it seemed a loud, vulgar interruption. His greeting was brisk.

"Is a friendly hello completely out of the question these days?" Doc Hayward asked with a laugh.

"I'm eating lunch at the Wisteria Inn."

"God, that dollhouse? You must be with Leslie since that's her new favorite place."

"I haven't seen her lately." He didn't want to talk about Les. "How's California and Diane?"

"California is the same every day—sunny. Diane, on the other hand, changes moods every hour. I think I'm getting too old to have much patience with pregnant women."

Doc's only daughter was the most precious thing in the world to him. Because Diane was expecting her first child so late in life, Matt knew the older man was anxious about the impending birth.

"Anything I can do to help?" Matt asked.

"Actually, yes. That's why I'm calling."

The waitress had delivered the bill, but in spite of the distraction Matt couldn't mistake the sound of worry in his mentor's tone. "Hold on a minute," Matt said, rising.

There was too much commotion at the table, and he was aware that the others were waiting for him to complete the call. While Nick signed the bill to the lodge's account, Matt signaled he would finish the phone conversation outside.

It was too cold to go outdoors. He stood near the pay phones in the lobby, trying to hear over the noise from the dining room.

"What's the problem?" Matt asked.

"Polly Swinburne went to see our new doctor in town."

For a moment, that information fell across the conversation like a tree downed in the middle of a road. A lot of people in Broken Yoke had come and gone out of Matt's life, but some of them he'd never forget. He swore softly. "Paranoid Polly went to see Kline?"

Doc chuckled. "I see you remember her."

"How could I forget? That crazy old woman scared the crap out of Nick and me as kids. Told us that the evil Soviet Empire had a weather machine and had killed all the sparrows in Birmingham. What the Soviets had against sparrows or Alabama we never found out, but we spent the entire summer building a fallout shelter back behind the woodshed."

"She *is* certifiable, I'm afraid," Doc agreed. "Too bad she also came into all that money."

"So Kline got hold of her?"

"Polly called the clinic about some rash she has on her chest, and Moira sent her over to his office. Before Leslie could call to give the poor man a heads-up, Polly was on the exam table. Next thing you know, she's telling Kline the rash was caused by the milk she's drinking."

"What's wrong with her milk?"

"Haven't you been reading the tabloids? Some terrorist group sprayed radiation on the grass. The cows ingest it, then pass it along to us in the milk. She's sure she has throat cancer."

Matt could just imagine what Kline must have thought. Broken Yoke's richest resident, spouting her latest conspiracy theory. The woman was basically harmless, and healthy as a horse. For years Doc had been putting up with the old hypochondriac. He might even have been fond of her in his own way. "Surely

Kline knew to check her out, pat her hand and then send her off?"

"Oh, he checked her out all right. Found nothing wrong, of course. But as soon as he realized she was nuttier than peanut brittle he tried to counsel her into getting professional help."

Matt drew a sharp breath between his teeth. "Not the best move. How did she take it?"

"I believe she called him the worst doctor since Hannibal Lector. She's contacted all her friends—"

"She *has* friends?" Matt couldn't resist asking.

"Her cash flow ensures a certain amount of loyalty. She's convinced everyone Kline's inept. She doesn't want him treating so much as a sniffle. Leslie says she fielded calls almost all day yesterday from patients."

"So what do you want me to do, Doc?" Matt asked, grinning into the phone. "Convince Polly that Kline isn't evil incarnate? I'm not sure she'll listen to me any more than she listened to him."

"No. I want you to baby-sit the clinic."

A small jolt ran the length of Matt's spine. He leaned forward, as though that could make the telephone signal stronger. "What?"

"I'm supposed to fly back next week right after Christmas, but I want to stay here until Diane has the baby. That's early January. I want you to take the patients who are now refusing to go to Kline's office."

"Why me?"

"Polly's always liked you. She won't raise a fuss over anyone being seen by someone born and bred in Broken Yoke, someone most of them know and a hot-shot surgeon to boot. I can't have them feel as if there's no one to go to, Matt, and Kline's already told me he'd be fine with that idea."

Matt frowned, clenching his teeth. "I can't."

"Why not?" the man asked in his blunt, straightforward way. "Aren't you on a leave of absence from Chicago? It's just a couple more weeks."

"It's not a matter of getting the time off."

"The old stomping grounds not a great enough challenge for a big-city fellow like you?"

"You know that's not it."

A group of diners went past him, loud and laughing. Matt turned away from the noise, knowing that he did not want to be having this conversation when his own family made their way to the front of the restaurant.

"I can't," he said again, when he thought he had privacy once more.

"Because of the hand?" Doc asked, clearly impatient now. "Hell, boy, who do you think you're talking to? I know you. You could handle anything in the clinic with one hand tied behind your back."

Doc had a lot more confidence in Matt's ability than Matt did right now. But then, the older man didn't really know just how badly Matt's life had tumbled away from him last year. How just *thinking* about all the ways things could go wrong put an endless, burning ache inside his gut.

He expelled a long breath and shook his head, as if his friend could see it. "Doc, don't ask this," he said. "You don't know…"

"Then suppose you tell me."

Doc wasn't going to give up, he saw that now. Matt calmed his breathing. When he spoke, he wanted his voice to be perfectly normal, though the blood in his ears threatened to betray him, pounding like a bass drum.

"I can't do it," he said. "Not yet. I don't have enough mobility for anything that requires fine motor skills. Range of movement for the flexor tendons is only about seventy percent right now—"

"I don't need your fine motor skills in the clinic," Hayward interrupted. "Kline's office can deal with cases requiring that. Call him if something comes up that you don't feel comfortable handling."

"Then you don't need me. Leslie can deal with everything else."

"You damn fool," Doc said roughly, and Matt was silent. With the exception of his father, Hayward was the only man who could talk to him this way. "Why don't you focus on what you *can* do, instead of what you can't? I need a doctor who has good instincts. One who knows how to read the truth between what's being said by the patient and what the tests show. Someone who knows when to act and when just to shut up and listen." The older man sighed in exasperation. "It may not offer the glamorous thrill you get from microsurgery, but those are the things that made you a great physician to begin with, Matt."

"Doc—"

"Hear me out. Yes, I want to stay out here with Diane. One way or the other I intend to. But you need to get back to business, and this just happens to be the perfect opportunity. Stop hoping this mountain of difficulty gets removed, Matt, and instead find the courage to climb it."

"Damn! You sound just like Pop."

"That's because I think of you as the son I never had. Always have."

Again, Matt fell silent, both touched by that comment and annoyed that Doc seemed determined to blockade him into a corner. There had to be some other way. This was a bad idea. A very bad idea.

He inhaled sharply, arching his neck back as if a solution might be written on the ceiling. Overhead, a ridiculously ornate chandelier spilled glass drops downward like frozen tears. God, he really did hate this place.

He was completely unaware that he'd sworn softly until he heard Doc's familiar laugh in his ear. "Is that a yes or a no?" the older man asked.

Tessa appeared in the lobby, followed closely by the rest of the family. They were shrugging into jackets, searching for keys and gloves and scarves. In another moment, they'd be beside him.

"All right," Matt said, swallowing the lump of uncertainty that seemed wedged in his throat. "I'll give you a couple of weeks. Then Kline's on his own, because I'm out of here."

"Wonderful!" Doc said, sounding satisfied and relieved. "I'll get in touch with Leslie and have her fill you in. She'll be delighted."

But later, when they were driving home, Matt wondered just how "delighted" Les was likely to be. Working side by side. Face to face.

The real question was—what had those few moments in his car the other night done to their relationship?

ONCE THEY REACHED the lodge, Addy, Tessa and Kari left Matt and Nick to get the tree off the top of the company van. Matt began unknotting the ropes that held the tree down on one side, while Nick tackled the other.

"You all right?" Nick asked, catching Matt's eye.

"Yeah. Why?"

"You seemed a little quiet on the drive home. Problems with Doc?"

"Not really." Matt explained, that he'd be staying a little longer than originally expected so that the clinic would have a doctor available until Doc Hayward returned from California.

"That ought to make Mom and Pop happy. They like having you home. I don't think you realize just how worried they are about you."

"I know they mean well, and I'm not trying to shut them out." Matt frowned. "It's just that I'm not a kid anymore. I can handle my own problems."

Nick had his side of the rope undone, and pulled it from under the tree. "I don't think they doubt your ability to manage your life, Matt. I think it's more the unexpected, uncomfortable realization that you might actually *have* problems like the rest of us."

"What's that supposed to mean?" Matt asked. He was becoming frustrated because the knot in front of him was so intricately tied that he couldn't find an opening to loosen it.

"Hell, they're used to Addy's mischief and Rafe's

wild ways. Even *I* gave them their fair share of gray hairs. But you…" Nick shook his head. "Boy wonder. The overachiever who could do no wrong. The darling of every teacher. I don't think you ever gave anyone a moment's worry. You've always seemed to lead a charmed life. Now suddenly, things are a little different."

"They won't be for long," Matt said in a determined tone. He was annoyed. His hand was stiff after the workout he'd given it this morning and wouldn't cooperate.

Nick came around to his side of the van and reached for the rope. "Let me get it," he said.

"I can do it."

"Stop being an ass," Nick told him without heat. "I'm not going to stand out here in the cold forever just so you can prove you don't need anyone's help."

Matt swung away from his spot near the front door, and settled back against the fender. He massaged his hand, trying to work more feeling into it. "Damned thing pisses me off sometimes when it refuses to do what I want."

Nick grinned at him. "Not used to that, I imagine."

"No, but I suppose I might have to *get* used to it. Find a specialty that doesn't rely quite so heavily on fine motor skills."

His brother gave him a close, sideways look. "You think it might come to that?"

"I don't know, Nick. I just don't know. Microsurgery is what I know and do better than anything. Honestly, I can't imagine what I'll do if it's beyond me now."

Immediately he was sorry he'd said anything. Every morning he turned his best face to the world, put on a stoic smile and hoped no one guessed how jittery he was inside about the future. But sometimes he couldn't stop his fear from spilling out. He wanted to tell Nick to forget what he'd said, to ignore it, but he was suddenly finding his throat unmanageable.

His brother stopped working on the rope and turned to face him. "Do you remember that summer when Pop took us on that hiking trip up Mount Winnona?"

Matt nodded, wondering where Nick was going with this. "Sure. I had a new camera and thought I was going to be the next Ansel Adams."

"Probably would have if you'd set your mind to it. But do you remember tracking that little herd of mountain goats, so you could get all the pictures you wanted?"

"Yeah."

"Then you should remember that one of them was missing a front leg. We felt sorry for it until we saw just how well it managed. It left us scrambling, I recall. Never missed a rock, never fell behind. It kept up with all the other goats just fine."

Matt grinned. "Is there a point you're trying to make here?"

Nick shrugged, his gaze direct. "My point is, that goat adjusted and did what it had to do to survive with the others. You will too, Matt. Whatever the results are with your hand, you'll find the way to make it all work out."

Matt nodded and ducked his head for a moment. It wasn't like his brother to give pep talks. Marriage to Kari was definitely mellowing him. The vote of confidence was unexpected, and Matt was touched.

"Besides," Nick continued. "You have one big advantage."

"I'm smarter than that goat?"

Nick snorted. "Well, I'm hoping that's the case," he said. "But in addition to that, don't forget, no matter what happens, you have the family behind you one hundred percent. You can't get any stronger support than that."

CHAPTER EIGHT

LESLIE HAD MADE the drive down to Denver to visit Perry because she had run out of excuses not to. She wasn't really sure why she hadn't come before now. He was generous and attractive, a man of means who could also be surprisingly down to earth. He was probably one of the few men she'd ever meet who could actually turn a woman's fanciful dream into a reality. It would be foolish to pass up the opportunity to further his interest.

So why couldn't she muster any enthusiasm?

After treating her to an expensive, leisurely lunch at Cherry Creek Country Club, Perry had brought her to his architectural firm's latest project—a thirty-thousand-square-foot mansion being built on ten pristine acres near Boulder. He seemed determined to give her the "grand tour."

Right now the mansion resembled a massive skeleton, nothing more than two-by-fours, sawhorses and sheets of dusty plastic. But when it was finished, it would be an ostentatious wonderland with a movie theater, a musician's mezzanine overlooking the dining room, two glass elevators, and probably more stained glass than Notre Dame.

Leslie knew she was supposed to be impressed—she tried to mouth the appropriate sentiments of appreciation—but she couldn't help thinking there had to be better ways to spend so much money.

She had never been afraid of heights, but climbing a staircase that was little more than fancy scaffolding made her stomach swoop and dive. She and Perry had nearly reached the third floor, and the stairs seemed to drop away into an eerie void. Without realizing it, her hand tightened on his.

He looked at her, offering a smile meant to reassure. "Don't worry. It's perfectly safe. And the view will be worth it."

He tucked her hand into the crook of his arm and pulled her close. This was not the reaction Leslie had hoped for. She wished he'd led her downstairs instead, where she could have admired this monstrous salute to someone's ego from the warm safety of the car.

Impossible to say that to Perry, of course.

He pulled her into one of the rooms, an area nearly as big as her entire house. "This will be the master suite," he told her, and led her to one of the windows that had been framed-out. Though it was cold enough to make Leslie glad she'd worn her warmest coat, sharp afternoon sunlight poured through the hole where glass would soon be placed.

"What do you think?" Perry asked, gesturing out the opening.

To take advantage of the view, the house had been situated on the property's highest point. From the master bedroom, both the city and the foothills were visible—a patchwork quilt of green and brown and white. In the distance, Mount Evans rose sheer and stately. Even in these stark, cold days of winter, there was a certain beautiful purity to the landscape.

This time she could be honest. "It's spectacular."

That seemed to make him happy. He pointed out the window again. "Can you see I-70 in the distance?"

The interstate winding out of Denver and into the mountains was no more than a pale ribbon. She could just make out cars traveling along it, glinting in the afternoon sunlight like schools of silvery fish. She nodded.

He draped his arm around her shoulder, pulling her close. "Sometimes when I'm up here, I look out there and think...in an hour I could be with Leslie. I could see what she's up to right now." His fingers caught her chin, lifting her face. "I often wonder what you're doing when you're not here beside me."

Leslie resisted the claustrophobic urge to escape his hold. She laughed lightly. "Lately, what I'm probably up to is sorting through Doc's files, trying to figure out his crazy system. You aren't missing a thing."

He frowned. She knew instantly that he had wanted a different response, perhaps some indication that she often felt the same desire to be with him. But that would have been a lie, and she couldn't let him believe it.

In some ways she wished she could, because loving a man like Perry would have been so much easier and safer than suffering through the bewildering emotional quagmire she'd found herself in lately.

Visiting him hadn't been her only motive for leaving Broken Yoke for the day. Her nerves were a jumbled mess. The night before she'd been unable to sleep and had awakened this morning desperate to find some measure of peace, some sort of distraction. Annoyed and frustrated with herself, she had decided that what she really needed was to put all thought of Matt D'Angelo behind her.

If only it was that easy.

How could she spend the day with Perry, who seemed determined to please her, who was charming and considerate, and still be so unmoved? It was an amazing thing to be wanted by a man like this, so why should he stir no more than feelings of friendship in her? It was frustrating. It was unfair to Perry. And that kind of insensitive behavior was completely unlike her.

But every thought, all memory, centered on those few moments in the darkened interior of Matt's car. She tried to reject the possibilities, to convince herself that she had misinterpreted everything.

And found that she could not.

She had always been the type to face the truth, no matter how unsettling. Nestled against Matt's side, she had felt him wanting her. She had sensed the current flowing between them, known the exact moment when his touch had no longer been one of comfort, but had changed into something new, leaving her mouth dry with panic. Those moments had seemed so impossible, had happened so fast. Was it any wonder she was confused?

Later that night, she had refused to turn on the lights in her house, refused to change clothes or make coffee. She had just sat in the living room, feeling dazed and vulnerable, bathed in shadow, trying to make sense of everything. But there had been no easy answers—all her resources had failed her in the end. All instincts of self-preservation had refused to rise within her.

Now she disentangled her fingers from Perry's, eager for an excuse to put distance between them. She found one. "That's going to be an awfully big skylight."

"The owner's an astronomy buff. He wants to be able to look at the stars from his bed. Why do you do that?"

She stopped staring upward and turned toward him. "Do what?"

"Change the subject whenever the conversation turns to us."

"I wasn't aware that I did," she said, embarrassed that he had seen through her efforts to distance herself. "But if I do, I suppose it's because it makes me uncomfortable."

Perry shifted, clearly unhappy with that explanation. He tilted his head at her. "*I* make you uncomfortable?"

"I didn't say that. I said the conversation makes me uncomfortable. The implication that there is an 'us.'"

"Isn't there?" he asked. "I've certainly been working toward that the past few months. I thought you were, too."

"Why do either of us have to *work* toward anything, Perry? Why can't we let things develop naturally over their own course and time? What's wrong with just dating, being friends?"

He came across the distance that separated them. Somehow Leslie kept from stepping away, though she wanted to when she saw the battle-ready tension in his face.

His hands cupped her shoulders. "I'm not looking for more friends, Leslie. Don't you know how much I've come to care for you? Do you think I brought you here simply to see what fine work my company is capable of?"

"I'm not sure why you brought me here."

His fingers stroked against her back. "I wanted you to realize…the possibilities. You don't belong in a one-horse town like Broken Yoke. You were meant to be living another life, and I can give it to you."

She shook her head. His eyes were so intense that a lump of misery rose in her throat. How little he understood what was important to her. "Material wealth isn't an issue for me, Perry. The right man doesn't—"

"Let me be the right man, angel."

She exhaled wearily. "It's not that easy."

"It can be," he whispered against her ear.

He pulled her closer, placing his lips against hers, and she did not try to stop him. His kiss tasted sweet and tender and slightly desperate. Her stomach fluttered for a moment. She wanted her body to bloom under his touch.

When it didn't, when she knew she could not pretend, she pulled her mouth away, feeling wretched and a little foolish. Perry's kiss could not erase the image of Matt from her mind. It did not make her heart jump with excitement. There was no desperate greed for more, as there had been with Matt.

Oh, Perry, she thought sadly. *I'm so sorry.*

They stood there for a while, as though suspended. When Leslie finally looked up at him, she thought she could read disappointment in his eyes.

"Well… Clearly the earth didn't move for you just now."

The temptation to comfort him was compelling, but, his statement being true, she found no answer.

He grimaced. "I have to admit, I'm not used to such a lukewarm response."

"You know it's not—"

Incredulity escaped him in a short laugh as he put up a forestalling hand. "God, don't make it worse by offering explanations or my ego really will be shredded. This doesn't mean I'm giving up, you understand. I didn't get where I am in life by letting small setbacks defeat me."

Leslie touched her fingers to his cheek, giving him a regretful smile. "You're a good man, Perry. You've been wonderful to me. But you can't create something that isn't there."

Determination suddenly lit his eyes. "We'll see," he said. "When I first saw this place, it was nothing but vacant land, you know? Two other companies turned the job down because the demands seemed too impossible. But I'm a man with vision."

"Perry—"

He stopped her, shaking his head. Then he caught her hand. She sensed that, for now, he was eager to put intimacy behind them. "Come on. Let me show you what else I can accomplish when I set my mind to it."

WEATHER-WISE, the next day couldn't have offered better conditions to pony-ski. It was one of those afternoons that sometimes leak out from the tight hold of winter, cold but not punishing, the air crisp but touched with warmth.

There'd been another dusting of snow overnight. Wolf Creek Meadow lay as smooth and pretty as cake frosting, its surface unmarred by even the smallest tracks of wild animals. The sun sparkled so brightly on the fresh powder that Matt's vision vibrated if he stared at it too long.

Addy had done a great job. She'd stacked blankets, snacks and thermoses of coffee and hot chocolate in Lightning River's van, then trailered Sheba and two of the other horses to the meadow. All three were outfitted with long lead reins for the drivers and longer tow lines for the skiers. She'd even added jingle bells to their harnesses, which gave the party a festive, holiday touch.

Pony-skiing was pretty much like sleigh-riding, without the sleigh. Two sets of reins were attached to the horse, one for the driver to control the animal's movement, a second set to tow as many as four skiers. No poles were used.

Because they had the most experience and were the better skiers, Nick, Addy and Matt were designated the drivers, which meant they skied up front. Tessa had invited Becky and a few other kids from school. Addy and Nick had each invited couples as well.

Unable to participate, Kari put herself in charge of the refreshments. Matt noticed her watching enviously from the sidelines as the skiers went gliding past. Nick took so many breaks to keep her company that everyone teased him unmercifully.

Les didn't show up, and neither did Perry Jamison. Matt resisted the temptation to ask Addy if she'd heard from either of them. If Les wanted to avoid him, there wasn't much he could do about it. Having agreed to work at the clinic, he would run into her sooner or later.

Instead of brooding, he concentrated on driving Sheba, making sure that he stayed upright on his own skis and towing the others safely around the meadow. Horses could be unpredictable, but the mare seemed cooperative enough. She tended to challenge the other horses when they came too close, flattening her ears and setting her head, so Matt stayed focused on holding her back.

Surprisingly, his bad hand didn't fail him. Though there were times when he felt the ache and strain all the way through his ski gloves, his fingers remained strong and responsive. Once, he was even able to manage re-threading Sheba's narrow belly band, which required the kind of dexterity he hadn't thought he possessed anymore.

The hours shaded into one another. He was tired, but a pure zest of satisfaction filled him with renewed energy every time someone came up for a ride.

After towing Tessa half a dozen times, Matt brought Sheba to a halt near Kari on the sidelines. They glided to a stop, then pulled out of their skis so they could walk freely. He tied the mare to the hitching post they'd fashioned out of a fallen tree. The animal breathed harshly, warm air streaming out of her flared nostrils.

Tessa joined him. She'd pulled off the protective helmet and goggles her father had insisted she wear. Her cheeks were bright from the cold and girlish pleasure.

"That was so cool, Uncle Matt. You're a better driver than Dad."

"Don't let your father hear you say that," Kari said as she approached them. She held a cup of coffee toward Matt. He took it gratefully, peeling off one ski glove to let the warmth bathe his fingers.

"He just won't go fast enough," Tessa complained.

The three of them looked toward the meadow. At one end Addy pulled a line of skiers around the far curve, creating a slingshot effect that sent the high, sweet sound of excited laughter echoing over the snow. Nick, skiing behind a pinto gelding and towing Becky, headed straight across the center. He was giving the girl a decent-enough ride, but hardly thrilling.

Matt smiled. "Nick's always been the cautious, over-protective one in the family. Big-brother syndrome."

Tessa turned back to Matt. "Is it true you once used a dead tree for a mogul and had to get three stitches in your chin?"

Matt shook his head, remembering that day. The deadfall had been significant that year due to severe storms, and the snow-covered trees made pretty tempting ski jumps. "That was your Uncle Rafe, not me. Even *I* know better than to try a stunt like that."

"I hope to meet Rafe one day," Kari said, taking a sip from her cup. "The family doesn't talk about him much."

Matt nudged Tessa. "Here come your dad and Becky. Why don't you see if he'll take the *two* of you around this time? Tell him you want to do a figure eight. Tell him I said to stop driving like a girl."

Tessa nodded excitedly and trooped away. A few

minutes later, the trio flew past them, knees slightly bent as they maneuvered the rutted snow. Nick waved at his wife as he went by, then gestured wildly toward his head. "Put your hat back on," he shouted.

Kari gave him a thumbs-up and ignored him. She grinned at Matt. "What a tyrant. I suppose he thinks I haven't got enough sense to know when my head gets cold."

"He worries about you and the baby."

"I know. It drives me crazy sometimes." She placed a hand against her stomach, smiling down. "Kinda nice, though, to know someone cares so much."

Their eyes met in a moment of complete understanding. Matt had a sudden, clear image of Nick and Kari's future, linked by years of small intimacies and gentle laughter. Even the sorrows would be shared with mutual trust, respect and understanding.

"I don't know what magic you've got, Kari. But I haven't seen my brother this happy in years. He's a lucky guy."

"Not half as lucky as I am to have found him," she said, and he watched her cheeks turn pinker. She swung her attention to the meadow for a few moments, then looked back at him. "So what's the deal with your brother Rafe? He seems to be the mystery man in the family."

"Nothing too mysterious about it, really. Rafe and Dad never got along, so Rafe decamped years ago and hasn't been back since. Don't most families squabble sometimes?"

"I can't imagine the D'Angelo family having that

kind of feud. Certainly nothing serious enough to keep Sam and one of his sons apart for years."

Matt's brow lifted. "You *have* met my father, haven't you?"

Kari laughed and ran her gloved hand down Sheba's dark neck. "Sam can be unreasonable and tough at times, but you know what I mean. Family is the most important thing in the world to him. To your mother, as well."

"True. Unfortunately, it's not the most important thing to Rafe, and until it is, we probably won't see him back here."

"Doesn't anyone ever talk to him?"

"Addy does, but he just barely communicates with her."

He watched his sister-in-law's expression turn sad. But he knew there was nothing to be done. Rafe had always been a stubborn cuss, and their father…well, no one could talk sense into him when he got in one of those moods. And with Rafe, that mood had lasted about twenty years.

So many years gone. Years neither of them will ever get back, Matt thought. Life had a way of escaping from a person. He knew suddenly, and with vivid certainty, that he couldn't allow any more time to be lost between him and Les. Whatever their relationship was—*or wasn't*—they needed to find out.

He walked around Sheba, checking harness buckles and repositioning lines that had twisted.

"How are you doing today?" Kari asked, glancing toward his left hand. Then, as though he might be offended, she added, "I mean, the day's getting colder, and I know how the chill can cut right to the bone sometimes."

Matt lifted his hand and wiggled it. "It's getting a

heck of a workout, but that's a good thing. Don't worry. It always lets me know when I need to let up."

"I'm sure it will be just like new in no time," Kari replied. As soon as she said it, she looked embarrassed. "I'm sorry. I'll bet people tell you that constantly, trying to be ridiculously upbeat."

He let his arms rest on Sheba's back as he smiled at her. "Yeah, they do. But here lately, it doesn't seem to bother me as much as it used to."

"Maybe that's because you're really starting to believe it yourself."

"Maybe," he said.

Kari looked past him, waving suddenly. "Here comes another customer for you. Looks like Leslie was able to get away after all."

He turned, his heart leaping stupidly.

Les was crunching across the snow, an old pair of skis he remembered from years ago perched on one shoulder. She was trim and sleek in a black ski bib and blue-striped jacket. A blue woolen hat the color of heaven covered most of her hair. Wraparound sunglasses made her look as worldly as a movie star.

"Hi," she greeted Kari and gave him a quick glance as well. "Addy left a message on my machine yesterday saying this was where the action would be today. Am I too late to catch a few trips around the meadow?"

"Of course not," Kari said.

The two women chatted briefly. Les waved toward the others out on the snow. Matt wondered if it was only his imagination that she seemed slightly wary of him. He gave her a long, speculative appraisal through his

An Important Message
from the Editors

Dear Reader,

If you'd enjoy reading romance novels with larger print that's easier on your eyes, let us send you TWO FREE HARLEQUIN SUPERROMANCE® NOVELS in our NEW LARGER-PRINT EDITION. These books are complete and unabridged, but the type is set about 25% bigger to make it easier to read. Look inside for an actual-size sample.

By the way, you'll also get a surprise gift with your two free books!

Pam Powers

Peel off Seal and
Place Inside...

LARGER-PRINT
FREE BOOKS
EDITION

THE RIGHT WOMAN

she'd thought she was fine. It took Daniel's words and Brooke's question to make her realize she was far from a full recovery.

She'd made a start with her sister's help and she intended to go forward now. Sarah felt as if she'd been living in a darkened room and someone had suddenly opened a door, letting in the fresh air and sunshine. She could feel its warmth slowly seeping into the coldest part of her. The feeling was liberating. She realized it was only a small step and she had a long way to go, but she was ready to face life again with Serena and her family behind her.

All too soon, they were saying goodbye and Sarah experienced a moment of sadness for all the years she and Serena had missed. But they had each other now, and that's what

She held

Printed in the U.S.A.
Publisher acknowledges the copyright holder of the excerpt from this individual work as follows:
THE RIGHT WOMAN Copyright © 2004 by Linda Warren. All rights reserved.
® and TM are trademarks owned and used by the trademark owner and/or its licensee.

YOURS FREE!
*You'll get a great mystery gift with
your two free larger-print books!*

GET TWO FREE LARGER-PRINT BOOKS!

YES! Please send me two free Harlequin Superromance® novels in the larger-print edition, and my free mystery gift, too. I understand that I am under no obligation to purchase anything, as explained on the back of this insert.

PLACE FREE GIFTS SEAL HERE

139 HDL D4AW   339 HDL D4AX

FIRST NAME / LAST NAME

ADDRESS

APT.# / CITY

STATE/PROV. / ZIP/POSTAL CODE

**Are you a current Harlequin Superromance® subscriber
and want to receive the larger-print edition?**
Call 1-800-221-5011 today!

▼ DETACH AND MAIL CARD TODAY! ▼

(H-SLPS-03/05) © 2004 Harlequin Enterprises Ltd.

The Harlequin Reader Service™ — Here's How It Works:

Accepting your 2 free Harlequin Superromance® books and gift places you under no obligation to buy anything. You may keep the books and gift and return the shipping statement marked "cancel." If you do not cancel, about a month later we'll send you 6 additional Harlequin Superromance larger-print books and bill you just $4.94 each in the U.S., or $5.49 each in Canada, plus 25¢ shipping & handling per book and applicable taxes if any.* That's the complete price and — compared to cover prices of $5.75 each in the U.S. and $6.75 each in Canada — it's quite a bargain! You may cancel at any time, but if you choose to continue, every month we'll send you 6 more books, which you may either purchase at the discount price or return to us and cancel your subscription.

*Terms and prices subject to change without notice. Sales tax applicable in N.Y. Canadian residents will be charged applicable provincial taxes and GST.

lashes and decided she mustn't be *too* angry with him for the other night. She was here, wasn't she?

"Where's Perry?" he asked when Kari headed toward the van to get a fresh cup of coffee.

She turned toward him at last. "In Denver, I imagine," she said in a cool tone that indicated there would be no further explanation. She flicked a glance toward Sheba, noting Matt gathering up the lead lines. "You driving?"

"Yep. Think you can hang on?"

"I don't know. The meadow looks like crud."

"Should have gotten here early if you wanted champagne powder."

She dropped her skis to the snow so that she could snap into them. He came around Sheba to offer a supporting arm, and surprisingly she took it. "I almost didn't come at all," she said. "I haven't skied much in the last couple of years, and I'm a little rusty."

He grinned at her. "So we're going to pretend *that's* the reason you almost didn't come?"

"Am I in the habit of pretending?"

"No. Not until recently."

He watched her throat work as she swallowed. He wished he could remove her sunglasses, but he suspected they served a greater purpose than just protection from the sun. Maybe he hadn't been the only one trying to teach his fantasies to behave the last couple of days.

"Come on," he said, helping her glide to a spot that offered deeper snow. "I promise to give you an easy ride."

"No whipping me in the curves."

"You'll think you're in a rocking chair."

"No galloping."

"God, why use Sheba at all then? We could probably *walk* faster."

"I mean it. Not until I find my legs."

"Agreed," he said, measuring out a good length of the
tow rope, then placing it in her hand. He motioned toward a small stack of colorful, battered helmets. "Want
a brain bucket? We brought them for the kids."

Her lips twisted in displeasure. Matt realized that
he'd become fixated on the shapes her mouth made
when she spoke. "Just drive," she told him. "I'll yell if
I want to go faster."

"Yes, ma'am."

Positioning Sheba ahead of them both, he snapped
into the bindings of his own skis. He was only ten ski
lengths in front of Les, but the distance seemed far
greater.

He glanced back. "Remember, if you don't want to
lose some fingers, don't wrap the rope around your
hand. And if you think you're going to fall, just let go.
I'll come back around for you."

Les nodded, looking as serious as a graduation photograph. He wished he could be beside her, but even
a horse as agreeable as Sheba needed someone to set
the pace.

"Get up, Sheeb," Matt called, and snapped the reins
along the mare's flank.

The animal responded with a snort and leaped forward. Matt sent a quick look back to make sure Les
hadn't gotten jerked off her feet, as often happened if the
person being towed wasn't prepared. She nodded, indicating she was fine, and he set Sheba into a smooth trot.

It wasn't long before he heard Les's whoop of excitement. He smiled, knowing she was feeling that exhilarating first shot of ice crystals against her cheeks. He knew how that felt. Like flying through a meteor shower. Pure joy.

They passed Nick and his team in a blur, then Addy's little group. Sheba tried to move into a gallop, but Matt held her back. Behind him he could hear Les calling out hellos as though they'd all gone out on a leisurely Sunday drive.

The meadow was like a huge, round bowl, and after circling it a few times Matt wondered if Les was ready to take a break. The snow was rutted and hampering in places. Tomorrow they'd all feel the beating their knees and legs were taking.

He glanced over his shoulder. "Ready to rest a while?" he called.

"No!" she shouted back. "More!"

He flicked the reins again. The harness bells increased their jingling as Sheba went quickly into a canter. Matt took one of the turns faster than he had the last time. Les propelled out to the side and almost ahead of him for a moment before she dropped back, laughing in delight. The meadow's boundaries were lost under snowdrifts, but he recognized one of the broad cross-country skiing trails jutting off to his left, its white terrain unblemished and deep. Featherbed fluff, the pros liked to call it.

He pulled Sheba onto it, and suddenly they were gliding through an enchanted kingdom of pungent evergreens that had been transformed into avenues of white castles. Matt's arms ached with the effort of keeping the mare on pace. The fingers of his bad hand cramped, but he refused to stop. It had been years since he'd explored any part of D'Angelo property. Living in the deep urban canyons of Chicago, he'd forgotten how beautiful and wild this land could be.

He was about to check on Les again when he realized the tow rope had lost tension and now bounced freely along the trail. He looked back to see that she was down, nothing more than a black smudge against the snow near the spot where they had left the meadow.

"Les!" he shouted as he jerked Sheba to a halt, then swung her in a tight turn.

Les didn't answer, but he saw her arms wave back and forth against the sunlight.

He brought Sheba to a halt beside her and slipped out of his skis to plunge through the snow that separated them. He went to his knees.

"Are you all right?" he asked, whipping off his gloves. "Are you hurt?"

She shook her head because her breath came in harsh gasps. "I lost…my focus."

He sank back in the snow, relief making his heart buck. A wandering sunray flashed on his glasses, obscuring his vision. He stripped them off, then reached down to remove hers. She looked up at him, completely lucid, her eyes sparkling.

"Thank God," he said. "I thought you'd hit a tree or something."

She lay stretched on the snow, breathing hard. "You maniac. Why didn't you warn me you were going to jog

off the course like that? I knew I couldn't trust you."
Then she grinned. "Can we try that again?"

He shook his head. "Not until my heart gets back in
my chest. I thought I'd killed you."

"It will take more than that to get rid of me," she said
with a gasping laugh.

He allowed himself a quick check of her features.
Those lips—had they always been the kind to set a
man's pulse leaping? He put his hand against her cheek,
brushing away ice crystals. "What makes you think I'd
ever want to get rid of you? I can't imagine a life without you in it."

She took hold of Matt's hand, stopping him before
he could stroke his fingers across her chilled flesh. The
silvery isolation around them suddenly quivered with a
slight, but perceptible change. There was that vibration
between them again. This time he welcomed it.

And wanted more.

"Help me up," she ordered, and she hardly seemed
to have enough breath to utter the words. "The snow's
seeped under my bib."

"I know how to warm you."

Before she could keep him from it, he stretched out
beside her, nearly over her, so that their faces were only
inches apart and he felt the soft, warm flow of her breath
against his cheek. Her body beneath his was delightful,
and he went still. So did she.

The moment stretched to the far side of friendship and
beyond. He placed his hands against her forehead, stroking
away the stray hair that had slipped from beneath her hat
and fallen across her brow. When she didn't protest, he

took his forefinger and brushed it with a whispery light touch across her lashes, down to the corner of her mouth.

She stirred then. "Matt, don't—"

"Why?"

"I don't want things to change between us." Her words sounded like dream-induced thoughts.

He smiled at her gently. "Sweetheart, they already have."

Matt knew exactly what he wanted. He wasn't going to spoil anything with reason or logic. Hell, logic had been surrendered long ago.

He lowered his mouth to her lips. They remained tightly sealed, offering no more reception than cold marble. "Let me, Les," he said, smiling at her with lazy good humor. "You know it's what you want. What we both want."

"We can be sensible about this," she replied, her voice so solemn and soft that he barely heard the words. "We can be rational—"

"It's too late for rational acts."

"Matt—"

"Stop." He caught her cold cheeks in his hands so that her eyes met his fully. "We have to know just what we're afraid of, Les."

He waited for her to agree, aching with anticipation and the effort of restraint. And then he stopped waiting. He kissed her.

The strong, classic beauty of her mouth remained hard against his, but Matt allowed his tongue to play at the seam of her lips, soft and curious, slow and suggestive. Her breath left her in a rush. She moaned a throaty response, just a sliver of sound, as though someone had tugged a thread and was unraveling her. The helplessness of that surrender buried what was left of his conscience. He didn't hesitate. He didn't hesitate at all, and very soon she was kissing him back, acknowledging the inevitability of this moment, welcoming his touch.

All his blood vessels seemed to burn with intense desire. He felt filled with a fierce, electric energy that begged release. When they had to surface from that kiss at last, Matt didn't know which one of them was trembling more.

Shaken, he rested his forehead against her shoulder.

Seconds seemed to stand still, while they were frozen in place like statues. Eventually Matt lifted his head. She was scanning the evergreens along the trail. He watched her carefully. For one of the few times in his life, Matt was absolutely speechless.

Something moved at the limit of his vision. He heard the sound of bells and realized that it wasn't Sheba's harness, but the pinto, coming up the trail with Nick close behind.

"You two all right?" Nick called out to them as he glided to a halt.

"We're fine," Matt said.

CHAPTER NINE

WHILE DOC WAS in California for the holidays, the clinic took patients only on Wednesday and Saturday. From the moment Matt arrived, the waiting room was full, so Leslie found very little time to brood about yesterday's kiss in the snow—not with Moira sitting at the reception desk and the three exam rooms occupied constantly. After a brief, awkward moment or two, she and Matt fell into the safe, hectic routine of patient care.

She had never worked with him before professionally, and it was nice to confirm what she'd always suspected, that he was a quick and intuitive physician. None of the talents he'd enjoyed in his younger years—a killer charm, the ability to make an empathetic connection with people—seemed to have deserted him. The time he'd spent so exclusively in the operating room had not robbed him of a bedside manner that rivaled Doc Hayward's. The patients loved him.

He dealt with several cases of the flu, a broken wrist, a penny swallowed by a three-year-old who wouldn't stop crying, a tourist's dislocated shoulder, a flare-up of bursitis from shoveling too much snow, a hysterical

Winnie Alameda who brought her husband in with chest pain and Clifford Powell's pulled muscle in his back.

He handled them all with the same brisk expertise. If his damaged hand gave him any trouble, Leslie never saw it.

They worked through lunch. By three o'clock she felt a little lightheaded as she stood at the medicine cabinet and hunted down samples of a muscle relaxant for Cliff Powell.

The door to exam room two opened, and Matt walked out with Cliff. "Christmas is a week away, and you don't want to be flat on your back for it, do you?" Matt asked. "You don't have to cut enough firewood for the entire winter all in one day."

The older man laughed. "Should have taken care of it sooner. But I didn't stockpile in the fall, so I'm paying for it now." He rolled his shoulders. "Guess I'm just getting too old to split wood for hours on end."

"You're in your prime," Matt told Cliff, "but it's easy to overdo. Tell you what. Nick and I will bring over a load of our wood. We've got so much lying around that guests are tripping over it."

That probably wasn't true, but Matt no doubt remembered that Cliff's landscaping business barely scraped by in the winter. The two men stood in the corridor, and while they talked, Leslie couldn't help noticing that Matt didn't look at all tired. In fact, he seemed energized. His dark hair danced under the harsh lighting. The faint shadow of afternoon beard stubble made him look sexy and too rugged for the white lab coat she'd loaned him.

Just watching Matt, her pulse pounded so hard it

hurt. What was happening to her? One kiss didn't mean anything.

She turned her attention back to the medicine cabinet, willing to chalk up that physical response to missing lunch. Willing to chalk it up to *anything* that didn't have to do with a rebellious heart.

Cliff was sent on his way, and Leslie stood at the back counter, finishing up notations on patient files when Matt came up behind her.

"Is that it?" he asked. "Nobody waiting?"

"There's a possible strep throat coming in at four-thirty." She pointed toward the closed door of the third examination room. Lowering her voice, she said, "We've got an unexpected arrival in number three. Polly Swinburne."

Matt grimaced. "Oh, damn. Don't tell me I'm about to get myself boiled in oil along with Kline?"

"I don't think she's here to complain. She won't say what's wrong. I've done the workup on her. Vitals are normal." She made a move to head back to the front desk. "Good luck."

He caught her arm before she could get away. "Oh, no, you don't," he said beneath his breath. "I need reinforcements, and you're elected."

"The woman's seventy years old. She can't hurt you."

"Tell that to Kline. He's probably *still* wondering why there's nothing but an echo in his waiting room."

They entered the examination room. Polly sat in one of the side chairs like a queen ready to meet her subjects. A tall, thin woman with ramrod posture, she'd held up well over the years. Only tight, silver curls and hands that were as gnarled as driftwood gave away her age.

Her head moved with a bird-like jerk. "I heard you were back. About time, if you ask me."

"Thank you, Polly," Matt said, lowering himself to the rolling stool. "I missed you, too." He spent a few moments reviewing the file Leslie had put in his hand. Finally, he closed it and patted the paper-covered examination table. "Want to hop up here for me?"

"No. I'm not a pork chop to be laid out on butcher's paper. I don't hop. The chair is fine."

Leslie hid a smile and moved over to the nearby counter. Even Doc sometimes lost his patience with Polly and her regal ways. It would be interesting to see how Matt dealt with her.

"Okay," he said with a smile. "What seems to be the problem today?"

"I have Jumping Frenchmen of Maine syndrome."

Jumping Frenchmen of Maine? Leslie read a lot of medical journals just to stay up on all the latest treatments and discoveries, but this was a new one on her. She glanced at Matt expectantly.

He didn't miss a beat. He tilted his head at Polly. "I didn't realize you had lumberjacks in your family."

"I don't," Polly said with a dismissive sniff. Her eyes narrowed, suddenly filled with surprise and a new respect. "So you've heard of it? You know what Jumping Frenchman is?"

"An extreme reflex disorder that causes you to be startled by an unexpected noise or sight. Originally displayed in Maine lumberjacks who came across the border from Quebec."

"That's it," Polly agreed with a quick nod. "That's

what I have. Do you think the Canadians are somehow infecting us?"

"I don't see how," Matt said mildly. "So you're telling me that you jump excessively, flail your arms, cry out, actually hit people with things when they come up behind you?"

"Yes."

"All right. This sounds serious, but let's be sure, shall we? Let's rule out anything else."

He began moving through the routine of checking her eyes, her throat, listening to her heart. This had always been Polly's favorite part of an office visit—she adored the attention. Matt was unbelievably patient with her, and even eventually managed to get her to sit on the examination table.

Thirty minutes later Leslie ushered the old woman out of the room and back to the front desk. She left Polly praising Matt's thoroughness to Moira and complaining once more that Doctor Kline, if he had a medical degree at all, had probably gotten it from the internet.

Leslie went back into exam room Three and began stripping the crinkled paper off the table while Matt finished making notes in Polly's file.

"I think she's disappointed with my diagnosis," he said.

Leslie nodded. "Presbycusis is a lot less interesting than Jumping Frenchmen of Maine."

"She's seventy-two. How could she not realize that hearing loss is inevitable at her age? She's probably needed a hearing aid for years."

"I've never heard of Jumping Frenchmen. Do you spend all your spare time reading medical journals?"

"Don't tell Polly," Matt said with a wink, "but I learned all about it from watching that television show '*Wacky Medicine.*'"

He tossed Polly's file on the counter, then stretched as though pulling the kinks out of his spine. "You're still coming up to the lodge tomorrow to celebrate Pop's birthday, aren't you?"

Leslie nodded as she balled up the paper, then tossed it in the waste can. "Your mom called to remind me. I'll need to stop by Dad's on the way up to show him how to use the new glucometer I bought him, but that shouldn't take long."

"Your dad has diabetes?"

"Type two, diagnosed a month ago. I don't think he's accepted it yet."

"Would you like me to discuss it with him?" Matt offered. "I could stop by on my way home tonight."

Leslie gave him a knowing look. "I can handle it, Matt. But thanks."

"Everything all right between you two?" he asked in an overly casual tone.

"It's fine. Really."

"When does he leave for his sister's?"

"Assuming the roads stay clear, the day after tomorrow. That's why I want to make one last visit before he goes." Leslie didn't want to talk about her father. In an effort to change the subject, she asked, "So how did you like your first day, Doctor D'Angelo?"

She discovered that she was waiting for his response with some vague hope that couldn't even be named. It was a foolish question, wasn't it? How could what they'd dealt with today compare to the life he'd had in Chicago and would have again one day?

"It felt good to be useful," Matt admitted. "Though I have to say, I'm not sure how Doc can do this year after year—the same people, the same types of complaints. There's not much of a challenge to this kind of medicine. I'd forgotten what solid citizens these people are. With the exception of Polly, I'd bet most of them go home at night and sleep in Norman Rockwell paintings."

His words were not intended to wound, but she felt a stirring of annoyance that she couldn't control. Maybe *he* couldn't imagine building a life in a small town, but it had served her well enough. "I think Broken Yoke has the same appeal for Doc that it has for me. These people depend on us for help. They're not just patient charts and insurance claims. They're our friends."

She knew her tone sounded cool and slightly censuring. Matt responded quickly. "That was an observation, not a criticism," he said. "I'm sorry if it came out wrong."

She shook her head. "No problem. I suppose I'm just edgy. You never know what grievance Polly's going to have. I'm relieved when she goes away peacefully."

"Think she'll follow up on my referral to an audiologist?"

"The way you finessed her, I think she'd check herself into the nearest mental hospital if you told her to. You're as adept at charming the ladies as you ever were."

"Am I?"

She heard the sly amusement of that question and felt his shrewd scrutiny. It made her nerves jump, and she gathered up Polly's file, eager to leave the room. "I'll see if our strep throat is here yet. He's the last appointment for the day. After that, you're home free."

He caught her arm. "Stay a few minutes," he said. "Moira will let us know when he shows."

"I have things to do. I want to finish up as soon as possible today."

"Why? Do you have big plans tonight? A date with Perry?"

"No."

"Brandon O'Dell taking you out?"

"Brandon? Good grief, no. Why would you think that?"

"I've heard he likes to visit the clinic a lot. That he might have a personal interest."

"He does. In Moira."

"Oh." He seemed to consider that information for a few moments. Then his eyes became somber. "Stop running away from me, Les. Why can't we talk?"

"We *are* talking," she replied warily.

He leveled a troubled gaze at her. "I'm not used to evasive answers from you."

"Well, I'm not used to such unexpected behavior from *you*."

"So you've been thinking about yesterday. So have I."

"Matt…"

He went on as though she'd never spoken. "I've been thinking that we ought to consider taking our friendship to a new level. A more intimate one."

Deep inside she'd known something like this was coming, but she still felt the shock of those words all the way to her toes. Her mind went into complete rebellion. Licking her lips, she shook her head. "I'm not sure that's wise."

He pulled her closer, his grip on her arm firm and unyielding. "Why not? Don't deny how you felt when I kissed you. I certainly felt the same way."

"You shouldn't have kissed me like that."

He gave her a look that was sinfully sexy. "Why would I ever kiss a woman any other way?" His eyes were laughing at her, but his tone was kind. "Come on, Les. What's so wrong about it? We've known each other a long time—"

"Exactly," she managed to get out. "Too long to ruin everything now. I won't give up friendship, especially not for a case of simple lust."

He blinked and stared hard at her. She found his gaze more than a little unnerving. His body held a masculine potency that managed somehow to please and intimidate her all at the same time.

"It's more than that, and you know it," he said. "I know you almost as well as I know myself. Do you think I would ever treat you like some casual, overnight fling? As if I'm bored and have nothing better to do?"

Filled with a cold dread, she looked away. She wished he'd turn her loose. It was so much easier to think when he wasn't touching her. The effect his nearness had on her was total and devastating, sapping her will to resist.

He caught a handful of her hair and gently brought her head back. She could see concern in his expression. Robbed of movement or speech, she let him touch his lips to her cheek and press his forehead against hers.

"There's nothing to be afraid of," he said, his voice like a gentle caress. "It's just me. Do you honestly believe I'd ever intentionally hurt you?"

"No. But that doesn't mean you won't."

He looked shocked.

"How can you think that? Do you know how I feel when I'm with you? I haven't been near a woman since Shayla was killed. I haven't wanted to be. But with you, it's… With you it's safe and sane and…wonderful, but in a new and different way. You feel like the only warmth in the world. You're my island of peace."

"I'm glad you feel that way," she said sincerely. "But it won't last."

"Maybe not, but what's wrong with enjoying what we have in the meantime? Neither one of us is looking for a long-term commitment." Feeling incarcerated in some dark, heavy place, she made a restive movement, but he only tugged her closer. "No, listen to me, damn it. Why can't we explore this? We're adults. We're free to do what we want. Don't you want to see where this can lead?"

She looked at him with dull agony. She wanted so badly to say yes. A reckless voice inside her whispered half-realized desires, crowding her mind with vivid images of how it could be between them. Her control nearly shattered, and saying no suddenly seemed unthinkable.

Luckily, the rational side of her brain, the sensible part of her she'd spent her whole life developing, refused to give in. Matt desired her, he needed her. He was a man trying to fight his way back to a normal life again, a man searching for comfort and understanding and relief.

But he wouldn't need that forever.

She wasn't fooled. Matt wasn't *in love* with her. Whatever else she might long for, she had no fantasies that he would stay here when the holidays were over. Hadn't he just implied that living in Broken Yoke held no appeal, offered no challenge? If they put aside all those years of friendship, if they temporarily gave in to something very primitive and beyond reason, what would she have left when it was over? Memories to be regretted instead of cherished. She would miss him and miss him, until there was nothing to her life but one point of irreducible pain.

If she said yes, she would be writing her own ticket to doom.

He was waiting for her answer. Her voice finally escaped from the knot of despair in her chest. "Our relationship is one of the truly good things that has ever happened to me, Matt. I guess I'm just not willing to take a chance with it. I'm not willing to take my place in the long line of women who have been romanced by you and then left behind. My answer has to be no."

She slipped out of his grasp and away from his reach, eager for the spell to be broken.

"Les—"

"I'm going up front to see how Moira's managing."

She left the room, forcing herself to go slowly so that she wouldn't seem desperate to escape. At the front window Moira told her that their four-thirty patient had called to cancel. She launched into a chatty discussion about Polly Swinburne's claim that the cruise-ship industry was being paid to sneak convicted felons into America.

For once Leslie found no amusement in Polly's never-ending conspiracy theories. She couldn't wait to go home. The office felt too hot, too smothering. Her facial muscles tightened as she nodded and smiled at Moira, but to her absolute horror, she felt tears burning behind her eyes.

She was almost relieved when the front door opened. Any distraction would be welcome.

The teenaged clerk from the hardware store two doors down came rushing up to the front counter, his eyes darting around wildly. "Somebody's gotta come quick," he said. "We got a customer bleeding all over the floor of the store."

The clinic kept two emergency first aid kits handy—one for dealing with possible heart attacks, the other for accidents. "Where's the blood coming from?" Leslie asked as she pulled the second kit out from under the counter.

"I don't know...his leg maybe? He was messing with one of the saws, took the blade guard off—" Trembling visibly, his lips white, the boy stopped talking.

Moira made a move to pick up the telephone receiver. "I'll call Kline."

Leslie was already heading toward the door. "No. Get Matt."

"But I thought—"

"Just get Matt," Leslie told her as she hurried after the teenager.

MATT LOOKED at his watch in annoyance.

Thirty minutes had passed, and still Kline had not shown up at the clinic to do the stitch work on Cliff Powell's leg.

The landscaper's cut was hardly life-threatening, but the man was a little woozy from loss of blood. The wound had been cleaned and irrigated, the field sterilized. Les had given Cliff a tetanus shot since he couldn't remember the last time he'd had one.

According to Doc's agreement, Kline was supposed to handle this kind of emergency—anything requiring stitches. So where the hell was he?

Powell lay back on his elbows, watching. His color was good. Matt suspected that, more than anything else, he was embarrassed by all the fuss.

"So how long is this going to take, Doc? I swear, I ain't gonna faint or anything. Let's get it over with. It's no big deal."

Matt ground his teeth together. Cliff was right. This would be a simple procedure he could do with his eyes closed no matter how uneasy he felt about his ability. It was stupid to waste any more time waiting for Kline to show.

He glanced at Leslie. She nodded, and he knew she didn't see any reason for him to be holding back, either. She seemed to be *willing* him to go ahead. *Just do it.*

So he did.

Less then twenty minutes later, he was sewing the last stitches in Cliff's leg.

"Can't believe I couldn't hold on to a little biddy saw," Cliff complained. "One minute I was testing it out, the next that damned muscle in my back went nuts. Made me drop it." He shook his head in disgust. "Darned humiliating to be carted over here like a newborn needing a diaper change."

"It could have been worse," Matt said. "You're lucky the blade didn't hit anything major. We'd have had to transport you to the hospital in Idaho Springs."

"Shoulda never taken the blade guard off. I don't know what I was thinking. Guess I wasn't, huh?"

"It happens to all of us."

"No offense, Doc, but I've been in this office more today than I have in a whole year. Sure hope this is the last time I see you today."

"I'm afraid we're not done with one another yet. You'll have to come back when the stitches need to be removed. About ten days."

Les came into the examining room. Earlier she'd helped prep the wound for suturing, laid down absorbent pads for irrigation and replaced sterile drapes that had become soiled.

"Your wife is here to take you home when we're done," she told Cliff. Then she turned toward Matt. "If you're managing all right, I thought I'd go over the post-op care with her."

"Go on," Matt said, nodding. "I'm fine here."

He continued stitching, while Cliff watched, apparently fascinated. The gash wasn't too deep, but it ran at least fifteen centimeters, with a jagged tip heading toward the back of the calf. The procedure was taking longer than Matt liked. If he'd performed this slowly in his hospital in Chicago, he'd have been laughed out of the operating room.

He caught Cliff's grimace, and his gloved hands stilled. "Anesthetic still holding up?" he asked. "You shouldn't feel anything but a slight pressure."

"Nah, I'm good. I was just thinking that I'm going to have one heck of a zipper when you get done."

"I'm afraid so." Matt looked at his handiwork—a fairly straight, even line of vertical mattress sutures. Not too bad, really. The needle holder in his dominant hand wasn't too much of a problem, but controlling the pick-ups with his left was awkward and slow-going. He needed more strength there, more mobility, and he could feel the protest of every sinew and tendon. "I warned you it might not be my best-looking work, didn't I?"

"It looks great, Doc. Straight as a corn row. 'Sides, after all these years of working outdoors, my legs aren't exactly my prettiest feature." Cliff gave Matt a broad grin. "Everyone says it's my smile."

Matt was tying off the last knot when Les returned. While he stripped off his gloves and rechecked Cliff's distal movement, sensation and circulation in the leg, she began removing the drapes and procedure tray, depositing the sharps into the disposal container.

"It looks great, Cliff," Les said as she dabbed anti-bacterial ointment on the sutures, then applied a sterile dressing. "I'll bet it won't even leave much of a scar."

Matt wondered whether that comment was for the patient's benefit or his.

After spending a little more time talking with Cliff, Matt left Les to finish up. In Hayward's private office, he sank into Doc's old leather chair. On the desk he saw Cliff's file, put there by Les no doubt, who knew he'd have to spend some time documenting the procedure—from technique to number of sutures to drawing a small picture of the wound as it had looked before he'd begun.

He smiled. Les knew her stuff. If she'd worked in Chicago, she might have made Director of Nursing in record time. They'd have been a great team in the operating room.

His bad hand ached, and he used his right one to massage it. In spite of the pain, he felt strangely pleased by this afternoon's work. With practice he'd get some of his speed back. And while sewing up a pretty basic gash under non-critical circumstances hadn't been particularly demanding, it was a start. It gave him hope.

His cell phone sat on the corner of the desk. When it rang, he snatched it up and heard Doc Hayward's voice.

"So how was your first day at the clinic?" the older man asked.

"It's not over yet. I'm still here. I just finished stitching up Cliff Powell."

Briefly he described what had happened to Cliff. Doc didn't seem surprised that the landscaper had suffered a mishap. Over the years, he'd sewn up more than one cut for the guy. Doc did, however, sound displeased that Kline hadn't shown up at the clinic.

"Where was he?" Doc asked. "He told me he could be there in five minutes if necessary. He can't just leave you high and dry when you need him."

"I don't know why he didn't show. I assume Moira called him. As it turns out, we didn't need him."

"It sounds like you managed beautifully."

"It wasn't a heart transplant, Doc."

"It still worked out just fine."

Matt lifted his bad hand, inspecting it as though he'd

never seen it before. "Yeah, it did. Surprised the heck out of me, I have to admit."

They discussed a few of the cases that had come in that day. Matt enjoyed the opportunity to talk professionally for a change. He'd missed that.

By the time he left Doc's office, he realized it was long past closing time. The lights in the examination rooms and back counter were off, but he could hear voices coming from the front desk.

Moira and Les were completing the day's work. Moira was at the copy machine. Les sat at the front desk, sorting through patient files. Because their backs were to him, neither saw Matt standing in the doorway.

Preparing to reload the copier, Moira tore open a fresh ream of paper. " I just don't want Doc to be mad," she told Les as she slammed shut the bottom drawer of the machine. "He was very specific about calling Doctor Kline's office in case of an emergency."

Les didn't even glance up from her work. "He can't be mad at you. I made the decision not to call him."

"I still don't understand why."

"We didn't need him. Matt managed just fine."

"But I thought—"

Les swung around on her rolling chair to catch Moira's full attention. "Look, Matt's a gifted surgeon. Cliff Powell was a good opportunity for him to reaffirm that he hasn't lost that gift. He just needs to rebuild his confidence. To know that, whatever difficulty his hand's giving him right now, it certainly doesn't have to mean the end of his career."

"I suppose that makes sense..." Moira agreed.

"Of course it does. Sewing up Cliff was a great way to get him pointed back in the right direction. It was the right decision for me to make, and even Doc would agree, I'm sure of it."

Matt's newly acquired feeling of satisfaction died a quick death. He felt sickened because he suddenly knew the truth. He knew why Kline had failed to show up. His heart pumped hard, but he could not feel anything but the knowledge in his brain that Les had manipulated him.

He was filled with a quiet, precise anger. It grew and spilled over into the room, so that in the next moment, both women looked his way. Moira went red with embarrassment. Les's expression was stricken and tight, as though she was stunned and unsure of what to do next.

Filled with a sense of betrayal, Matt had no thought for anything except maintaining control. He walked over to the desk and slapped Cliff Powell's file on top of all the others.

"It's late," he said to Les. "If you don't have any more charity work to throw my way, I think I'll go home."

CHAPTER TEN

"DAD..." Leslie paused, searching for a handle on her patience. "You're making this more difficult than it needs to be."

They were seated at her father's kitchen table. The diabetes test kit sat in front of them; the new glucometer for testing his blood sugar lay in Quentin Meadows's palm as if it were a snake she'd just asked him to hold. They'd been through the test sequence three times, and he still didn't seem to understand how the procedure worked.

He tossed the glucometer on the table with a snort of derision. "Why don't you just chain me up so I can't reach the kitchen and be done with it?"

Leslie leaned back in her chair, determined not to snap at him. It wasn't easy.

Her car hadn't wanted to start this morning, and the roads had been tricky to maneuver due to two inches of fresh snow. The dry cleaners had lost her favorite pair of slacks. And if she didn't leave within the next two minutes, she'd be late getting to Sam D'Angelo's birthday party. Add to that the unpleasant way she and Matt had parted yesterday at the clinic, and she wasn't feeling particularly tolerant right now.

"This isn't to keep you from eating," she said with a sigh. "It's a tool for you to use. You have to be more conscientious about monitoring your blood sugar. That's the only way you'll manage it."

"Monitoring!" he said with a snort of displeasure. "Like some damned criminal. I don't like having to keep track. Too much to remember."

"Which is why I've brought you this new one so you can get used to it before you leave tomorrow. It keeps track for you."

Ignoring her father's sour look, Leslie leaned forward to pick up the equipment again. One more time. He'd get the hang of it with practice. She just had to remember that he'd always been resistant to any change in his routine. And though he'd never admit it, he was probably still frightened by Doc Hayward's diagnosis.

Slowly she went through another few tests with the control solution that came with the glucometer kit, then helped him draw a sample of his own blood. He seemed to understand at last.

"See," she said when he'd successfully gotten a reading. "That wasn't so horrible, was it?"

"No, I guess not," he admitted.

"Aunt Tanya can help you if you forget how to use it. Uncle James has been a diabetic for years."

"Great. She can have two invalids on her hands for Christmas."

Leslie had to laugh at that. "You're hardly an invalid, Dad, and neither is Uncle James. The two of you always got along well. You can compare notes." When he said nothing to that, she gave him a close look. "Aren't you looking forward to this trip?"

"I know *you* are."

"Don't try to make me feel guilty about this. Aunt Tanya's eager to have you come and spend time with them. You can use a change of scenery, and working on the new house will keep your skills sharp."

"Cheap labor," he muttered.

She shook her head in frustration and set her jaw, refusing to let him get to her. This trip would do him good in so many ways. He needed to feel useful, to spend time with more people, and since he seldom seemed to enjoy spending time with *her,* being with a sister who still cared about him seemed the ideal solution.

Finally, she rose. Her father saw her out to her car, but just as she was about to say goodbye, he placed his hand on her arm. "Why don't we go to Maloni's tonight? You can make sure I don't eat dessert."

"Oh, Dad, I'm sorry. I can't tonight. But tomorrow why don't we have lunch together before I take you to the bus station?"

"Why can't we do it tonight? Some hot date?"

"Not exactly." Knowing the way her father felt about all the D'Angelos, she considered leaving it at that, but she realized that he had spotted the small wrapped present on the front seat of her car. "I'm going to a birthday party up at Lightning River Lodge. Sam D'Angelo's turning sixty."

Quentin expelled such a harsh breath that a bouquet of cold air swirled in front of them. His watery blue eyes went to ice. "You'd rather eat cake and ice cream with a bunch of strangers than spend time with your old man."

"They aren't strangers. They're…"

"*Family?* Is that what you were going to say?"

"No—"

"You know how I feel about those people, and yet you continue to rub it in my face that you care more about them than you do your own father."

"I've never said that."

"Didn't have to. You think I don't know how much time you spend with them? I've got eyes. I hear things."

She looked away for a moment, filled with equal parts of guilt and annoyance. It was true, she didn't spend much time with her father, but whose fault was that, really? She'd certainly put forth the effort.

She looked back at him, determined to keep things pleasant. "Dad, please don't do this. The D'Angelos have been nothing but kind to me from the day I met them. They have never, *ever* tried to turn me against you. They couldn't. I'm your daughter, and I always will be."

He jerked away when she laid her fingers on his arm. "Sam D'Angelo tried to turn your mother against me, and he won't be happy until he turns you against me, too. And have you forgotten what his son did? Raising a hand to me in my own house! When you're standing there in the middle of *that* family, singing 'Happy Birthday' to *that* man, you remember what I've said."

He stalked away, marching through the wet, dirty drifts of old snow as though he was completely unaware of them.

"Dad…"

"I don't have anything more to say," he snapped

back over his shoulder. "Try to remember to pick me up tomorrow."

In another moment, the front door of the trailer closed behind him with a bang of anger.

All the way up the mountain road, Leslie indulged in harsh self-examination to see if she could feel truth in any of her father's words. All right. Some of what he'd said was true. She *did* think of the D'Angelos as family.

From the very beginning they had offered the sort of kindness, contentment and love that had always been missing from her own world. Easy laughter and bad jokes, but most of all, a warm, stable peace. Was it any wonder that she would continue to be drawn to them?

That didn't mean she didn't care about her father. She loved him.

There were moments in her past when she knew he'd tried to make a good home for his wife, to be loving and supportive to his daughter. But she'd long ago accepted that alcohol—not his family—had ultimately given Quentin Meadows the release he seemed to need. When he drank, Leslie knew he felt unencumbered by harsh reality.

He'd made no pretense about hating Sam D'Angelo. Leslie's mother and Sam had grown up next door to one another when his parents had still owned their tourist cabins in Broken Yoke. They had never developed a closeness like the one Leslie shared with Matt, but they had remained friendly over the years. Her mother had once admitted that Sam had been furious with her choice of a husband, but he had never withdrawn his friendship.

Leslie knew her father was subject to attacks of petty jealousy and unreasonable resentment. She mustn't allow him to spoil this day, which, because of Matt, already promised to be difficult enough.

Her stomach felt hollow when she remembered the look in Matt's eyes as he'd left yesterday. Shocked. Angry. So…betrayed.

The weight of a wordless dread threatened to engulf her, but she refused to give in to it. Looking back, she supposed she could have handled the situation differently, but it was too late now to second-guess.

Eventually Matt would realize that she'd only tried to help him. He wanted his old life back. He wanted to return to that operating room in Chicago. And as much as the idea of him leaving made her heart cramp inside her chest, she wanted that for him.

What good would it do for him to stay here if he was miserable?

Determined to be upbeat, she parked in the lodge's lot, grabbed Sam's gift and strode toward the front entrance.

She hardly needed her coat today. After last night's snow, the afternoon sunlight was surprisingly warm and reviving on her shoulders. Winter bushes lining the driveway bloomed with melting snow roses, and farther along the lake path the bare trees spread black lace branches against the sky. It was a perfect day for a celebration.

There were a few lodge guests around: a couple sliding skis and poles onto the top of their car, a trio of kids having a snowball fight on the front lawn while their parents laughed and manned a video camera. Leslie smiled and waved as she passed a teenaged girl making a snow angel while her boyfriend looked on.

Like all the resorts in the area, the lodge would be busiest on the weekend, and the weeks before Christmas were often the most hectic of all.

As the days to Christmas wound down, however, the place would get less crowded. The D'Angelos were firm believers that families ought to be together at Christmas time, and room bookings were discouraged during the last days before the holiday so that minimum staff was required. Anyone staying overnight on the actual holiday would be encouraged to join the family for dinner, but the lodge would be almost deserted, an unofficial day off for everyone.

George at the front desk nodded a welcome as Leslie went through the dining room and into the kitchen. Dozens of loaves of freshly baked Italian fruitcake cooled on wire racks on the huge wooden table. Around Christmas Matt's aunts, Renata and Sophia, sent a loaf home with every guest.

Beyond the kitchen, where the D'Angelo's private quarters lay, she heard the sound of laughter. The party had already started.

Everyone was in the living room. The coffee table had been pushed out of the way to make room for Sam and his wheelchair and a healthy stack of presents. All around him were the touchstones of D'Angelo family history—a comfortable accumulation of books and old pictures and small treasures—but more importantly, the people he loved most.

As Leslie entered, she was greeted as though she

was one of those people, a member of that inner circle. She had never found words to tell them what their acceptance, these times, meant to her, but she had a feeling they knew.

Nick rose to take her coat, and Addy handed her a glass of punch. As conversation began to whip cheerfully around the room once more, her eyes sought out Matt.

She found him sitting in a quiet corner, listening to Renata. He nodded a few times, but made no comment. Leslie knew him well enough to guess that it was a masquerade performance for the older woman's benefit, that he was barely listening at all.

Unwilling to let him ignore her, Leslie refused to look away. When he finally did sense her presence and glanced her way, he lifted his hand in a friendly acknowledgement and gave her a tight smile. His eyes, however, were cool and distant. Her heart sank, and she felt his rejection like a frigid draft down her back.

Feeling as though she were made of glass, Leslie crossed the room and went to Sam. "Happy Birthday!" she said with bright enthusiasm as she held out her present.

"About time you got here," he scolded. "We've all been waiting for you."

In Matt's case, she doubted that was true, but she would not let his attitude ruin this day for his father. She would not.

THE PRESENTS had been opened and fawned over with whoops of excitement and aahs of appreciation. The cake had been devoured with appropriate compliments for Rosa's talent. Sam had made a very sweet, very heartfelt speech about how thankful he was to have so many family members close at hand.

Matt had barely said two words to Leslie.

Barely spoken to anyone, really. Most of the time he had seemed lost in some inward maze of concentration. It was so unlike him that even Tessa had asked if he was feeling all right. Though polite, his answer was so abrupt that Leslie felt irritation grab hold of her. It was one thing to be angry with her. But he didn't need to take it out on his family.

She tried to ignore him, tried to focus on the conversation she'd been having with Nick and Kari about plans for the coming baby, their getaway trip to Aspen this weekend. But the discussion was so personal that in no time she felt left out. It wasn't their fault. They were in love. So much so that it made her throat ache just to watch them together.

"I think I'll get another cup of coffee," she said, finding an excuse to leave Nick and Kari to each other.

She went into the kitchen, where an industrial-size urn held an endless supply of coffee. As she tipped cream into her cup, she heard the double doors swing open. She turned and discovered that Matt had entered.

She took a deep breath. "Matt—"

"No coffee, thanks," he said and continued through the room. From a line of pegs near the back of the kitchen he grabbed his down jacket. He went out the back door. He never even glanced her way.

She felt a sense of having been treated unfairly. Striving to keep from heading out the door to confront him, she stood rigidly erect, staring out the window as he made his way down the narrow path that led to Lightning Lake, head down, hands shoved in his pockets.

Caught up in her thoughts, she didn't know how long she stood there before she became aware that she was no longer alone. She glanced over her shoulder to find Sam wheeling up to her side. She forced a smile.

"You're in big trouble," he said.

She couldn't bear to let him see how much Matt had hurt her, and how angry she was. "He'll get over it."

"Who?"

She frowned. "Aren't we talking about Matt?"

"No. I was referring to your present—the CD collection."

"What's wrong with it? I thought Doris Day was your favorite."

"She is. But Rosa says her voice is too syrupy. We once had a three-day disagreement over whether "Que Sera, Sera" should ever have won an Academy Award for Best Song."

Leslie laughed, glad to have something else besides Matt to think about for the moment. "Should it have?"

Sam gave her a look that said such a question was ridiculous. "Of course. But I'll tell you a secret," he said, taking a quick peek toward the living-room door. "My favorite album went missing last summer. I grilled every member of this family, but no one confessed. I'm convinced Rosa was the culprit. Now thanks to you, Doris is back in the house." He winked. "We'll see who has the last say in this."

"Great," Leslie said with a resigned sigh. First Matt.

Then her father. Now Rosa was probably ready to shoot her. She folded her arms, casting a regretful look out the back of the lodge. Matt was long out of sight. "What's having one more person mad at me?"

"So now tell me what's going on with you and Matt," Sam said.

She turned her head to look at the older man. "Was it obvious?"

"You both seem preoccupied and quiet today. And just now when I said you were in trouble, you thought I was referring to Matt. Is there anything I can do to help?"

"Thanks, but I doubt it. I suppose I'll just have to wait for him to come around."

"Mind if I offer you a word of advice?"

"Of course not."

"Don't let him shut you out. Whatever feud there is between you, get it out and settled. Matt has always been easygoing, but lately he spends entirely too much time brooding." He shook his head. After several long, thoughtful moments, he added, "I know my son. He has never minded being in the spotlight. He enjoys being in the thick of things. He has always loved being around people, especially his family." Sam gestured out the window. "He does not take himself off to be alone like an unlicked wolf cub."

She looked down at Sam sharply. He was sixty today, and yet suddenly he seemed older, his forehead creased with decades of anxiety. "You're very worried about him, aren't you?"

Sam nodded. "The *family* is worried about him."

"But isn't it understandable? After everything that happened last year, he's bound to be changed."

Sam's full, chiseled mouth twisted in displeasure. "I concede that it was a horrible time in his life. But it's not the load that breaks a man down, Leslie. It's the way he carries it. Rosa says he has no appetite, that she's caught him awake at all hours of the night so she knows he hardly sleeps. As a result, *she* hardly sleeps. He has no right to put his mother through that kind of torment."

"He would never hurt any of you deliberately," Leslie said, compelled to defend Matt in spite of her anger with him. "He's just very concerned about his future in medicine."

"Of course," Sam said. "But I fear there may be something else on his mind. I believe he blames himself for what happened in that diner."

"But that wasn't his fault."

"I know."

She glanced back out the window. The sun threw deep afternoon shadows among the trees, then swept them back up again as clouds crossed the sky. "I wish we could talk about it," she said. "But he's upset with me right now, and we don't seem to be able to discuss anything."

"That alone says something," Sam said with a tired sigh. "You two rarely fight. You've always shared a special relationship, perhaps more special than either of you know." Before she had time to think what he meant by that, he touched her arm, drawing her gaze. His eyes gave her a long, searching look. "Now more than ever,

my son needs you, Leslie. Don't let him wall himself
off. Make him listen. You may be the only one who can."

LESLIE GAVE Matt half an hour to return on his own. A
brisk hike around the lake took that long, and in today's
velvety sunshine, the melting snow might make the trail
slow going.

She helped gather dirty plates and glasses, then col-
lected crumpled ribbons and empty boxes as Tessa filled
a trash bag with torn wrapping paper. She gave Addy a
hand moving the furniture back into place. Finally, with
a last glance at her watch, she pulled her coat and scarf
off the kitchen peg and went out the back door in search
of Matt.

One way or the other, they were going to talk. *Now.*

When she reached the rim of the lake, she shaded her
eyes against the glare and scanned the area. On the far
side, a deer with sun-tipped antlers pawed the frozen
ground. The snow was piled like a white bracelet around
the shoreline. The water lay in a chilling sparkle in front
of her, like the glass of a fogged-over mirror. There was
no sign of Matt.

Then she spotted the footprints on the snow-covered ice.

They led out to the lodge's ice-fishing hut, a small,
portable building that Sam had constructed years ago
out of treated spruce. In years past, after the ice had frozen to a depth of four inches, the hut had been dragged
out from under its protective tarp and set up so that Sam
and the kids could fish for trout. In spite of the fact that
it was designed for comfort—warmed by a portable

heater and a thick covering of rugs placed over the ice—the guests rarely used it.

But someone had trekked out there, and who else but Matt was around? Gingerly, Leslie stepped out on the ice, found her footing, and began the trip across the frozen water.

She opened the hut's door slowly. It creaked noisily on piano hinges, but a wave of warm air fanned her immediately, so she knew the hut was occupied. It had only one very small window, so it took a moment for her eyes to adjust to the gloom.

Then she saw Matt sitting in a camp chair on the other side of the room. His hands were empty, dangling loosely between his legs. He glanced up.

Had he ever looked at her like that before, with such weary dread? She couldn't recall it, and her nerves ripped like silk.

"Catching anything?" she asked. Her voice sounded rusty and hollow in the silence.

"I wasn't trying to."

She shut the door quietly behind her. At least he'd spoken to her.

She let her gaze roam. The hut could hold six people if you didn't mind getting cozy. It hadn't changed much since she'd been here last. A small propane heater glowed in one corner, a huge, wicked-looking ice drill took up another. There were rods and reels, nets and a gaff for hauling the big ones out of the hole. The hole itself was covered.

"I remember when your father hosted an ice-fishing tournament out here one winter. You ended up catching the biggest trout, and everyone claimed the contest was rigged."

He looked at her again. "Did you want something, Les?"

His face remained blank. His eyes were so cold that a slow prickle of panic went up Leslie's spine. In spite of it—or maybe even because of it—her resolve set like steel in that moment.

Enough, she told him silently. *Enough.*

"Do I have to *want* something in order to talk to you?"

"If you've come to apologize for yesterday—"

"Apologize!" She'd been prepared for anger and argument. But not this. She took a step further into the room. "If anyone needs to apologize, it should be you, Matt D'Angelo."

"How do you figure that?"

"You were very rude, walking out of the clinic that way."

"Rude? Considering the conversation I'd just heard, I think I was remarkably restrained."

"So we're alone now. You don't have to be restrained. Just say whatever you want."

He settled back in the chair. "I don't think that's a good idea."

"Well, I do. Don't hold back."

He shook his head. "Go away."

"No. Not until we get this settled. In fact, why don't I start? I honestly thought what I was doing was the right thing. You were there. Kline wasn't. I knew you could handle that sort of emergency in your sleep."

He appeared to give her words serious consideration, but she groaned inside, knowing he wasn't really listening. She watched him pretend just as he had with his aunt earlier.

"Makes sense…" he said at last. "*If* I really believed that convenience was what had motivated you." He got up, coming across the distance that separated them to stand right in front of her. "You know damn well it wasn't just a case of me being nearby. You decided I needed to be thrown a bone. You decided I needed to feel good about myself. I'm disappointed that you couldn't have engineered a better challenge. A first-year resident could have breezed through sewing up Cliff."

"I wasn't throwing you a bone. I only pushed you into doing something you would have done eventually anyway. I know you're desperate to have your old life back, that Chicago is where you want to get back to as soon as possible. What's so horrible about trying to help you accomplish that?"

The color seemed to darken in his eyes as they narrowed. "I'm the one who needs to make that decision. Not you. You shouldn't have done it. I don't need your pity, Les. I sure as hell don't *want* it."

His words sent a jolt through her body. "Pity? Why on earth would I pity you? Let me tell you something. Up until now, your life has been a very easy journey through open doors because you're charming and handsome and smart. You never had to work for grades or friends or recognition."

He swung away from her, bracing both hands against one of the walls. "I can't do this right now," he said, his head hanging low between his shoulders as though he were trying to catch his breath. "I'm not feeling very understanding, and if you're smart you'll save this lecture for another time."

"This isn't a lecture. It's a long-needed reality check. The shooting was a terrible blow. But aside from the sheer horror of what happened, you've had to face a few unpleasant facts, and you don't like it. You thought you were invincible. Well, guess what? You're not. You're just like everyone else. You can make mistakes and run into roadblocks in life and generally get the short end of the stick sometimes. But it doesn't have to be fatal. It just means you have to do what the rest of us mere mortals have to do. Find a way to fix it. And if you can't, then you find a way to live with it."

She put the brake on her words, getting a breath or two to calm her temper. They seemed headed for an impasse, and she wouldn't allow that to happen. To emphasize what she was about to say, Leslie put her hand on his arm, and when he flinched at her touch, she ignored it.

"Matt, I know you'd never deliberately hurt the people who love you," she said. "But right now you're doing just that to your family. They're worried sick about you. If you can't pull yourself together, can't you at least *pretend* for their sakes?"

He shook his head at her, and the look in his eyes was so filled with misery that it nearly slapped the breath out of her. "You just don't get it. I'm pretending all the time these days. In so many ways. And I'm sick of it."

"You don't have to pretend with me, Matt," she said more calmly. "I think I know what you must be feeling—"

He turned on her. An electric antagonism seemed to jump between them. He gave her a hard, straight look. "You *don't* know what I'm feeling. If you did, you wouldn't touch me…"

"I've known you long enough—"

"You don't know me at all."

Those words sounded more icy and impenetrable than the frozen lake beneath them.

A cold, clammy finger of fear clutched her heart, but she had come too far to turn back now. "If you can't find a way to deal with what's happened to you, then I do pity you. Because you'll be throwing away a life that still has so much value in it. That still has meaning. And *that* really will be the greatest loss."

His jaw tightened. He seemed so remote, as if he didn't want her anywhere near him. But why? Always in the past, they'd been able to sort through their differences.

He blew a harsh breath, as though she were a child who refused to cooperate and he had reached the end of his patience. "Everything you say is true. *Nothing* you say makes any difference. Let's just let it go."

"I can't."

"Damn it, Les. Leave me alone."

"No, you mule-headed idiot, I won't. You're a man I've believed in all my life. I'm not going to stop now."

"Listen to me," he said fiercely, his hands out in supplication. "I don't want you to believe in me. I know what you want me to be, but I can't. I just want you—" He broke off, his clenching fists so hard that the bones of his knuckles looked as if they might break through the skin, "…to leave me alone."

She felt exhausted and drained of hope. Desperately Leslie grabbed the wrist of his injured hand and hung on tightly when he tried to lower his arm. "It's only your hand, Matt. It's not you. Look at it. Yes, it's not perfect, but do you know how much worse it could have been?"

"I don't want to hurt you. Let...go."

"No. Look at it. Tell me why this should be the end of who you are."

"It isn't, and I know that. Right at this moment, what I'm feeling has nothing to do with my damned hand."

"Then what?" she asked.

"Let go."

"No."

"Turn loose, damn you."

"Or what?" she asked defiantly.

"Or...this."

With a twist of his wrist, it was suddenly Matt who had hold of her, not the other way around. He pulled her off-balance, and they were instantly so close that she felt his breath on her lips. Leslie made one small frantic sound, and then Matt's mouth crashed against hers, absorbing her shock and kissing her with a wild, raw energy so erotic that she shivered.

CHAPTER ELEVEN

YOU'D NEVER deliberately hurt the people who love you.

With frightening clarity, Les's words slid into Matt's mind as he kissed her.

He knew he ought to turn her loose. He knew he mustn't do this. But he was nearly blind with longing, victim to an overpowering passion. All he could think about was being lost inside her and never having to leave.

He realized that he'd been making this choice for so long, a little at a time, until there was nothing left to decide anymore. Until there was nothing left but this. She had belonged to him for years.

She remained still and dazed in his arms, and he let the rough-soft tug of his whole mouth convey everything he wanted to share. His lips touched the hair that rippled around her temples like satin.

"If you think you have the words to stop this, then for God's sake, find them now." He tightened his hold. "Because I can't anymore, Les…I can't. This feels so…right. You know it does. Don't deny it. Don't deny your heart."

He pulled back, watching her warily, as though she could be a wild creature he might startle into flight. He didn't know what he would do if she rejected him.

She must have caught the reflection of his thoughts in his face because she shook her head—not in rejection it seemed, but in relieved acceptance for what they both knew: Destiny had been leading them down this path for years. It was too late to turn back.

He'd taken off his coat because the heater had warmed the hut sufficiently. Les's hands ran down his shirt, exploring his chest with tentative fingers. He had envisioned this scene again and again over the past few days, and now at last he was experiencing it. He groaned, his throat so constricted with yearning that he couldn't speak. He shut his eyes, letting the feel of her hands on him sink all the way to his bones.

When her lips came feather-light against the hard line of his jaw, his pulse lurched. No woman had ever had this trigger-quick effect on him before. That it should be Leslie, his sweet, sweet Les…

He opened his eyes, catching her head between his hands. In the rusty light of the lowering sun, she was all peach and golden tints. Her eyes flared up to meet his, full of wonder and anticipation. He kissed her again, the hunger rising within him like a wild tide.

Because of yesterday, he'd wanted to stay angry with her. But just seeing her today, he'd known he couldn't. His emotions wouldn't settle. His senses wouldn't cooperate. He had felt as though he were unraveling from one end everything he had so carefully woven from another.

He could not stop wanting her.

His hand tugged the red scarf from her throat, moved under the coat to push it from her shoulders even as they were both sliding down to the thick rug that covered the ice.

For an instant Matt cursed the inadequacy of their surroundings. He wanted more for their first time. He wanted the golden sands of some paradise for her, filled with the song of jeweled birds and flowers by the armload. But in the next moment, as Les yanked his shirt from his waistband, he could not remember anything of what he wanted at all, could not think of *anything* beyond the feel of her hands along his ribs.

When they were naked at last, panting and groaning over clumsy fingers and stubborn buttons, Matt shifted her beneath him, dragging her into tight contact with his body.

He explored her with his lips and tongue, delighted when the trim flesh of delicately defined muscles quivered under his touch, enchanted by the constellation of freckles that lay across her breasts. The arch of her neck, the shape of her hands, all of it was so unbelievably familiar, but yet not. It made his throat go dry.

In return, her teeth nipped lightly at his mouth, then her tongue stroked a provocative apology. This time it was *his* breath that came fast and uneven.

"Les…" he gasped out. "Les, do you know…how long I've wanted…"

"I know," she said, giving him a hectic, hazy, flickering smile. "So what are you waiting for *now?*"

His experienced fingers parted her legs, stroked and soothed, finding their way to the warmth offered by the tight, throbbing furnace between her thighs. She arched and pushed hard against his hand almost immediately. There was suddenly no time for delicacy and gentle wooing. He groaned and entered her, and she answered with another involuntary surge that took the remaining breath from him.

He met her. Pressed harder. Plunged to the last inch of penetration.

He felt the tiny spasms shudder through her, and moments later he realized that they were his as well. The sheer bliss of it—such sweet flashes of agony— made him want to cry out. He could not seem to get enough air into his lungs, and yet he heard his own hoarse voice through the black rush of blood in his ears, calling her name over and over again simply for his own pleasure.

When it ended, she collapsed under him, shaking and apparently, too breathless to speak. Matt brushed the back of his fingers along the curve of her cheek, but he was in no better shape than she.

He moved to lie beside her, pulling her close. Les snuggled against him as if there was nowhere else she would rather be. Pleased and filled with an overwhelming tenderness, he planted soft kisses along her cheek, her temple. His fingers wove into her hair, lightly, and after a while he felt her body relax against his as she drifted to sleep.

There was so little time to be together. Sunset soon. When the moon came up, they must dress and find some way to explain their absence to the family. For now, it was enough just to lie here together.

The soft rhythm of her breathing, the warm coziness of this ridiculous lover's nest worked its magic on Matt as well. He felt himself floating into some lost dreamland, caught between sleep and the press of time in an exhausted contentment.

Les murmured his name.

Just before he lost consciousness himself, he smiled and tucked her closer against him. This woman had knocked out a window in the solid, stone wall he'd built around his soul, letting the sun shine through. She made him feel as though life was wonderful. Every particle of it.

Oh, Les, he wanted to say. *Why did we wait so long? This is some kind of miracle, isn't it?*

Against the soft shell of her ear, he whispered those very thoughts. He whispered words he had never spoken to any other woman. He whispered that he had been looking for her forever.

IT CAME to Leslie at last. There was no resisting it.

She loved him.

Surprisingly, that admission was not nearly as terrifying as she had feared. If anything, the words had a calming effect, like finding the solution to a long-postponed puzzle.

For so many years she had fought her need for him, letting time drift on, letting the unspoken desire that lay deep within her be buried and ignored.

She had settled for friendship, never believing she could have more. She knew Matt was a man who could break any heart he was handed, so she had protected hers. She had told herself friendship was enough, and all the time, deep in her heart, she had known it was not.

Could it be that she had finally found what had eluded her all her life?

Of course, Matt hadn't said he loved her. His hopes for their future might have nothing in common with hers. This could all be a dream, but if it was, she didn't want to wake. Not yet.

Instead, Leslie focused on the sure feel of his hands on her bare skin. Matt was awake, caressing her with a rough, new urgency that drove every thought from her mind. She turned into his shoulder where the scent of him filled all her senses.

Through the tiny window she saw the last, fading rays of a pink and golden sunset. "We'll have to go soon," she whispered against his chest. "My car's still in the parking lot. They'll wonder where I am."

"Let them," Matt said, and gave her a kiss that threatened to deprive her of resistance.

"Your reputation may survive this, but I'm not sure mine will."

"Do you care so much?"

"No."

His smile held a touch of triumph as he pulled her under him. Earlier he had found a stack of blankets in one corner of the hut, clean and smelling sweetly of cedar.

He looked down at her, moving to put most of his weight on his hands. "Why have we waited so long for this?"

Unable to answer, she shook her head. There were so many reasons, but all of them seemed ridiculous at the moment.

He stroked a finger across her bottom lip. "Do you remember the day I first kissed you? We were watching the hockey game."

"Of course I do."

"You jumped away from me like a scalded cat."

"I know," she said, feeling a flush rise within her. "I can barely think about it without turning a dozen shades of red."

"What's changed for us? How did you go from finding my touch the most repulsive thing in the world…" His fingers drew a gentle pattern down to her bare breast, "…to this?"

Leslie was stunned. "Repulsive? Is that what you thought?" She exhaled a short laugh. "Oh, Matt. How could two people who know each other as well as we do have been so blind?"

"Tell me."

She bit her lip, embarrassed even after all these years to talk about it. "In those days, I was so hopeless around boys. I'd never been kissed. And there you were, the most popular boy in high school, the boy every girl wanted, acting as though you really wanted to kiss *me*."

"I *did* want to kiss you." He bent to touch his lips to her shoulder. "I think I will never *stop* wanting to kiss you."

"Well, I was terrified to let you see how ignorant I was. I even thought you might be trying to get back at some girl who'd had the audacity to turn you down. You weren't used to being rejected—by anything or anyone."

In the dusky light, she barely saw his frown. "God, Les, you make me sound awful. I never felt that the world revolved around me back then."

"Well, I certainly did," she told him, "and I didn't think you were a risk I could afford to take. If you'd laughed or gotten mad—I thought everything we had...could be ruined."

She could see she'd surprised him. He studied her face intently for a long time. Finally, he shook his head. "I'm so sorry for that. I hope I would never have treated you that unfairly, but obviously you believed I might."

"I was too afraid to find out. You don't know what it was like, Matt. Before you came along, there was no one who cared about me. You brought me into your enchanted circle, you showed me I could be more than the place I came from. Back in those days, if you had withdrawn your friendship for *any* reason, I'm not sure I would have survived."

His hand found her cheek. He kissed her long and deeply, until her heart reeled with the sweetness of it.

After a little while, he said, "You would have survived beautifully. You're tough and sensible, and you never took crap from anyone, least of all me. I admit, I was stung when you didn't seem interested. But I also remember thinking, 'Les is different from the others. You can't play with her feelings, you jerk.'"

"So you backed off."

"What else could I do? You wouldn't look at me. You seemed so... uncomfortable." He smiled down at her with such indescribable tenderness that she fell a little more in love with him. "But I swear to you. Somewhere inside, I've always wanted you. I've always wanted us to end up just like this."

She wound her arms around his neck, tugging him closer. "Such a waste of years," she said against his ear.

"I don't want to waste any more of them."

"Neither do I."

This time Leslie initiated the kiss, slow and luxurious, until need blossomed between them once more. The world seemed to dissolve away from them.

Where would they go from here? she wondered. Could she come right out and ask? No. She couldn't. She would let her body rule the moment, and forget the chatter in her mind.

Some of her internal tension must have communicated itself to Matt because he gave her a look that seemed to assess her from the inside out. "Les? Are you all right?"

Say you love me, she begged silently. She realized that she wanted to hear those words so badly that it terrified her.

She mustered a smile for his benefit. "I'm fine."

The door to the hut suddenly rattled under the force of urgent knocking.

"Matt!" Addy's voice cut through the stillness. "Are you in there?" Matt barely had time to pull a blanket over them before his sister came rushing inside. "Have you seen Leslie? Her car's still here, and— *Oh!*"

Sizing up the situation quickly—it would have been nearly impossible *not* to—Addy took a step back, though she didn't look away.

"Damn it, Addy!" Matt swore. "What's the point of knocking if you're going to barge in anyway?"

"Sorry. It never occurred to me—" She broke off, pretending that there wasn't anything unusual about finding two people making love in an ice-fishing hut. "Your father's up at the lodge," she said to Leslie. "He's demanding to see you." She turned a worried gaze Matt's way. "Pop's arguing with him, and since Nick and Kari have already left for Aspen, I thought I'd better get you. I think he's been drinking."

All the lovely moments with Matt died a quick, quiet death with that announcement. Addy waited outside the hut while Leslie and Matt dressed hurriedly. Their haste might have been amusing if they hadn't been so tense. Leslie knew her father's presence could never be construed as a good sign, and if he really *had* been drinking...

She just had to pray that Addy was wrong about that.

They went up the slope from the lake in near darkness, sliding and stumbling on the snow-crusted path in their haste. Matt's long strides put him far ahead of both women, and by the time Leslie hit the lodge's kitchen door, she was out of breath and her lungs felt seared by the cold air. Addy was right behind her, breathing equally hard.

The D'Angelo kitchen was crowded with family members, but Leslie spotted her father right away. Weaving on his feet, he stood over Sam D'Angelo's wheelchair, his fists clenched at his side, "...where the hell do you get off, talking to me like that," he was saying. "Do you think I don't know what your game is?"

Matt was just inserting himself between the two men, facing her father. Before he could say anything that would make the situation worse, Leslie rushed forward. "Dad, I'm here. Let's talk."

Sam D'Angelo looked furious, too, his features dark and mottled. Behind him, Rosa, Renata and Sofia were a solid wall of support. "Get him out of here, Matt," Sam told his son. Then he sent a disgusted glance toward Quentin. "You will leave this property now, or I will have you arrested."

Leslie reached her father's side. She could smell the sour odor of whiskey on him, and, even if that hadn't given him away, one look at his flushed features confirmed the worst. "Dad, please…let's go somewhere and talk."

"Why?" Quentin Meadows snarled as he grabbed her arm. She gasped when his fingers dug into her flesh. The wildness in his eyes made her heart stumble with pain. "So you can tell me how wrong I am? So you can take his side?"

"There are no sides to take. I love you."

Matt laid his hand on top of her father's. His features were set in hard, uncompromising lines, unnervingly intense. "Let her go, Meadows."

Quentin turned her loose and swung his attention back to Matt. He swayed, and when he spoke, the words were bruised with bitterness. "Oh, you'd like to take another poke at me, wouldn't you, you damn meddler? Meddlers, the whole lot of you." He gestured violently toward Sam. "And he's the biggest of all!"

"You're a disgrace, man," Sam flashed back. "Pull yourself together. If not for your own sake, then for your daughter's."

"Shut your damn mouth. I don't need your advice!"

"*Someone* needs to knock some sense into you! Isn't it enough that you abandoned your wife when she needed you most? Are you going to abandon your daughter—"

With a cry of outrage, her father struck out in Sam's direction with flailing fists. The liquor had left Quentin uncoordinated, and Matt had a tight grip on his arms. His punch never reached Sam, but that didn't seem to discourage him.

Leslie sucked in a harsh breath as the two men grappled with one another. "Dad! Stop!" she begged him, pulling on one of his arms. "Please, stop."

"Sam!" she heard Rosa D'Angelo shout. "Stay back!"

Focused on her father, Leslie was barely aware of Sam's chair rolling forward. She had no idea what he intended to do. He seemed equally furious.

Matt was desperately trying to control Quentin without hurting him. When her father lunged, Matt fended him off with a shove backward. Quentin lost his footing, then tried to catch himself on the edge of the kitchen table. He succeeded only in sending two large trays of fruitcakes catapulting. Unfortunately, as he fell, he landed on the footrest of Sam's wheelchair. His weight unbalanced it, and Sam spilled out onto the floor with him.

There was a chorus of horrified cries from the D'Angelo women, then they rushed forward. Sam was sprawled on his hands and knees. Clumsy and confused, Quentin could do nothing more than let loose with a fresh string of curses. Pieces of fruitcake, spilled silverware and broken dishes lay everywhere.

Clearly out of patience, Matt yanked Leslie's father up by the back of his flannel shirt and dragged him away from the mess. He pinned Quentin against the metal door of the walk-in cooler. "Addy," he called to his sister. "Get me the key."

Realizing Matt's intentions, Leslie pushed hair out of her eyes and latched on to his arm. "Matt, no. You can't lock him in there."

Matt didn't try to hide his anger. "Right now, this is the best place for him," he snapped. "It's a cooler, not a freezer. With all the alcohol in his system he'll be fine. Hell, maybe he'll even sober up quicker."

"Please," Leslie said desperately.

He ignored her. Addy appeared with the key, and while Quentin shouted and cursed, Matt pushed him into the cooler and slammed the door after him. He turned the key in the lock and deposited it in the pocket of his jeans.

The women were trying to help Sam get to his feet.

"I'm all right, I'm all right," Sam said, shaking off their help with an irritable snap of his hand. "Stop fussing! Matt—"

"I'm right here, Pop."

Matt helped ease his father back into the wheelchair. As soon as the older man was settled, Leslie knelt beside him, taking his hand in both of hers. "I'm so sorry, Sam. Please, please, try to understand. He didn't know what he was doing."

Sam was still out of breath. Leslie could see his pulse pounding hard in his throat. Behind them they heard Quentin's muted, enraged yells as he beat his fists against the cooler door.

"Your father needs help," Sam said sharply. Beneath her fingers, Leslie felt his hand trembling. "You should never have to deal with behaviour like this."

"I don't. He never drinks around me. He just has

such a blind spot when it comes to this family. He begrudges the time I spend with you."

"Well, is it any wonder you'd come here, when—"

"Sam," Rosa said, stepping into the conversation. The consummate peacemaker, she laid her hand along his arm. "I want you to come to the bedroom with me and lie down for a while."

"I don't need to be babied—"

"Well, I do. This has been way too much excitement for me. My heart feels like it's going to pound right out of my chest."

She didn't look nearly as unnerved as she claimed, but Sam's agitation quickly turned to concern. "All right, Rosie. All right."

Rosa began pushing Sam through the double doors that led into their private quarters, issuing orders as she went. "Addy, you and Renata start cleaning up this mess. Sofia, stop wringing your hands and go check on things out front. Find out if anyone heard the racket and report back to me if we have problems. We might not have many guests right now but the ones we do have are not paying to listen to a free-for-all."

When Rosa and Sam had left the kitchen and everyone else scattered to do damage control, Leslie went to Matt's side. The sight of his tensed jaw gave her a feeling of dread in the pit of her stomach, but she could sense that his anger had abated a little now that the worst was over and no one had gotten hurt.

"What are you going to do?" Leslie asked.

His brows went up, as though he found the question ludicrous. "You mean, am I going to call Sheriff

Bendix and have him haul your father off to jail? I ought to."

"Matt…"

"It could have been serious, Les."

"I know. But it wasn't. Your father seems fine."

He grimaced. "Probably more embarrassed than anything else."

She certainly could understand *that*. "I'm sorry. I never dreamed anything like this would happen. How could everything have been so wonderful just a little while ago, and now…?"

Quentin had stopped banging on the door. They could hear him cursing in frustration, demanding to be let out. It was humiliating to listen to, reminding Leslie of the worst years she'd spent as a teenager growing up. Matt wasn't about to crumble at her father's appeals, and both Addy and Renata were trying to pretend they couldn't hear a thing.

Feeling cold and unnerved by it all, Leslie hugged her arms close against her chest.

Matt reached out to run his hands up and down her arms, as though trying to warm her. "It will be okay, Les. When your dad calms down and sobers up, he can go home."

She nodded her thanks. "I promise, somehow I'll make him understand that he has to get control of his drinking once and for all."

Matt frowned. "I don't want you anywhere around him for a while." When she opened her mouth to protest, he shook his head sharply. "Don't argue about this. *I'll* drive him back to his place, not you. On second thought, since the presence of any D'Angelo seems to be an issue, maybe I'd better have Brandon take him. He's ex-military. He can handle him."

She agreed, the stern set of his features defeating her.

He took a long breath, clearly relieved that she'd accepted his plan. Some of his stiffness seemed to leave him.

The cooler was silent now. "He sounds like he's given up," Leslie said.

"Good. Another few minutes and I'll check." He caught Leslie's hand in his. "Stay up here with us for a few days. I don't like to think of you being by yourself. Not when your father is so unpredictable."

She felt a defensive flare light her insides. "He's my father, Matt, not the Boston Strangler. He'd never hurt me."

He gave her a sweet smile. "Maybe I have other motives for wanting you close by."

"Oh."

He straightened a little as Renata went out the back door carrying a black trash bag filled with fruitcake. Matt glanced around, shaking his head at the damage. Addy was busy picking up spilled silverware across the room.

"God, what a mess," he said. "It looks like we had a food fight in here."

In a low tone that only Matt could hear, Leslie said, "The fruitcakes are a total loss."

"Not much of one," Matt replied in an equally subdued voice. "I don't know anyone who likes the stuff. They might have made handy weapons, though, if I'd thought to use them."

"I'm so sorry…"

"Stop," Matt told her, brushing his fingers across her

cheek. "This is not your fault. It's just too bad your father chose today to go to war with Pop." With a quick glance in Addy's direction, he gave Leslie a brief, soothing kiss. "I could think of several wonderful ways to mark the occasion, but this…" He inclined his head toward the kitchen, "…would not have been one of them."

"It *was* nice, wasn't it? Before, I mean."

"Nice!" he complained with a sardonic smile. "Hell, you'd better come up with a better adjective than that for what happened down on the lake. No, better yet, let *me* come up with something appropriate." He laid kisses across her knuckles, looking up at her from under lashes that were ridiculously long. "It was spectacular. Mind-blowing. Incredible. How's that for starters?"

Before Leslie could say anything, Addy spoke up from across the room. "For Pete's sake, either take it upstairs or pick up a broom."

Leslie and Matt laughed.

Addy walked over to them. She waved her hand back and forth between them. "So how long has this been going on?"

"None of your business," Matt said.

"We can explain," Leslie added.

Addy grinned. "I *know* how it works, Leslie. I just want to know what took the two of you so long."

Before either of them could say anything, Rosa D'Angelo came barreling through the double doors. Her face was absolutely devoid of color. "Matt, come quickly. I think Sam is having another stroke."

CHAPTER TWELVE

THE REGIONAL HOSPITAL in Idaho Springs was the same one Sam had been taken to when he'd had his two previous strokes. Though small, it seemed to Matt to be well-equipped and efficiently run, even late at night, when emergency-room staffing could sometimes be problematic.

The last few hours had been pure insanity. The rush to the hospital. The late-night consultation with both a neurologist and a cardiologist. Matt pushing to secure his father a bed on the crowded Coronary Care Unit, even when his blood tests and ECG didn't appear to warrant it, and an MRI seemed to rule out another stroke.

"I'm sure we're looking at no more than angina brought on by stress," the cardiologist had told Matt and the rest of the D'Angelo family after he'd examined Sam. "I think we'll send him home tonight with nitroglycerin tablets and plan to do some follow-up testing on Monday."

So definitely not another stroke, thank God.

But Matt hadn't been willing to take any chances. "I'd like him admitted overnight. Perhaps a consult in the morning for an angiogram." Then he'd given the doctor his credentials and the man had agreed without further argument.

Doctors didn't like having their directives questioned, and Matt could see the guy resented his interference. But tonight he didn't care about that. Tonight he was *willing* his father to live. Funny how different it felt when you were on the other side of that doctor/patient dynamic.

Now he sat by his father's bedside, watching his chest rise and fall with each deep breath. Sam was sedated, stabilized, and though his color was good and the heart monitor indicated no arrhythmia, Matt's father had never looked so diminished.

In the middle of the night a hospital seemed so peaceful. A temporary illusion, as Matt well knew. He had been in hospital rooms exactly like this one hundreds of times, visited patients to give them news—both good and bad—on too many occasions to count. He'd even been a patient himself and had hated every minute of it.

There was no peace here. There was just…the waiting.

His father stirred. His eyes opened halfway, glazed with medication. "Rosie…"

Matt inched closer to the bed so that Sam could see him without effort. "She'll be right back, Pop. She's getting coffee. We sent everyone else home, but we're going to spend the night with you."

"But they don't think it's another stroke?"

"No. Nothing to worry about." Plenty of time in the morning to discuss everything.

"Ticker…giving out, then?" Sam's stronger hand lay

across his chest. On top of the sheet, his fingers jerked spasmodically, unconsciously shaping themselves to be held, and Matt grasped them lightly.

"No. We'll get you on some medication, and you'll be back driving everyone crazy in no time."

"Damned…inconvenient…" Sam said with a frown.

The words trailed away as his lashes lowered, and he sank into sleep once more. His features looked very gentle and unguarded, and yet very old. The lamplight brought out with microscopic cruelty every fretful line of his face, every glinting gray hair.

Matt settled back in his chair and exhaled wearily.

Since coming home he'd grown closer to his father. In some ways, their physical limitations were so similar—Sam struggling to regain full use of his arm and leg, Matt trying to improve the mobility in his hand. As he'd promised, he'd talked to Sam's doctor, and a new regimen had been set. Lately father and son had exercised side-by-side, planned objectives together and celebrated small victories.

They'd both benefited. Their common goals made them a good team. And perhaps more than anyone else in the family, Sam understood the frustration of having to face facts that not even the most indomitable will-power could change.

On the other side of the bed, an intravenous drip fed heparin into his father's system, dissolving blood clots and preventing new ones from forming. The family was going to get through this latest emergency. Sam would be fine. Matt would make sure of that.

It was a relief to feel more confident at last. He certainly hadn't felt that way when he'd seen his mother, pale and frantic, coming through the kitchen doors. When he hadn't managed to keep a tight leash on that son of a bitch Meadows.

God, he really did loathe that man. How did Les deal with his crap year after year?

Les. He wished she could be here with him right now. He wanted to hold her, just be with her. Something ached in his chest every time he pictured the two of them together.

He was thirty-one years old, and he'd never been in love. Not really. Not in any way that counted. And he certainly didn't need to be in love now, not with everything in his life still up for grabs. But Les…Les had brought him to the most intense, intimate experience he'd ever known. She could tumble him over the edge if he wasn't careful.

What was he going to do about her?

He closed his eyes and rubbed his forehead, but a moment later, his attention snagged on the sound of his father's deep-throated groan. Sam seemed restless, as though his dreams weren't to his liking. Matt leaned closer, repositioning the oxygen canula into Sam's nostrils.

"Shh," he said in a tone of soft command. "Just rest. Everything's going to be fine."

Sam's eyelids flickered open, but his thoughts seemed cloudy, unfocused. "Have to…tell her," he mumbled, barely coherent. "I told you…should have listened…Told you he was dangerous."

Matt smoothed a strand of wayward hair back from his father's forehead. As independent as Sam was, he was like a child when it came to wanting his wife nearby in times of crisis. "She'll be here soon," Matt told him.

Sam moved in agitation. "No. Tell her…Leslie deserves…to know…" The heart monitor beside the bed registered only a fractional change in rhythm. "No more… secrets."

Secrets? What was he talking about? What did Leslie deserve to know? Matt stroked his father's cheek, determined to keep Sam calm. "I'll tell her," he promised. "Rest now. I'll take care of it."

"Not…fair to the…girl. Celeste…you have to… All these years. It's…so wrong not to tell."

Matt fell silent. Celeste was Leslie's mother. Since her death five years ago, Sam had seldom mentioned her name. Why would he be so worked up about her now? And *what* was so wrong and needed to be told?

His father's head swung sharply on the pillow. He blinked at Matt like a baby owl, but there was no lucidity in his gaze. He clearly wasn't seeing his son at all. "I'll help… Important she knows…Celeste. Tell her about…John…how he…" The rest of his words tumbled away, lost in a whispering confusion.

Some unnamed fear began to wind around Matt's chest. "Who's John?" he asked softly. "Tell Leslie *what* about John?"

Sam scowled as though impatient. His gaze loosened and swam. "John…her father. Not…Quentin."

The words dropped like stones into a well, and Matt's heart hit the roof of his mouth. He could only look at his father, startled into speechlessness.

Quentin Meadows was not Leslie's real father?

And Leslie didn't know? From her actions and from the little he could piece together of Sam's words, that much was obvious. How long had his father kept this secret?

A dozen questions raced in Matt's brain, but now was not the time to ask them. Sam needed his rest, and even at this moment he was slipping back under the sedative.

But tomorrow maybe…when things had calmed down. When the clear light of day would make everything seem normal.

He turned sharply as the hospital-room door opened with a soft whoosh. It was his mother, bearing two cups of coffee from the machine down in the cafeteria.

She took one look at Matt's face. "What is it?" she asked, her fear evident in her voice. She was beside him in an instant, looking down at her husband. "What's wrong?"

Somehow Matt managed to answer calmly. "Nothing," he replied. "Nothing's changed. Everything's fine."

But it wasn't. Everything seemed displaced. Surreal. Everything was most definitely *not* fine.

LESLIE WAS DESPERATE for news of Sam's condition, and wished now that she had gone to the hospital with Matt and the rest of the D'Angelos.

Instead, Brandon O'Dell from the front desk had driven her father home in his car, while she had followed them. At the trailer a half-asleep Quentin had been tucked into bed like a naughty child. Brandon had offered to watch over him the rest of the night and the next morning. Thanking him, Leslie had done as she'd promised Matt she would. She had driven home and tried to rest.

An effort that proved to be a dismal failure.

Matt had called her late. He had reassured her that the problem didn't appear to be another stroke, but they were admitting Sam and would run more tests in the morning. He promised to keep in touch with news just as soon as they knew anything definite.

No matter how hard she tried, she couldn't get the mental images of that horrible incident with her father out of her head—the frozen shock on all their faces, the way Rosa had hidden her concern and nerves behind a mask of calm command. Most of all, the anxiety she'd seen in Matt's eyes as he'd hurried the family out the door and into the company van.

Why didn't someone call? She glanced at her watch. It was already 7:00 a.m. Surely the family knew something by now.

As though she had willed it, the phone rang, making her jump before she snatched it up.

It wasn't Matt. It was Perry.

"It doesn't sound like I woke you," he said.

"You didn't."

"Good. I know it's early, but I wanted to catch you before you made any other plans. I'm coming up to Broken Yoke for the weekend."

"Why?"

He laughed. "That's not very welcoming. You're supposed to say, 'Wonderful, Perry! When can we get together?'"

"I'm sorry. I'm a little distracted. I can't see you this weekend. The clinic's open on Saturday."

"All right," Perry said, stretching out the words as though he didn't quite believe her. "That takes care of eight hours. What about the rest of the time? We could do something on Sunday."

"I can't," she said, her voice flat.

"Give me a good reason."

"I gave you *good* reasons when I was in Denver," she replied, trying not to let her annoyance show. "I just don't think we have a future together, Perry."

"We'll see. I'll stop in at the clinic."

She started to argue that comment, then decided it was pointless. "Okay. Don't say I didn't warn you." It was the best answer she could think of at the moment. "I have to go. Things are a little hectic here this morning, and I'm expecting a call."

When he finally hung up, Leslie sat on the couch with her legs tucked under her, just staring at the phone.

She couldn't help thinking that it would be easier if she could fall in love with Perry. He truly seemed to care about her. While Matt... Loving Matt the way she did certainly didn't mean everything was going to be wine and roses from here on out. Since they'd had very little time to talk, she didn't have a clue what his intentions were.

Or even if he *had* any.

She got up, determined to find distraction in activity. Waiting for the phone to ring didn't make *anything* better.

Her father would probably be up by now, feeling hungry and out-of-sorts if past hangovers were any indication. But he should be safe to be around. It had been so long between his last bout of heavy drinking and this one. Leslie wanted to talk to him, find out what she could do to help.

Last night she had also accepted the fact that until she could figure out what to do about her father, there was no way he could make the trip to Salt Lake to spend Christmas with Aunt Tanya. Leslie had called her aunt, offered an excuse but very few details, then promised to be in touch. The woman was used to her brother's unpredictable ways and hadn't sounded surprised.

Leslie drove over to the trailer, and the first thing she noticed was that her father's battered old truck wasn't in the driveway where Brandon had parked it last night. Stomach tightening, Leslie went quickly up the icy walkway and knocked on the door.

Brandon opened it, looking a little surprised. "You must be psychic. I was just trying to call you."

Her heart stumbled. "Where is he?"

"He just left."

"You let him go?" she asked, more sharply than she intended.

"He's a grown man. He was sober. He's not under arrest."

"No, but…" She glanced worriedly in the direction of town, thinking of every bar and convenience store that stood between here and Broken Yoke. "If he's gone to buy a bottle…"

Brandon shook his head. "I don't think he's doing that, Leslie."

"How do you know?"

He plunged his hands into the pockets of his jeans, looking down for a moment before answering. "I think I know what that looks like—a man who's determined to find a drink."

She realized the truth in that statement. She'd nearly forgotten that Brandon had fought his own battle over alcoholism since coming to live here. "I'm sorry," she said. "Where do you think he's gone, then? Did he say *anything*?"

"No."

"Does he know about Sam?"

"He knows. I told him this morning."

"I have to find him." A sudden thought occurred to her. "Will you go up to the lodge just in case he should show up there? Make sure that he doesn't disturb anyone?"

"Of course."

Fifteen minutes later, Leslie had driven past all her father's favorite hangouts in Broken Yoke. They weren't open yet, but that didn't mean he wouldn't find a way to get what he wanted if he was determined. Unlike Brandon, she didn't have much faith that Quentin wouldn't try to find solace in a fresh bottle.

She had just about run out of places to look when she spotted his truck. It was parked just past town on River Road, at the base of the dilapidated remains of Lightning Overlook.

Years ago, some well-meaning town committee had decided that what Broken Yoke needed was a rest area where tourists could stop to enjoy the view of Lightning River, the valley and the surrounding mountains. Land had been cleared, picnic tables had been purchased, and a pine-and-flagstone observation tower had been built atop the granite cliffs.

The building was lovely, but it had never lived up to its potential. Tourists were lazy. The climb up the notched steps was so steep that few people went that far, settling instead for the quick, easy snapshots they could grab at the base of the cliffs before jumping back into their cars.

When the area's tourist flow dried to a trickle, the town stopped setting aside funds for maintenance on the overlook. The observation deck fell into disrepair, covered with graffiti, the wood rotting and dangerous, until finally the place had been boarded up and forgotten.

Leslie couldn't imagine why her father would come to this spot. He'd never mentioned it, not once.

She got out of the car, pulling her coat closer around her as a chilly breeze tugged at it. She stayed away from the edge of the slope, knowing that the snow was deep there and the wind whipping up from the bottom of the valley would be even colder.

"Dad!" she called, circling her hands like a cone around her mouth. The word bounced back at her a dozen times before disappearing on the raw air.

She scanned the area around the low stone wall of the overlook. Beyond it, snow had erased the world entirely, leaving a crisp, blank page on which nothing moved. No birds in the bare trees. No soft thud of snow dropping from weary branches. Everything was so still. Far below, even the river seemed silent, frozen in place.

She looked up at the open balcony of the observation desk…and saw her father.

He leaned against the railing, his hands dangling over the edge. Leslie's heart skidded to a halt. Unexpectedly, insanely, she thought that he was be about to jump.

"Dad, come down," she yelled quickly. "I need your help."

She didn't wait for his reply. She took off for the flagstone steps that had been placed at the base of the tower, slipping on treacherous ice more than once. The boards across the entrance had been removed, and she went swiftly past them, her heart hammering.

The spiral staircase was enclosed in a column of stone, dark and unfriendly. Halfway up she tripped, banging her knee against the lip of the next step and falling hard in her haste.

The staircase was the equivalent of three flights. She was out of breath by the time she reached the top. All she could think about was getting to her father.

The landing opened up, revealing a dusty pine floor covered with the grime of many years and a few signs of transient occupants. If the observation deck had been glassed in at one time, it was no longer. The wind blew directly into the balcony opening, swirling down the staircase with a faint, ghostly moan. There were no furnishings, only a long wooden bench along one wall.

Her father sat there, and he looked up as she rushed forward.

A long moment passed. Even in the murky light Leslie could see the harsh tension in her father's ruddy features. His hands were balled into fists on his thighs. His hair was wild, as though it had lost a tussle with the wind.

She approached slowly, quietly, and sat down next to him.

"What are you doing here, Dad?" she asked, giving him a brave, determined smile. "You should be resting."

He didn't respond right away, only shifted slightly on the bench. After a long time, he said, "I know you mean well, but I want you to go home. I don't want you here. We can talk later."

Leslie searched for her anger toward him, but couldn't find it. His behavior last night might have been inexcusable, but he was still her father. She reached out a hand to brush a strand of hair away from his brow. "Let me help."

"No!" He caught her wrist, pulling out of her reach. His eyes were hot with despair, and he seemed completely unaware that his grip was so tight and painful that she'd probably have a bruise tomorrow. "Go away! Leave me alone. You *can't* help."

She refused to give in. "I'm not leaving you," she said calmly. "I want us to talk this out. *Now*."

For a long time he just glared at her. Then he let her go with a heavily expelled breath. His jaw clenched, but he seemed suddenly resigned to her interference. "You've got your mother's stubborn streak."

"So you've said before. I'm still not leaving."

He gave a lazy shrug to indicate she could suit herself. A dull flush of color lay across his cheeks. Sensing that he would not give in to conversation easily, she let him be.

Hugging her coat closer, she rose and walked to the balcony. Whoever had planned this particular angle for the observation deck had known what they were doing. The view of the valley was stunning, and the mountains were impressive monoliths in the background, sharp and clear in the distance. The kind of sight that could almost stop your heart.

The tower itself blended in well with its surroundings. It was a shame it had become such a forgotten relic of Broken Yoke's more hopeful past. "I'll bet this place was beautiful once," Leslie said and meant it.

"It was," her father agreed. "I built it."

Leslie turned back to him. "What do you mean, you built it?"

"Back before your mother and I were married. Construction boss." His voice was low and steady, and when he looked up, Leslie saw the hard glitter of pride in his eyes. "It was one of the first steady jobs I ever got. Lasted almost eight months from start to finish. The town had big plans for this place." She watched her father's mouth tighten, turn into no more than a grim slash. "*I* had big plans for my life because of what I accomplished here."

She was too stunned to move. In all their years together, her father had shared so little of the past.

"You've never told me that before," she said to him.

He shifted again, uneasily. "No reason to. By the time you came along, all those grand plans were as worthless as a bucket of spit."

She wondered what he was thinking in that moment. So many years gone wrong. Had he taken passionate gambles that had failed miserably? Foolish little chances that had somehow turned ugly? Was he remembering what it felt like to be young and strong and full of hope?

He looked at her with such precision that it made her shiver. "The day after the ribbon-cutting ceremony for this place, I asked your Mom to marry me. Right where you're standing." He exhaled gruffly, his version of a laugh. "Even got down on one knee like some lovesick knight in a book of fairy tales."

"Mom must have loved that," she said, surprise making her voice sound foreign to her own ears. "She was always a romantic at heart."

"She was the best thing that ever happened to me, and she deserved a lot better than what she got. I was crazy about her." Her father's gaze fell to the floor. His feet moved in an arc along the pine boards, creating a sandy rasp beneath his boots. "It's no good to need someone more than they need you," he said, so wearily that it broke Leslie's heart.

She didn't know what to say. He wasn't the kind of man who had ever been easy to speak to. Or get close to. In years past, there had been days when she'd actually hated him. Sometimes, during the worst times, he had seemed like a complete stranger. But he had never stopped being someone whose love she'd longed for.

She wanted to be angry with him, but she couldn't. Her mother was gone. He needed help. He was just a man with no resources left to confront each disappointment in his life.

The silence had stretched too thin. Leslie went to his side, sat down and took his arm. She could feel the coldness in him even through his thick coat. "It's all right, Dad…"

He turned to look at her. Across his face ran a parade of emotions, and while she watched, his eyes filled with tears. "I'm sorry," he said. "Sorry about what I did yesterday. I've been thinking about it all morning." He shook his head wildly. "It wasn't me. You know that wasn't *me*."

"I know."

"Problem is, I haven't been me for so long, I don't know *who* I am anymore. I want to get it right, but I feel like everything inside is on a wire that just keeps getting twisted tighter and tighter."

The lines in his face looked deep enough to have been carved by a knife. Wrapping one arm around him, Leslie stroked her hand across his cheek. "We can fix this, Dad. We can."

"I've done enough damage to last a lifetime." His face crumpled in a wave of pure misery. The tears streamed from his eyes, unchecked. "I'm nothing but trouble for you, Leslie. No good. No good at all. Sometimes death seems like such a peaceful, easy answer."

That needed a breath or two. Her heart made slow, heavy sweeps in her breast.

Determined, she caught his chin so that their eyes could meet. "You will never say that again. You're my father, and I love you."

The look in his eyes was beseeching. And afraid.

"It's *not* too late," she said firmly, for both their sakes. "We can get through this. I'm going to help you."

THE RESULTS from Sam's angiogram were conclusive. There was no need for immediate concern.

Although he'd suspected as much, Matt felt relief trickle into his system as the cardiologist told Sam that, with medication and a few lifestyle modifications, there should be no repeat of the angina attack that had brought him in last night.

His father seemed heartened by that news, though resentful that more changes were needed in his diet and exercise regimen. True to form, he complained that he was already being made to do more in that area than any one human being ought to have to.

After the doctor left, Sam didn't waste any time.

He looked at Matt, determination glinting in his gaze. "Let's go home," he said, making a move to get out of bed.

Matt gently pushed him back. "Take it easy, Pop. All in good time."

"Weren't you listening? He said I could go home. So get me out of here." Dissatisfied with his son's lack of urgency, he turned toward his wife, who was already gathering personal items from the dresser. "Rosie, get me out of here."

Matt's mother didn't look any more intimidated than her son. "The doctor said he could have you discharged in about an hour."

Sam made a displeased sound, bristling defiance.

Personally, Matt was just as eager to get his father back home. There were things he wanted to talk to him about, questions that needed peace and quiet. A *lot* of questions.

"What's the big hurry?" Matt asked.

"I have things I want to take care of."

Shaking her head, Rosa came to her husband's bedside. "What things? If you think you're going home to take up where you left off, you're mistaken. You're not going to overdo—"

"Ebbene!" Sam said, waving away the beginnings of her argument. "But before you lock me up like a lab rat that needs to be studied every minute, I want to stop in Broken Yoke."

"Why?"

"There's someone I need to see."

"You're not going to talk to Leslie's father," Matt said.

"Certainly not," Rosa added. "There's nothing more that needs to be said between you two stubborn fools."

Sam plucked at a strip of adhesive tape the nurse had placed on his arm when she'd removed the IV. "You're right about that, Rosie. It's time for action now. Before we go home, I want to stop by Bendix's office."

Bendix was Broken Yoke's sheriff, a man Sam disliked intensely. Matt and his mother exchanged a surprised glance. "Why?" Matt asked.

As though daring anyone to argue, Sam tilted his chin up and glared at them. "Because I intend to press charges against Quentin Meadows."

CHAPTER THIRTEEN

SAM HAD long ago accepted that regaining his health would be a hard-won battle, that recovery was going to take a lot longer than he liked. But waking up this morning to find out from some wet-behind-the-ears cardiologist that his heart was now in the process of adding insult to injury…this angina thing…well, that had been the last straw.

He was tired of being a victim. It was time to fight back.

To Sam's way of thinking, there was only one person responsible for this latest setback, and that person was Quentin Meadows. As much as he hated the idea of making Leslie unhappy, he had to teach Meadows that he couldn't fool with Sam D'Angelo and get away with it.

He was pleased that the family evidently realized that he meant business. All the way to Broken Yoke, they'd been quieter than little stone gods. They knew better than to argue with him. They knew he wasn't about to change his mind, and they wouldn't dare try to make him change it.

Quentin Meadows was going to be behind bars by sundown.

Sam drew a deep breath as Matt pulled the van in front of Broken Yoke's tiny police station. Bendix had been complaining about the size of his office for years, but with crime almost non-existent, he got hooted down at every town council meeting.

But tonight, Sam thought, tonight he'd have Meadows to keep him company.

He waited for Matt and Rosa to get out so they could help him. But instead of coming to open the sliding side door, his wife gave Matt a short, mysterious nod, then slammed the front passenger door. She headed off down the snow-shoveled sidewalk toward the pharmacy that sat next to the police station, while Matt stayed behind the wheel and didn't turn around.

"Where's *she* off to?" Sam asked.

"She's going to get your prescriptions filled."

"Why? Ray's always been willing to have someone deliver them up to the lodge."

"Because I asked her to leave the two of us alone."

"What for?"

"So I can talk you out of making a mistake." Matt turned in his seat so he could look at Sam. He inclined his head toward the police station. "You don't want to do this, Pop."

Sam hated it when his children opposed him. It made him more aware of how impotent he'd become in his own family. Nobody listened to a word he said anymore, and frankly, he'd had just about enough of it.

"That's where you're wrong," he said, letting his exasperation show. "*Somebody* needs to do it. You make a dove of yourself, son, and the hawks will devour you.

Well, I'm not going to let that crazy bastard think he can devour *me*. Now help me out."

"No."

"Then I'll do it myself," Sam snapped, reaching for the door handle.

He heard a slight click and realized that Matt had engaged the child-proof locks. "I want to talk to you for a few minutes, Pop," his son said in a calm, reasonable tone.

Sam's blood felt as though it had been infused with hot lava. He yanked on the door handle a few times. *"Cafone!"* he cursed. "Unlock this door this instant!"

"Nope."

"Unlock it, or I'll…I'll…"

"You'll what?"

"I'll cut you out of my will," he sputtered. "You won't get a dime."

His son had the audacity to shrug. "Money isn't everything."

"You'll think differently when your brothers and sister get it all and you're left with nothing. You have no right to keep me a prisoner in here. This is America. You can't just—"

"I know about Meadows not being Leslie's real father, Pop."

Sam's threats stumbled to a halt as those words bore down on him like an old freight train. "What do you mean?" he asked on a tight breath. And then, in an effort to recoup lost poise, he said, "I don't know what you're talking about."

"You were sedated last night, but that didn't keep you from talking."

"I never talk in my sleep. Ask your mother."

"Celeste Meadows told you that Leslie's real father was someone named John. You encouraged her to tell Leslie. I take it she never did."

Sam regarded Matt from under a furrowed brow. He'd never been a facile liar. An unsettling discomfort grew in his chest, a feeling of weakness, of frustration. Resigned, he said at last, "I don't know if she did or not. I suspect she didn't."

"How long have you known?"

"Since just before Celeste died. I've never told another living soul. Not even your mother."

The interior of the van remained quiet for a long moment or two. Finally, Matt nodded slowly. "I know the basics. Trust me enough to tell me the rest."

"It's old history, Matthew. The way the world works nowadays, it's not even shocking."

"I'd still like to hear it."

Sam closed his eyes and let his head fall back. Even after all these years, the images were still so clear in his mind. He could see them all, that close circle of friends—so young and full of promise. All those old memories had stayed with him, bright and valuable, like ancient coins held in his hands. What harm could it do to share them now?

"Nick was still in diapers," he said. "Your mom had just found out she was pregnant with you. We were building the lodge on land I'd inherited from your grandparents, but we didn't have a lot of money in those days." He smiled, remembering just how tight times had been. "More ideas than sense, I guess you could say.

When it looked like the money was about to run out, I called a few old college buddies. Back then, you never asked why a friend needed help, you just showed up. John Wentworth was starting to make a name for himself as an architect, but he came up from Pueblo right away. Didn't hesitate to pitch in. Worked like a dog right beside us."

"Sounds like you had good friends."

"We had a lot of them, even around here. Celeste came up every chance she got. She sewed drapes with your mother. Painted. Never complained a bit."

"Did Meadows come with her?"

"No. He never cared for the fact that we'd been close as kids, and he was working two jobs to keep food on their table. He wasn't a heavy drinker back then, but he'd grown up wired for trouble. He was always the jealous type, wanting Celeste right by his side when he wasn't working."

"But she came anyway."

"She and John…I didn't see it then, but I guess the two of them fell in love."

"And she got pregnant."

"Yes."

"Did she tell John?"

Sam shook his head. "Never had the chance. One weekend the weather was bad. It was slowing everything down, so John decided it was a good time to go home to check on things. He took a little puddle jumper that barely got off the ground in the rain. A few minutes after takeoff, it plowed into the Front Range. Killed everyone on board."

Matt blew a long breath. Finally he said, "So Leslie's father never knew he had a child on the way."

"No. Celeste never said anything to anyone. Not even to me."

"How did you find out the truth?"

Sam felt his muscles tense, remembering those final days of Celeste's life as though it had only been yesterday. "She asked me to come see her…toward the end. She told me the truth. Wanted to know what I thought she should do. She'd never told Quentin the truth, and I didn't think she should. But I did think she should tell Leslie everything, let her make the decision."

"Did you say that because of your dislike for Meadows?"

"I'm sure that was a factor," Sam admitted. "I have no use for that man. Celeste's marriage was no bed of roses. And you know as well as I do how he treated Leslie. But mostly, I thought Celeste owed it to her daughter—to let her know what a fine man John had been."

Matt shook his head. "Why did Celeste marry Quentin in the first place?"

"You'd never know it to look at him today, but when he was young, he had a certain rough, dangerous mystery about him that some women found attractive. Celeste's parents were strict. I think she couldn't help but find him appealing. And to be fair, he treated her special, seemed to adore her. But after he hurt his back and started drinking, everything soured."

"I don't think Celeste took your advice. I don't think Leslie knows the truth."

"How can you be sure?"

"She would have told me by now. Our relation-ship…she trusts me." He sighed. "I don't give a damn about Meadows. But you realize…if you press charges against the man she thinks of as her father, you'll only be hurting Les."

"That man is dangerous."

"I agree. But there are other ways to handle this. We can insist that he get professional help."

Sam glanced out the window, unwilling to be swayed. "A few months in jail will get his attention a lot quicker."

"Were you in love with his wife?"

The unexpected question made Sam's head jerk around. He pinned his son with a shocked, angry look. Speaking carefully, he said, "How dare you ask me such a thing?"

"I'd be happy to see the son of a bitch out of Les's life, too, Pop…but your need to see Meadows pun-ished…aside from what happened yesterday, it seems… personally motivated."

"I have loved your mother from the day we met," Sam told his son in crisp, measured syllables. "I have never known any woman who could hold a candle to Rosa. Your question is an insult to her and to me."

There was an uncomfortable pause. "I'm sorry," Matt said at last. "I know you love Mom. So if that's not it, then isn't it possible that you want to do this, not because it will help Meadows, but because it will help you?"

"Don't talk in riddles."

Matt slid forward, until he could place a hand on one of Sam's knees and draw his full attention. "I know what it feels like," he said in a soft, controlled voice. "Wanting to take out all your frustrations. Wanting to make someone pay for the things that are missing in your life and might never be replaced."

"This is nonsense."

"Is it? Nobody wants to feel vulnerable, Pop. Sometimes I think about how senseless Shayla's death was, what I've been through this past year, and the anger just wants to spill over. But if I let it, it will poison every other part of my life. All I'll be left with is the hate."

Sam glared at his son. "Shall I assume you're changing careers? That you're leaving microsurgery for psychiatry?"

Matt gave him a small smile. "I'm not going to pretend that I have all the answers. It's a work in progress. Do you think I'm any less stubborn than you are? However, lately Les has really made me question myself…" He frowned, then shook his head. "Although why she puts up with my moods is a mystery to me."

Sam hesitated only a moment. Might as well say what he was thinking. "She puts up with you for the same reason Rosa puts up with *me*. She loves you."

He knew that might not be what his son wanted to hear, but it was long past the time when he should hear it. Life was too short to let the good things slip away.

Matt folded his arms, giving Sam a look of warning. "Don't try to sidetrack me. All I'm really asking is this—will you consider the possibility that Quentin Meadows isn't the one you're really mad at?"

The question just lay there as Matt waited, and Sam turned to stare out the window. On the door to the police station, someone had hung an enormous Christmas wreath. Probably Bendix, trying to make the place look a little less stark.

Sam couldn't help imagining Meadows in jail. That certainly wasn't the way anyone ought to spend the holiday, he supposed, but ultimately that kind of shock might do the bum some good. He needed to be forced to face some ugly facts about his behavior. Forced to get his life together once and for all. Before it was too late.

The strained silence in the van seemed suffocating. Sam's body felt thin and brittle to him suddenly. Ready to break. Matt was wrong. This wasn't about misplaced anger at all. This was about meeting problems head-on, as Sam had faced every obstacle in *his* life.

In a deadly calm voice, Sam said, "I want to get out of this van now. Either you help me, or I will flag down a stranger on the street. One way or the other, I'm filing that complaint."

THAT EVENING, Leslie heard the car pull up in her driveway. When she looked out the window and saw that it was Matt, she headed for the door. She had it open before he'd even reached the front step.

He came into the foyer and took off his coat so she could hang it in the hall closet. He didn't say a word. He didn't have to. He looked exhausted. His clothes and hair were mussed. There were circles under his eyes and the dark stubble of a new beard along his tightened jaw.

"How is he?" she asked nervously.

"Didn't Mom call?"

"Just to give me the basics."

"He's home."

"That's great. What's the diagnosis?"

"Stable angina brought on by stress. The angiogram was clear. No worry there."

She realized she'd been holding her breath and inhaled sharply. "Thank God. This has been one of the longest days of my life. You look exhausted. Would you like some coffee?"

"Lots of it," he said, following her into the darkened kitchen. "The stronger the better."

She turned on the light over the stove and pulled coffee out of the cupboard, along with mugs for both of them.

"How's your father?" Matt asked as he watched her measure grounds into the filter and then switch on the coffeemaker.

"Filled with remorse for what he did."

"We need to talk about that."

She nodded. "I know. But he realizes that his behavior was inexcusable, and that he can't go on this way. I've promised to help him."

"I'm not sure it's going to be that easy."

Something in his tone made her look at him. "I can handle it." She didn't want to get into a difficult discussion with him over her father. "Have you eaten? Do you want me to fix you something?"

He came across the kitchen, catching her against the sink and hauling her up against his body. "No. All I want right now is you."

Caught by surprise, her lips parted under the pressure of his kiss. It seemed as though she had been waiting for this all day. Never mind all those internal lectures she'd given herself about being patient, about not expecting what Matt might never offer, not longing for something beyond his power to give. He was here now. Touching her the way she wanted, creating a kind of magic with every feather-light stroke, and she could not think of a single reason to tame this moment between them. She kissed him back with a passion she had once thought impossible.

Just when she began to wonder if they might actually make love right here on the rug, Matt lifted his head.

Even in the dim lighting, she could see that his eyes were alive with amusement. "I guess that settles the question of whether or not you missed me today."

"Every minute," she replied. "Did you miss *me?*"

"Every minute."

He showed her just how true that statement was by kissing her again. His lips found the side of her neck, the line of her collarbone as he pushed aside the opening of her blouse. Again her mouth...her mouth, it tingled under his gentle assault.

Oh my, Leslie thought. Maybe they really *would* make love on the kitchen rug. The idea was deliciously exciting.

When she laughed a little, he stopped long enough to give her a teasing, dark look. "Laughter is not the response a man wants when he kisses a woman," he told her. His voice was husky with the telltale remnants of passion. "What's so amusing?"

"I was just thinking that when you walked in just now you looked as if you might want to make it an early night. You looked so tired. But you seem to have found hidden reserves somewhere."

"It's amazing, but I'm feeling suddenly revitalized."

Her fingers clutched against his chest as he dipped his head to nuzzle the underside of her chin, then warmed it with his tongue. "This spot," he said softly. "How did I miss this yesterday?"

"You were distracted."

"Still am," he replied, and his voice sounded as shaky as hers. His fingers were tugging at the buttons of her blouse. "Why do you buy so many things with buttons?"

"I never will again."

"Good."

One of his hands caressed her hip, pressing, lifting, so that she came up against his hard arousal. Words were impossible suddenly. The only thing that would form in her mouth was a sigh as her breath came up hard in her throat. Her head fell back, and she closed her eyes in pleasure as he tugged lightly at the soft flesh of her throat.

Her hands lay along the back of his head. He captured them, bringing her fingers to his lips so he could kiss each one separately, sucking, nipping, then running his tongue against the very same spot. Her nerves were jumping, jumping with anticipation...

It took her a moment, a very *long* moment, to realize that Matt had gone still.

She opened her eyes to discover that his smile had faded. He lifted her hand, turning it over, and the intensity of his gaze was frightening to see.

"What's the matter?" she asked.

He ran a light fingertip across the inside of her wrist. "Where did you get this?"

At first she didn't understand what he meant. Get what? Then she realized that the slight discoloration had caught his notice. The evidence of her father's tight grip on her wrist lay like a brand on her skin.

"It was an accident."

Matt stepped away from her, flipped on the overhead light, then returned to her side. He studied the marks intently, tilting her wrist toward the light. "What kind of accident?"

"I went to see Dad this morning—"

Something dark and angry rose immediately in his features. "Your father did this?"

"Yes, but he wasn't really aware of his strength." She dropped her eyes for a moment, embarrassed to admit her fear that her father might have been about to throw himself off the observation tower balcony. "You don't understand. There were extenuating circumstances."

"I'm sure there were. Extenuating circumstances are a pretty popular excuse for drunks."

She stiffened. A cold front couldn't have changed the atmosphere more. "That's uncalled-for."

He pulled away from her so quickly that Leslie felt the air move between them. He leaned back against the sink, his hands braced against the countertop. "For God's sake, Les, do you know how many times I've had to do reconstructive surgery on women and kids who fell victim to 'extenuating circumstances?'"

Their gazes locked and held. She felt her heart drop,

because the moments of happiness between them were moving further and further away.

"I'm *telling* you it wasn't intentional." Her voice was hard, but barely more than a whisper.

Matt shook his head. "That doesn't matter. I've given that bastard more benefit of the doubt than any man like that has a right to expect. Because you've asked me to."

"It won't happen again."

"You're right about that at least, because I'll be damned if I'll let him abuse you this way. Why do you continue trying to protect him!"

"Why shouldn't I try to protect him? He's my father."

"The hell he is."

She watched him as he turned and snatched the coffee cups off the counter, then tossed them into the dish drainer so roughly she felt sure they had broken. He snapped off the coffee maker, breathing hard, his nostrils flared like those of a horse that had just finished a punishing race.

And all the while, his words were sifting into her consciousness.

"What is *that* supposed to mean?" she finally asked.

Matt didn't look at her. Leslie marveled at how completely different he seemed, unwilling or unable to communicate with her at all.

He raked an angry hand through his hair. "I meant he's not the kind of father he needs to be," he said.

Her heart felt shredded. They were worlds apart now. "That's not what you meant. Don't lie to me. *Tell me* what you did mean," she pressed.

The moment stretched into forever. Finally, his eyes met hers. "He's not your father, Les."

"What are you talking about? Of course—"

"Your real father was a man named John Wentworth. He was a friend of Pop's from college. He came up here to help build the lodge, and he and your mother fell in love."

A cold, deathlike feeling sent goosebumps up and down Leslie's arms. Her world tilted for a moment. Her breath caught in her chest. *Something wrong there,* she thought. She shook her head, stunned by the knowledge that Matt, the man she loved, could turn into someone she didn't know at all. "Why would you say such horrible things? Do you hate my father that much?"

For just a second his worried glance clung to her desperate one. "If you don't believe me, then ask Pop. He got the whole story from your mom a short time before she died."

In slow, careful words, Matt explained how he'd found out the truth. How he'd strong-armed his father into a larger explanation. Stunned, Leslie listened and tried to absorb it all. She tried to envision how it must have been for her mother and this other man—John Wentworth—but something inside her wouldn't allow the images to coalesce.

When Matt finished, she simply stared at him, barely conquering the shudder that threatened to destroy her poise completely. "Does my father know?" she asked, hardly aware that she'd said the words aloud.

Matt came to her, trapping her between his hands. "No. Pop said your mother never told him."

"Where is this man now? This John Wentworth?"

"He's dead," Matt said, then explained as best he

could about the plane crash his father had told him about. After a pause, he said, "I'm sorry. This isn't the way I wanted you to find out. I'm tired and worried about Pop." He brought the back of his hand up to stroke her cheek. "And every time I think about what a loose cannon Quentin Meadows is—the harm he could do to people I care about—I guess I go a little crazy."

"He really does intend to get help this time, Matt. Professional help."

"It may be too late for that."

"Why?"

"Pop plans to press charges."

She felt momentarily light-headed and suspected that every drop of color had left her face. "He can't," she said, her voice full of real and imagined horrors for what that could mean.

"Try telling that to my father."

"No, *you* try telling him. He listens to you."

"I *have* tried. But you know how stubborn he can be."

"Yes, and I know how persuasive *you* can be," she countered. Then she gave him a hard, fierce look. "You could talk him out of it if you really wanted to."

He stiffened, as angry now as she was. "I can't."

"You *can't?* Or you *won't? You'd* love to see my father behind bars, wouldn't you?"

"Truthfully?" Matt asked with a raised brow. "Yes, I wouldn't lose any sleep over it. The man has never been any good, Les. He's a violent alcoholic, he doesn't care about anyone but himself. I've watched you spend years trying to please him, trying to build a relationship that's just never going to exist. You've said that yourself." He exhaled heavily. "Well, now you don't have to try to make it work. He's not your father. You owe him damn little when it comes right down to it."

She pulled out of his grasp, shaking so hard now that she thought her knees would collapse. She swallowed the sickness in her throat, knowing that whatever foolish fantasy she had imagined for the two of them, none of it, *none of it* would ever come true.

When she had put a good distance between them, she swung around to face him. "You think that's *all* it takes? I just scratch out the name Quentin Meadows on my birth certificate and pencil in John Wentworth?" She would not have believed that her voice could sound so tense and brittle, so utterly devoid of warmth.

"I'm not saying that," he told her gruffly. She could tell he was barely hanging on to his own temper. "I'm saying that if he continues to spiral down the way he is, then you're under no obligation to be there for him anymore."

For a long moment, she stared at him, too appalled for speech.

Finally she said, "Don't you get it, Matt? I'm not going to stick by my father because I *have* to. I'm going to stick by him because I *want* to. And if you think I could do anything else, then even after all these years we've known each other…you don't know me at all."

CHAPTER FOURTEEN

CHRISTMAS WAS just three days away, and it should have been a happy, festive time. Instead, that day at the clinic started out just the way Matt expected it would. Awkward. Tense. Miserable. And it rolled downhill from there.

Four more cases of flu came in, sneezing and coughing all over him every time he got close enough to stick a tongue depressor in someone's mouth. The Sanchez twins, eight-year-old whirlwinds with matching ear infections and a mother who looked as if she was at her wit's end, terrorized everyone in the waiting room. Moira arrived late, looking flushed and glassy-eyed, then threw up in a trash can, the victim of what Matt suspected was a mild case of food poisoning.

Not a great day so far, and a very slim chance of getting better.

Les's attitude was the thorniest problem of all. All morning long—except when professional conduct required it—she pretended he didn't exist. He was surprised when she actually sought him out in Doc's office to let him know Moira had gone home, leaving no one to run the waiting room.

Matt tossed the patient file he'd been reading onto the

stack already teetering on the desk. "Oh, sure," he said with light sarcasm. "When the ship's about to sink, all the mice desert it."

At the very least, that should have gotten a smile from her. But today—nothing. For hours now there had been just this cold, dispassionate stranger, her expression a mask of restraint, her voice—when she spoke to him at all—as animated as if she'd been reading a bus schedule.

Think, Matt told himself. *Find a way to reach her.*

Nothing remotely inspired came to him. He rejected trying to justify his position that she was being foolishly sentimental about a man who was not even her father, and a dangerous drunk to boot. Giving it more words would only give it more life, and Les was unlikely to change her mind about that anyway. An apology might smooth the waters between them, but she would be sure to spot the slightest disingenuous note in his voice.

The only bright spot in the whole day was that, so far, Sheriff Bendix had not arrested Meadows.

The sheriff knew Sam. What sense was there, Bendix asked Matt when he called, in doing all that paperwork if he'd just have to *un*do it if Sam changed his mind? Although it wasn't exactly the by-the-book police procedure a big city would have followed, Bendix had decided on a twenty-four-hour cooling-off period. Now, in addition to being furious with Matt and Rosa for trying to talk him out of pressing charges, Sam was just as angry with the sheriff.

Would anything go right today?

He watched Les head for the door. No cease-fire in

the hostilities, it seemed. Before she could leave, Matt called out to her.

She turned. He looked into her eyes and saw a stone wall, but he refused to give up. "Mom sent down lunch," he told her, keeping his voice friendly and flexible. "Her special lasagna. Want to share?"

"Thanks, but with Moira gone, I'll be swamped. I think I'll skip lunch."

Her words held no warmth. They lacked even the mildest interest. They turned his heart over.

You shouldn't skip lunch, he wanted to say to her. *Bad for you.* But considering how little she welcomed any advice from him right now, she wasn't likely to be receptive.

"No problem," he said. "I'm used to working through lunch myself."

He was almost relieved when the telephone rang. Since a call could be picked up anywhere in the clinic, Leslie grabbed the extension on Doc's desk. She listened for a few minutes while Matt watched her mouth and remembered how much he craved kissing her.

"That was your mother," she said when she replaced the receiver. "Brandon's bringing a guest down. A little girl who fell and gashed her forehead. They should be here in a few minutes."

"Anyone waiting up front?"

"No. We're good until Ron Eberly shows up at one-thirty. He had a laparoscopic appendectomy a week before Doc left town, and he might be developing an abscess. We can push that back a little if we need to. Even without Moira I should be able to handle both the

front and the exam rooms—*if* no one else comes in unexpectedly. I'll get us set up in number two."

He nodded, and she left.

Matt looked down at his left hand, flexing his fingers
and watching the play of muscle and tendon beneath the
skin. He knew he was lucky to have back as much mobility as he did, but he couldn't kid himself. A child with
a facial wound who might need sutures could be a
touchy job requiring the kind of fine motor skills he just
didn't have. That he might *never* have again.

Knowing what he had to do, Matt reached across the
desk and pulled Doc's Rolodex in front of him.

Less than ten minutes later, the kid came through the
front door of the clinic, carried in the arms of her wor-
ried-looking father and followed by her equally frantic
mother.

Brandon came in right behind them, introducing the
Jackson family to Matt and Les. The little girl, a four-
year-old cutie named Chrissie, was crying softly, and
her eyes—what Matt could see of them from behind the
bloody towel pressed against her face—went wide with
fright as soon as she saw his white lab coat.

Les lost no time in trying to calm the child. "Hello,
sweetie," she crooned to Chrissie as she stroked curls
away from her forehead. "We're going to fix you right
up. Don't you worry."

She smiled reassuringly to the Jacksons and then led
the family through the waiting-room door and back into
the exam room she'd set up.

"She fell climbing the railroad-tie stairs out by the
lake," Brandon explained to Matt as they followed.

Chrissie's father glanced back over his shoulder. "I've told her a dozen times to take her hands out of her pockets when she goes up stairs. It happened so fast, she couldn't stop herself once she started to fall."

Jackson laid the child on the examination table, and as soon as Matt lifted the towel to look at the wound she started crying harder, holding out her arms to her mother.

Matt could feel the tension coming off both parents. He knew they'd had an excellent view of his damaged left hand before he'd slid it into a glove, and under the bright exam light, the network of scar tissue had made it look a lot worse than it actually was. He'd bet they were wondering just how skilled those hands of his were.

The gash lay diagonally between the girl's eyebrows, no longer bleeding. It was short, but pretty wide and deep. Chrissie was a beautiful child, without so much as a freckle to mar her flawless, pale skin. Although she was lucky to have missed damaging either eye, even with the most skilled suturing a small scar would be unavoidable.

He smiled at the little girl, then nodded toward the Jacksons. "We'll have to put in a few stitches, but I think that will be the worst of it. Probably ought to get an X-ray, too, just to make sure there are no fractures, but I doubt if she'll have anything more than a headache from this."

The mother bit her bottom lip, and the father looked relieved. Probably eaten up with guilt that this accident had happened to Chrissie on his watch.

"Will you have to put her out?" he asked.

"No, we can do this with a local anesthetic."

He was about to explain the procedure to the parents when Dr. Kline came into the room. He looked no older than Matt. Kline had a self-assured manner and an easy smile.

"This is my associate, Dr. Kline," Matt said, and introductions were quickly made all around. "He's actually going to take care of this for you. I'll be assisting him. All right?"

The parents nodded eagerly. Maybe they were just glad to have two doctors looking after their daughter instead of one. Kline slipped on a pair of gloves, and while he examined Chrissie, Matt caught Les's eye.

Her glance flickered over him in a disappointed, unspoken comment. He knew she was surprised that he had called Kline to take care of this instead of handling it himself. Her lips parted, but before she could speak Matt turned his attention back to the parents.

"Chrissie's going to be fine. There will be some forms to fill out, and we'll need a full medical history." He turned toward Les. "Will you get these folks started on the paperwork so we can have them home by dinner?"

She didn't like it, he could tell, but she smiled a tight smile anyway. "Of course, Doctor."

He'd never heard her sound more professional.

Or more distant.

IT WAS HOURS before Leslie could talk privately with Matt.

Chrissie Jackson was sewn up with seventeen stitches, most of them placed internally, then sent back to the lodge with her grateful parents. Kline finished off the chart and then hung around to talk to Matt for a while. Leslie was left to watch the front desk, but fortunately, the flurry of activity they'd seen that morning did not repeat itself in the afternoon.

When closing time rolled around, Leslie went into Doc Hayward's office. Matt was at the desk, reading a printout of blood work that had come from the lab on one of their patients. He glanced up as she walked in. When she closed the door quietly behind her and leaned against it, his eyebrows rose in a what-took-you-so-long? look.

Knowing there was no point in dancing around the issue, she gave him a hard look and said quickly, "Why did you call Kline?"

"Oh. So you're talking to me again?"

"Of course I'm talking to you. In fact, I've got *plenty* to say."

He gave her that cocky grin that had broken the hearts of more girls than she could remember. "Figured you would," he said, tossing the report on the desk. "Are you going to give me the entire lecture, or can we just cut to the nickel version of how I mustn't throw my career away, how I just need to build up my confidence?"

She crossed the room, planting her hands wide along the edge of the desk. "I don't know how you can joke. This is serious, Matt. Kline didn't do anything you couldn't have done. You know that."

He gave her a sad smile. "You're wrong," he told her in a quiet voice.

"No, I'm not. You just have to—"

"Les, stop. Hear me out. All right?"

She subsided. Mostly because Matt seldom looked

as serious as he did right at that moment. She straightened, crossing her arms. "All right, but it had better be one heck of an explanation."

He shook his head. "You're always hard on me in a way no one else ever dares—except maybe Pop."

"That's because I...care about you," she said, realizing how stupidly close she'd come to risking disaster.

"I know you do," Matt said in a soft voice. "The same way I care about you."

Oh, not true! she wanted to shout. *Not even close to the same way you feel about me.*

She knew a declaration of love from her would only complicate things further. She knew he had tender feelings as well as a raw hunger for her. But *love?*

He had glanced away as though uneasy, and for a moment there was only silence and a sense of naked vulnerability for them both. There had been a time when telling her best friend that she cared about him would have been easy to do. But sex had changed everything for them, she realized. Just as she had feared it would.

"So tell me why," she said, determined to keep to the plain, sensible things her mind could deal with and forget about what her heart might want.

He turned his attention back to her. "The week before I walked into that diner last year, I spent seven hours in an operating room putting a nine-year-old boy's face back together. Some damned fool left a back gate open and a dog got out. The mutt literally ripped off half the kid's face. It was some of the most extensive damage I'd ever seen. And do you know what that boy looks like today?"

She shook her head, though she knew he didn't really expect her answer.

"It's miraculous. The only real scars he has are in his mind, and he's getting counseling for that. But I brought that kid back from the kind of traumatic injury that could have ruined his life forever. It was some of the best work I've ever done."

"That doesn't surprise me. You have a rare, God-given talent and the intelligence and determination to know how to use it best."

"That's the first time we agree today. Someone should mark that down." He got up and came around the desk, then hitched himself onto the corner of it so that one leg swung freely. "I'm not going to be modest about the kind of microsurgeon I've been. I've had some terrific success." He held out his damaged hand. "But this—no pun intended—is the hand I've been dealt right now. And though I agree with everything you said the other day in the hut—I *am* lucky because it could have been so much worse—I can't pretend or wish or hope that it's good enough to handle the really fine work. The truth is, it may never be good enough again, no matter how hard I push myself."

"It will be. With time."

"Maybe. But today we weren't talking about the back of Cliff Powell's leg. We're talking about the *face* of that child, one who's going to be quite a beauty someday. I couldn't give her less than the best, Les. Haven't we both seen scars that made us wince because they were so poorly laid? She didn't deserve that." He looked directly at Leslie. "I suppose I could have taken a chance.

I would have, if it was just me we were talking about. But it wasn't. I wasn't willing to take a chance like that with Chrissie Jackson's face."

Leslie stood a moment, wrestling with the obvious truth of that statement. "All right," she conceded. "I guess that's a legitimate concern. But you *will* get back to where you want to be, Matt. I know it."

He gave his head a weary shake, and the look on his face said there was more to come, none of it likely to make her any happier. She suddenly felt cold, inside and out.

"I've been giving this some thought, Les. The truth is, I think the person who really can't deal with what's happened to me...is you."

She jerked. "What?"

He held up his hand again, so that it was eye-level, right between them. "I think, no matter what happens, I'll be able to handle this eventually, but you can't. Because it means I'm not perfect."

She'd made a restive movement away from him, and he slipped off the desk to come beside her. "You promised to listen."

"I take it back."

"Why? Because the truth isn't something you like to hear? I can't be the perfect doctor for you, Les. I can't be the perfect *anything*. Somehow, a long time ago, you began to see me as some kind of white knight, the fellow who could do anything, no matter what. But I make mistakes—just like I did last night by telling you about your dad. Just as I did the night I insisted on stopping at that diner for a lousy cup of coffee. Shayla would still—"

He broke off and looked away for a moment, then turned back to her, taking in air. "I haven't always made the right choices," he said in a quiet tone. "Most of the time I haven't had to give my decisions much thought because things have always been easy for me. But whatever my future holds, you have to accept the fact that I can't be who you want me to be anymore."

"I don't want you to be anyone but you."

"That's not quite true, Les."

"I'm beginning to think your hand is fine," she said with a touch of anger. "That it's your brain that needs fixing. Why is this suddenly *my* issue? I've never asked you to be anything but what you are."

The door to the office suddenly opened. In one hurried movement, she and Matt stepped apart. "Hellooo," Polly Swinburne called out. "The office wasn't locked and the lights were still on, so I took a chance someone was here."

"We're here," Matt said. With one regretful glance in Leslie's direction, he added, "What's up with my favorite patient?"

Leslie was amazed that he could sound so unruffled by the woman's appearance. Maybe his heart hadn't been pounding as hard as hers.

For the first time in her life, Leslie saw Polly Swinburne blush. *My God*, Leslie thought. *No one is immune.*

Polly came to the desk, setting down a dish covered with foil. "I wanted to say thank you for the excellent care I received the other day. You were wonderful, Doctor." As an afterthought, she threw a quick glance toward Leslie. "You, too, dear. As always."

"That's what we're here for," Matt told her. "Did you make that appointment with the audiologist I referred you to?"

"Oh, that very day. I'm sure you're right, though it does my ego some damage to think I'm losing some of my hearing." She touched the edge of the casserole dish. "I wanted to bring a little something to show my appreciation. Meatball Surprise, one of my best recipes. I'm quite an excellent cook, you know."

Matt lifted a corner of the foil. "Smells wonderful."

Paranoid Polly looked pleased, then her features slid into absolute seriousness. "I use only the finest ingredients. You won't find any of that mad-cow beef the English keep trying to foist on us."

"That's good to know," Matt said, and Leslie had to hide an amused smile behind a small cough.

"I was thinking that, if you liked this, I could bring something else by occasionally. I realize your mother is a wonderful cook as well, but perhaps for something different… My banana cream pie has taken prizes."

"No one beats Mom when it comes to cooking Italian. However, I'd never refuse banana cream pie."

Polly looked so thrilled that Leslie would have swore she heard a girlish giggle come out of the old woman's mouth.

Matt cocked his head at her. "Are you sure you want to spoil me like this, Polly. You do realize, don't you, that I'm only here temporarily? In another couple of weeks, Doc Hayward will be back from California, and I'll be back in Chicago."

Back in Chicago.

Such simple words, and yet they stopped Leslie's foolish hopes from rising. Any illusion she might have had about Matt staying, the possibility of a future here for the two of them…well, obviously none of that was going to happen, was it?

Somehow she got through the next few minutes. She listened to Polly Swinburne express her disappointment, watched Matt soothe the old woman in that wonderful way he had of dealing with people, the way he handled *any* obstacle in his life.

Back to Chicago.

Hope had fallen away with those words, and Leslie was finding it almost unbearable to remain in the same room. When Polly finally made a move toward the door, Leslie quickly offered to show her out. She couldn't stay any longer. She couldn't look at Matt. Or talk anymore, when there was clearly so little left to be said.

Back to Chicago.

That's where his life was now. That's where his career had its best chance of survival. If she really loved him, that's what she should want for him, shouldn't she? Happiness. A sense of fulfillment. But not here in Broken Yoke. Not here, with *her*.

Whatever they'd shared had been wonderful, but it could never have lasted. All of her fears had really come true, after all. For her, giving in to love had permanently altered their relationship. In the future, her need to share Matt's life would have to be adjusted somehow. As for the past…

It had been short and sweet and wonderful, but it was over.

CHAPTER FIFTEEN

SAM DIDN'T KNOW why he considered Leo Waxman one of his best friends. He was nothing but a long-winded air bag who didn't know when to shut up and get on with the job.

Leo had finally come up to the lodge to finish the wiring he'd started two weeks ago. Sam sat in his wheelchair, watching him work. No. Watching him *talk* was more like it. Occasionally he'd mess around with the fuse panel that hung near the back door of the kitchen, but he didn't seem to be making headway.

At the moment, Leo was tailoring a fingernail with his teeth. Sam fumed. It was ridiculous! He shouldn't have to pay good money to watch the man give himself a manicure.

"Are you going to finish this job *today?*" he asked, as he brought his wheelchair closer.

Either Leo didn't hear the belligerence in Sam's voice, or he chose to ignore it. "Maybe," he said.

"I don't understand what's taking so long."

"That's because you're not an electrician."

"From what I've observed, you aren't much of one, either."

Leo made a face at him. "I wish you'd never given up all the good things in life. You were a lot easier to get along with. But I guess it means you'll live longer." Rosa was working at the kitchen table, chopping onions for the lodge's specialty dinner that night. Leo called out to her, "Doesn't that make you feel lucky, Rosa? Knowing this old crank's going to be here forever?"

"Not lately," his wife said.

That response didn't surprise Sam. Even Rosa had been a trial to be around lately. She'd hardly said two words to him since he'd informed her that he intended to press charges against Quentin Meadows.

Sam turned back to Leo. "Giving up wine, women and song doesn't make you live longer. It just makes it seem that way."

Leo laughed and went back to work, although not with any more enthusiasm or speed. Before too long, he launched into a long discussion about his dog Brutus, who had been exiled from the lodge's interior since the Christmas-tree fiasco. Sam, who had never cared for dogs and preferred a quiet, non-demanding cat, groaned inwardly and tried to tune him out.

No such luck. Leo stopped working on the fuse box and now stood waiting for Sam to reply to some question that hadn't even registered. "What?" Sam asked irritably.

"I said, what do you think I should do? Should I breed Brutus with the Gunderson's bitch?"

"Hell, no. I think you should have Brutus the Wonder Dog stuffed and mounted, then open up a damned museum so you can charge admission. Finally make him good for *something*."

Since Leo was as crazy about Brutus as he was his grandchildren, that comment didn't sit well. He scowled at Sam. "I don't think that's funny."

"Well, I don't think a man ought to be more in love with his dog than he is with his own family."

Leo stared at him long and hard. Sam was aware that Rosa had stopped chopping onions at the table. Even his sister-in-law Renata, who usually knew when to mind her own business, was no longer clanging dirty dishes in the big metal sinks across the room.

"What's wrong with you today?" Leo asked.

"Nothing's wrong with me. Nothing that a good electrician couldn't fix."

"Are you complaining about the way I do my work?"

"I guess I would. If I'd ever seen you *do* any work."

"Sam!" Rosa said behind him.

Leo stood over him, hands on his hips. "You ornery jackass. I've got a good mind to let you hire someone else to do this job."

"If there's a *good mind* in that empty head of yours, I'd like to see it."

"What are you saying?"

"Jump in the lake. Go fly a kite. Take a hike. You can choose any one of those and make me deliriously happy."

"That's it." Leo hauled on his coat, picked up his toolbox and strode across the room. On his way out of the kitchen, he said to Rosa, "I'll come back when His Royal Pain in the Ass takes a nap."

"I don't take naps!" Sam shouted after him.

Rosa got up. Without a word, she moved to the back

of Sam's wheelchair and began pushing him toward their private quarters.

"Where are we going?" he demanded.

She didn't say anything until they had reached the living room. With the curtains drawn, it was dressed in shadows. It needed a fire snapping in the grate, he thought, but that duty was usually left to Nick or Matt. These days, nearly everyone in his family could do everything better than he could.

Rosa sat back on her heels at the side of his chair and placed her hand along his arm. "I want you to sit here for a while. Think about why you just had an argument with one of your best friends."

Sam made a mulish sound of displeasure. "I'm not being put in time out like some kindergarten brat. Besides, I know why. He talks too much, and he doesn't work."

"That's not the reason and you know it." He had looked away from her, and she caught his chin, forcing his eyes back to hers. He felt suddenly ashamed because he saw nothing but concern and love in her gaze. "You can't do this anymore, Samuel. This is not you. You can't fight with everyone just because you hate yourself right now."

He opened his mouth to protest, but she shook her head at him. "Be quiet and listen to me. You're mad at your body, and I don't honestly blame you. But do you really believe that makes you less than what you have always been? The man I love lives here…" She pressed her hand against his heart. "And here…" Her fingers brushed lightly against his temple. "He has a fierce heart and a gentle soul, but I haven't seen much of him lately."

She straightened and gave him a quick kiss on the lips. Then she headed toward the double doors once more. "Don't come back to my kitchen until you've found that man again."

Sam sat still for a moment after she left, dumbfounded. Then, with a muttered curse, he began to roll his wheelchair back out to the kitchen. Rosa had no business trying to bully him.

Halfway there, he jerked his hands off the chair's power box and stopped. When his wife wanted something, she usually got her way. Besides, he wasn't at all sure she wasn't right about one thing, at least. He did need to be alone for a while.

Sighing, he maneuvered over to one of the windows and threw back the curtains. From this angle, a little sliver of Lightning Lake was visible through the trees. Since his strokes he'd seldom gone out there. The uneven terrain played hell with the wheelchair.

He thought about all the concessions he'd had to make because of his illness. The way it chipped away at him, until there wasn't all that much left. He was no more than a walking hospital. Rosa was right about that, too. He did hate his body. And he hated any reminder of just how much it could fail him at times.

He supposed that was one of the reasons he'd been so determined to see Quentin Meadows behind bars. Yes, the man was no good. Yes, he was dangerous. But worst of all, he had made Sam feel impotent and ineffectual in his own home. Coming at him like a rottweiler, standing over him the way he had the other day. If Matt hadn't intervened, the whole thing might have gotten a lot uglier. As it was, spilled out there on the kitchen floor like a damn baby, Sam had looked like an idiot. A man's family shouldn't have to see him at such a disadvantage.

But maybe he *was* being unreasonable about this whole thing. Matt had been right. Putting Meadows behind bars would give Sam a lot of satisfaction, but it would hurt Leslie. And he liked that girl. Liked what she did for Matt. Always had.

Maybe there was another way to make Quentin Meadows shape up. A way that didn't have anything to do with taking out Sam's own personal frustrations. He might not have much physical strength left, but he still had a little gray matter in the old noggin, didn't he?

Over the years he'd made a lot of friends and connections. He knew people. A couple of the most influential doctors in Denver had been coming to the lodge for years. Maybe it was time to call in some favors. Between that and Matt's own influence in the medical community, surely they could find a way to get help for Meadows—and quickly.

Leslie would have to agree, but Matt could help with that. Matt could probably talk her into anything.

He rolled to the side table where the telephone sat, pulled out the address book under it, and looked up Leslie's phone number. Might as well get started. See how she receptive she was.

After that, he supposed he'd have to call Leo. Apologize, probably. One good thing about Leo, he never held a grudge. Of course, he'd probably work the conversation around to the Wonder Dog again.

Dio mio! The things Sam had to do in order to keep the peace around here.

MATT HAD LOCKED UP the office and was almost to his car when he heard someone call his name. He swung around and found himself face to face with Perry Jamison.

Perfect, he thought. A great way to end a crummy day.

"Good to see you, Matt," Perry said pleasantly, offering his hand. "You're looking well."

Great. How could you actively dislike a man who seemed genuinely glad to see you? "Thanks," he managed to say as they shook hands. "I suppose you're looking for Les."

"I was, but..." Perry cast a quick glance over his shoulder toward the darkened clinic. "It appears that I've missed her."

"Afraid so. She seemed to be in quite a hurry to get out today."

That was an understatement, if ever there was one. She'd left arm-in-arm with Polly as though they were best friends. Judging by the look on her face as she'd left, she probably didn't want any further opportunities for discussion between them. But he wasn't going to say any of that to Jamison.

"Actually," Perry said. "As long as you're here, can I buy you a cup of coffee? I'd like to talk to you."

"I really ought to get up to the lodge..."

"It's about Leslie."

Matt stopped searching his pocket for his car keys. Anything Perry had to say about Les might interested him.

He pointed toward Downhill Donny's, one of the bars on Main Street. "How about a beer instead? I think I'm ready for one."

It was still early enough that Donny's was reasonably quiet and uncrowded. They had no trouble finding a booth in the back, tucked against a wall covered with Donny Robinette's memorabilia from his days as a competitive downhill racer.

The beer was cold and welcome. Matt was halfway through his before he settled back against the seat and raised a brow at Perry. "So what's this about?" he asked.

Perry played absently with his coaster. "I suppose I should get right to the point. You know Leslie and I have been seeing one another for several months."

"Yeah."

"She's really a very special woman."

"You won't get any argument from me on that score."

Perry lifted his head, giving him a sharp look. "I'm in love with her."

Matt's stomach did an odd flip. It seemed a fitting end to a rotten day, having to sit across from Les's boyfriend and listen to all the sweet little details of his love life. Matt didn't see why he'd been elected. He and Perry weren't friends. Hell, they were barely acquaintances.

He signaled for Donny's attention. Time for the check. Time to get the hell out of here. "I'm not sure I'm the right person to talk to…" he began.

Perry ignored Matt's efforts to escape. "Unfortunately, Leslie's feelings for me don't seem to be quite as definite."

During their time together in the ice-fishing hut, Matt had been unable to resist asking about Les's feelings for Perry. She'd made it clear she wasn't in love with him.

He'd been so delighted by that statement, he'd kissed her even harder.

Matt had half risen in his seat, but now he settled back down. Did the guy know that Matt and Les had...? He caught Donny's eye, indicating he wanted another beer instead of the tab.

Matt polished off the rest of his drink. Perry went back to drawing wet circles on the table with his bottle. He seemed uneasy, unsure—nothing like the sharp, confident businessman Matt had met before. Is that what being in love did to a person? If so, he could actually feel sorry for Perry.

Donny brought a second beer for Matt. He downed a few swallows and watched Perry continue to nurse his first one. Since the man seemed content to let time pass without talking, Matt took the opportunity to take a closer look.

Whatever else he might be, Jamison was no slouch. His clothing accentuated his reputation for money and power. The designer haircut and professional manicure added to the image. Addy claimed that half the eligible women in Broken Yoke were just waiting to have a chance at him if Les would turn him loose.

Finally Perry pushed his beer away and looked up at Matt. "I suppose this is where you come in."

"How do you figure that?" Matt asked. Then a thought dawned on him. An unbelievable thought. "What? You want me to plead your case to her?"

"I'm well aware that you're her best friend. That the two of you have always shared a rather...special relationship." He smiled a little. "But relax, Doc. I'm perfectly capable of making my own case to Leslie, and I'm not in need of your blessing."

"Then what *are* you in need of?"

"Recently I've sensed something…different in Leslie. I can't put my finger on it, but I'd like to find out the cause. It will help me decide how to proceed."

"Les has had a lot on her mind lately."

"I think it has something to do with her feelings for you," Perry said quietly. "And I'd like to know what your feelings are for her."

Matt pulled back a little. He considered telling Perry to mind his own business, but something about the man's unwavering gaze wouldn't be denied. He decided to hedge. "As you've just pointed out, our relationship is special. We've been friends for years, and that's not something I want to see change."

"But are you *in love* with her?"

"I don't see that it's any—"

"Is that why you've come back here?"

Matt broke off as the sharp kick of truth nearly took his breath away. A long time ago, his father had made the comment that the heart plans nothing, that love just sneaks up on a person when they aren't looking.

All these months, when Matt had been eaten up with guilt over Shayla's death, when he'd felt his career slipping out from under him, his need to see Les, to be with her, had been rising in him as steady as mercury in a thermometer. He wasn't here because he needed to rest, or regroup or even to spend Christmas with his family.

He was here because this was where *she* was, the one

person in the world he wanted to be with. Not as a sister. Not as a co-worker, or even a best friend. Leslie Meadows was, and always had been, the woman he loved.

And the hopelessly sad part of it was, he wasn't at all sure she felt the same way about him.

He'd been silent so long that Perry took it to mean an unwillingness to discuss it. "All right," the man said. "Let me ask you something else. Do you think *she's* in love with *you?*"

Matt considered that for a moment. Finally, he took another swallow of beer and met Perry Jamison's eyes with man-to-man frankness. "I think Les has been in love with me for years," he said. "But not the way you think. She's in love with an ideal. Someone who doesn't exist."

"I see."

"Do you? Then you're doing better than I am, friend."

"So you have no claim on her."

No claim. Damn, but he hated the way that sounded, the way it made him feel. He wished he *could* be her dream man, but he couldn't be.

He felt the sudden drop of his heart at the thought of someone else touching her the way he had touched her, hearing that sweet moan she made when the sex was soft and slow or the way she arched with pleasure when it turned fast and raw. She had the warmest smile of any woman in the world, and it belonged to him. No one else.

And yet, the cold, hard truth settled down inside him, where it lived its own sad life. Les didn't belong to anyone. Least of all, him.

"No," he said when his breathing steadied. "I don't have a claim on Les. No commitments. No promises."

Perry looked pleased with that answer. "Good," he said. "Because I think I can make her happy."

Matt clamped his teeth together and resisted the urge to reach across the table and deck the guy. How could he refute Perry's claim?

In that moment, it seemed to Matt that if you put the two of them side by side, Jamison would come out way ahead. He knew where he was going, knew what the future held, and how to get it. Les, who'd cornered the market on sensible, organized thinking, would find that combination unbeatable.

Matt sighed, pulling a few dollars out of his wallet and laying them on the table. He had to get out of here. Right now.

"I want Les to be happy," he said. "She deserves the best. Maybe that's you or maybe it's not. She'll make that decision herself, but I only know one thing for sure. It isn't me."

He slid out of the booth.

CHAPTER SIXTEEN

UNABLE TO SLEEP for thinking of all the ways he'd screwed up his relationship with Les, Matt got up early the next morning and went down to the lodge's exercise room. He was relieved no one was around. He didn't feel like making small talk. He didn't honestly feel like exercising, either. What he felt like doing was pounding his fist through a wall.

What a jackass he'd been. Sitting there yesterday, practically giving Perry Jamison carte blanche to go after Les. He might as well have handed her over to him on a silver platter.

But that had been the whole idea, hadn't it?

Find a way to keep Les at arm's length? Because what she wanted out of life, what she *deserved*, just wasn't in his power to give. So why should he be surprised to feel that sharp pain around his heart?

Disgusted with himself, Matt ran quickly through the exercises that were eventually supposed to work miracles on his hand. It didn't take long before he decided something more punishing was in order. Something that would require full concentration. He stretched out along the workout bench and began doing presses with the barbell.

His muscles burned, but he didn't stop. About the time he was almost out of breath and his arms were quivering, he realized that someone had come into the room. In another moment, a face, upside down, loomed directly over him.

It was Les, and it took no more than a single glance to see that she was furious.

"Let me get this straight," she said in a tight, crisp voice. "You *gave* me to Perry Jamison?"

He frowned up at her. "What?"

"Don't play dumb with me, Matt D'Angelo."

"I'm not playing dumb."

"No, I suppose not. You really *are* clueless, aren't you?"

Replacing the barbell carefully on the rack, Matt levered himself upward to straddle the bench. "Could we start this conversation over? I don't know what you're talking about."

She moved to stand in front of him, her fists planted on her waist. "Perry came to see me last night. He said you two had talked, and that you'd told him he could *have* me. Like two kids trading baseball cards. I hope you got something wonderful in exchange."

"It wasn't like that. I didn't say he could *have* you. I said I didn't have a claim on you. That you had always made your own choices."

"So that distinction is supposed to make me feel better?" Her voice dripped scorn.

"At the time—"

She held up her hands to stop him from going into any further explanation. "I think we need to get a few things straight."

He pulled his towel off the end of the bench, and Les sat down, angling toward him. While he wiped his face and bare chest, he met her intense and blatant scrutiny—and slid every emotion behind a shield.

"All right," he said at last. "I'm listening."

She drew a deep breath. "I've been up all night thinking about everything that's happened recently. Thinking about Perry's offer of marriage, and—"

"Perry proposed?" That bit of news came as a surprise. Good old Perry hadn't waited long to pop the question.

"Yes, but that's not important now. I told him no. I told him we shouldn't see each other anymore. That it was just never going to work."

"You did?"

"I thought you were going to listen."

"Sorry."

Her nearness was like pure electricity circling closer and closer, but he knew it was time to shut up and just let her vent. He watched her look away, saw the way her slim throat worked as she swallowed. This was the woman he dreamed about every night, but he didn't dare touch her.

"Look," she said finally. Some of her fury seemed to have settled. "I wasn't going to be ridiculous about this. I'd almost convinced myself how it ought to go. Between us, I mean. I was going to let you go back to Chicago without saying a word. I was going to try as hard as I could to go back to being just friends. To forget that we'd ever been…anything more than that."

"If that's what you think is best, Les," Matt hedged.

"Don't be so agreeable. I'm not letting you off the hook that easily."

"I assume there's some point you're trying to make here."

"I'm *making* it," she protested. "My point is, last night I thought I had it all sorted out in my mind. I knew what I should do. But then, I looked up, and guess who I saw on top of my dresser?"

"I'm afraid to guess."

From the side pocket of her purse she withdrew a small object and held it out. He didn't recognize it at first. It had been years since he'd seen the damned thing and he'd thought it had long been deposited in some trash can.

"Do you remember giving this to me?" she asked.

It was one of those cheap plastic figurines one could get in almost any toy store. This one was of a boxer. Muhammad Ali, maybe? He couldn't remember. When you pushed your thumb against the button on the bottom of the stand, the boxer's fists shot out in a one-two punch.

He took it off her palm and tested it out. The thing had to be fifteen years old, and yet it still worked. Remembering how it had come to be in Les's possession, Matt couldn't help smiling a little. "Of course I remember. I gave it to you on the day you flunked your driving test."

"Right. You told me that I should quit doubting myself. That, just like a boxer, I had to keep my dukes up to protect myself, take my lumps like a big girl and keep swinging. Do you remember that?"

"We were teenagers. You were crying buckets over

parallel parking, for God's sake. I was desperate for something positive to say."

"Well, it worked. So well, in fact, that I've kept it all these years. Any time I've faced something that looked impossible, every time I've had to deal with the really horrible stuff, I've only had to look at that little guy to know I can make it."

"You always could, Les." The idea of her keeping this stupid toy was rather sweet and unexpected. "You don't need a dime-store talisman to get you through the tough times. It's part of who you are."

"Maybe that's true, but last night, when I looked at it, I finally realized that I'd almost forgotten the most important lesson I learned that day."

"And that would be…?"

She ducked her head for a moment, studying her hands as though she'd never seen them before. Then she lifted her head and gave him a look that sent everything inside him into rebellion. "I learned that I can't give up," she said softly. "That the love I have for you is one I have to fight for."

"That's not—"

"Perry Jamison isn't the love of my life, Matt. You are."

They stared at each other in silence until he willed himself to say something. Anything would be better than letting her continue to look at him this way, as though her heart would break. "Les—"

"I love you," she told him in a softly textured voice. "Part of me always has. I know that all of me always will."

He rose and moved away from her. His mind was staging a full-blown stampede. She was such a beautiful temptation, but he drew back from the need to take her into his arms, drew back with a rush of discipline that was as sharp and unwelcome as it was necessary.

He only turned to look at her when a reasonable distance separated them. "Les, don't do this," he said. "If Perry isn't the one for you, then there's someone else out there who will be. Someone who can make you as happy as you deserve to be."

She shook her head. "There will never be anyone else for me but you. You haven't won my heart from any rivals, Matt. You've won it from *me*. That's never going to change. Even if you never feel the same way I do."

She got up and walked slowly toward him. When she stood directly in front of him, his blood felt suddenly thicker and hotter. He knew it had nothing to do with exercising. Warmth spread through him as if he'd taken a swallow of expensive brandy. He wanted to touch her so badly that he had to keep his hands clenched on either side of his body.

Don't do it, he thought.

Les's forehead puckered, and her smile was filled with sorrow. "You aren't in love with me, are you? It really was just sex all along."

The tension between them electrified the air. He could not take his eyes from her face. It sent a fierce sense of shock right through him to realize that he could feel happier than he'd ever been in his life, and yet defeated at the same time.

But he couldn't let her think that it had all been about the sex. Driven by something as untrustworthy as pure emotion, he reached out to capture a delicate curl that had fallen against her cheek. He let his hand play against her skin, watched her flesh beneath his fingers go pink.

"Do you really think that's what it was?" he asked. "Don't you know that there's never been a moment in my life when I *didn't* love you?"

She blinked. She looked stunned. "Then why are you making this so complicated for us?" She sounded calm, but the pulsing muscles in her jaw betrayed her.

Her steady gaze demanded an honest answer. "Because my life *is* complicated right now. Damn it, Les, I've spent years planning for a future that's got every possibility of drying up. I don't know if the worst is going to happen. I don't know what the alternatives will be if it does. I just know that it's unfair to ask *any* woman to share that kind of uncertainty."

She gave him a long, speculative appraisal through her lashes. "Fine," she said at last. "Then don't ask. Do you think I need some kind of long-term commitment from you? I don't. I want now."

"I want it, too, Les. But—"

"I used to count on you for everything, Matt, and you never let me down. But I don't *need* you anymore. I *want* you."

"How can you? You know me so well. I'm selfish and self-indulgent and arrogant—"

"Don't forget bossy and stubborn," she added with a smile. Then she shook her head quickly. "It doesn't matter."

"It *will* matter. Eventually. You think this is what you want, but—"

"I don't *think*. I *know*. I know we've been through so

much together that we deserve this little bit of happiness. For however long it can last, we've earned it. Don't you see that, Matt?"

There were a thousand things he wanted to say to her. A dozen arguments he knew he should make. But all he could see was Les, standing in front of him, offering a truth that rippled through him again and again.

They *did* deserve to be together. He *did* love her. And in his selfish inability to ever resist going after what he wanted most, he couldn't let her go.

He pulled her close, moving his hands through her hair and down her back. "God, Les, I wish I could be half as certain of things as you are."

Her hands spread over his bare chest in a slow caress that wound through his blood like a river of fire.

She caught his face in her hands. "Just be certain of this. I don't care that you're not perfect. I know you just the way you are. All that's right in you. All that's wrong. And there isn't a single part of you that I don't love."

He smiled down at her. "You mean that, don't you?"

She met his glittering gaze head-on. "Kiss me, and I'll show you how much."

CHAPTER SEVENTEEN

THE HOURS UNTIL Christmas Day passed so quickly that Leslie couldn't imagine how they had slipped away. No, she wasn't being honest. She knew *how.* She knew *who* was responsible. The truth, well…it didn't flatter her one bit, but she thought she had a reasonable excuse.

How was she supposed to think of anything when someone like Matt was in her life—kissing her until her mouth was blurry, sending her hot, private looks that could make her toes curl even in a room full of people? Making love to her in such wonderful new ways that it seemed as though the world had tiptoed away and left her floating in a soft, silver sea.

She knew it couldn't last, of course. She and Matt were both aware he would return to Chicago, and she supposed that they both accepted that fact.

By some unspoken agreement, they didn't talk about it or try to reason out a way to make a long-distance relationship work.

Briefly she considered the possibility of making her own move to Chicago. But just as quickly, she rejected the idea. Even though she might manage to find work that would be equally as satisfying in Chicago, just how needy would she look to Matt, traipsing after him like a lovesick teenager?

He would hate that. And she'd hate herself for doing it.

She wouldn't allow herself to wonder if, by this time in her life, she shouldn't have had more sense than to fall in love with a man who wouldn't stay.

It didn't matter, she told herself. *Now* was what they had, and she could hold on to that just a little while longer, couldn't she?

The next morning she drove up to the lodge to join the D'Angelos for their Christmas celebration. The resort was nearly deserted with almost no cars in the parking lot. The dining room was closed until dinner time so the family could exchange presents and be together.

Since she and Matt had made no secret of their relationship, the rest of the D'Angelos made no secret of their approval. It was lovely to think of spending the holiday surrounded by so many people she cared about, and she tried not to think about her father. There was no way she could be with him today.

The moment Leslie entered the family's private quarters she was swallowed into the noisy, festive atmosphere near the tree. The decorations sent old-fashioned glowing enchantment leaping around the room. She delighted in inspecting them more closely before Matt took her hand and led her to the spot he'd saved for her on one of the cozy loveseats near the fireplace.

Kari handed her a small glass of wine with a sugar cube melting in the middle of it—a holdover tradition from the days when Sam's Italian parents had been the ones to host Christmas. "Wish this baby would hurry up and get here," she said, absently rubbing her extended belly.

"Are you very uncomfortable?" Leslie asked.

"No, it's not the baby. It's Nick. He's impossibly overprotective. Trying to have any fun right now with him around is like going fishing with a game warden."

Since Nick had joined them in the middle of the conversation, Leslie didn't take Kari's complaint seriously. Evidently neither did Nick. He handed his wife a glass of milk, and Leslie caught a look pass between them that only two people in love would share.

She settled back on the seat with her present to Matt on her lap as everyone opened gifts in no particular order. While Leslie watched and laughed, in many ways she was aware only of Matt. His hand was against the underside of her hair, playing with the flesh at the nape of her neck until, in no time at all, she was nearly breathless with pleasure.

She turned her head to look at him as Sam and Nick debated the idea of expanding the workout room next year to include more spa services.

"Behave," she said under her breath. "We're supposed to be listening to your father."

The corner of Matt's mouth lifted, though he kept staring straight ahead. "Can't help it. All this talk about massage therapy is giving me ideas."

"Leslie," Sam said suddenly. "How is your father?"

Caught off guard, she jumped a little. She realized that with Matt's hand creating havoc with her nervous system, she'd completely lost the thread of the conversations around her.

She gave Sam a hope-filled smile. "I spoke to him last night, wished him Merry Christmas. He seemed well. His counselor says he's right on target."

Matt and Sam had helped her get her father into an alcoholic-rehabilitation program in Denver. Six weeks of intense behavior modification and counseling. He'd been far more receptive to the idea than she'd ever expected. He was really trying to get his life together.

"Excellent," Sam replied. "I'm sure it's a good sign that he's cooperative."

"I'm hopeful. It seems strange, but I miss having him around, even though we seldom visited one another."

"Perhaps the program will show him ways to strengthen your relationship."

She could only pray that it worked out that way, that this new treatment was successful. As interested as she was in learning more about her biological parent—John Wentworth—Quentin Meadows would always be the man she considered her father, flaws and all.

Addy, who'd been passing out presents to everyone, came over to hand her father a small package. "Here's one for you, Pop."

Sam seemed surprised. "But I've opened all of mine." He shook the box. "Who is this from?"

Addy's dark eyes sparkled. "A mystery gift," she said with a mischievous grin. "Open it and find out."

Sam ripped away the bow, then tossed it on the floor where it joined the tangled rainbow of ribbon and crushed paper. He lifted the lid and frowned down at the contents. Withdrawing a cream-colored envelope, he tore the seal and pulled out a folded piece of paper. "It's a letter," he informed everyone around him.

"Who's it from?" Nick asked.

While everyone waited, he read the contents. His reaction was stony silence, and as his eyes widened just a little, Rosa was already finding the seat beside him, placing her hand on his shoulder. She seemed uncharacteristically nervous, and Leslie suspected she already knew what the letter said.

When he finished reading it, he looked up at the family. He seemed stunned. "Rafe," he said. "It's from Rafe. He's coming home."

All the adults fell silent, waiting for Sam's reaction. Everyone knew that the relationship between father and son had been strained.

Tessa, however, with a teenager's typical love for drama, was excited. "Cool!" she exclaimed from her spot near the tree. "How did you get the letter, Aunt Addy?"

Addy never took her eyes off her father as she spoke. "Rafe sent it to me," she told her niece. "He wanted me to deliver it since he wasn't sure how anyone else would feel about him coming back. But you're happy about it, right, Pop?"

"He wants me to call him."

Rosa squeezed Sam's shoulder. "What are you waiting for?"

Sam eyed her sharply. "You know about this?"

Rosa's face was flushed with excitement. "Of course. I have hardly been able to wait for you to open it. This is the best present we could ever receive, Samuel. Don't you think so?"

Sam's head tilted back, his nostrils flaring a little. "We haven't spoken to one another in years."

"Then you won't run out of things to say," Rosa said with her usual air of practicality. "Call him. Call him right now. Enough time has been wasted."

With Rosa close on his heels, Sam rolled out of the room, heading for the privacy of their bedroom. Everyone watched them go in silence. As soon as Rosa closed the door behind them, the room erupted in conversation.

"You should have told us," Nick said to Addy.

His sister threw up her hands. "Hey, don't shoot the messenger. Rafe told me not to say anything to anyone except Mom, and if she approved telling Pop, just to do it. Whatever bad blood is between them, it's long past time it got settled, if you ask me."

"No one was asking you," Nick said without real anger. "But I've never known that to stop you."

Leslie knew that Nick, who had left the military to take care of the family business after Sam's stroke, resented the fact that Rafe had not come home to see their father. He might not welcome Rafe's return.

"I wonder what brought this about," Nick said.

Matt shook his head ruefully. "Let it go, big brother. It's never too late to start over or change. Rafe may have discovered that. Maybe you should, too."

Nick looked as if he might argue that advice, but Leslie saw Kari slip her hand into her husband's. A short time later the two of them were tucked against one another on the couch, having a quiet discussion.

Matt rose unexpectedly, holding out his hand to Leslie. "Let's go out to the lake."

"Now?" she asked, then tapped the wrapped package still on her lap. "We haven't exchanged our gifts."

"Bring it. I need to talk to you."

She didn't like the sound of that, the way his features suddenly looked serious. While he picked up his present to her from under the tree, she shrugged into her coat, feeling an uneasiness take hold in the pit of her stomach.

He took her hand and led her down the steps to Lightning Lake where they settled on a fallen log at the edge of the frozen water. She tilted the package she'd brought against her leg, and Matt placed his gift to her at her feet. It was a large box, big enough to hold a wide-brimmed hat.

White waves of snow were piled around the shoreline. The morning was crisp, but surprisingly mild, and Leslie let the sunlight filter through her lashes. It was a perfect spot for enjoying a view of the lake and mountains beyond it, but when Matt wrapped his arm around her and nuzzled her neck, she closed her eyes and let her senses wander.

When he kissed her, she felt his warmth as her warmth and welcomed it. For a little while, they communicated in a language of easy gestures and soft sighs. Leslie tried hard to prolong the moment, not wanting the world to come back, not wanting to do anything but stay in the tender comfort of Matt's arms.

She couldn't, of course, and she knew it. She pulled away at last and cleared her throat because it seemed suddenly as though some lump of apprehension had wedged itself in her windpipe. "You wanted to talk?"

He seemed reluctant. His hands were wrapped

around hers. She'd forgotten her gloves, and now Matt rubbed his fingers back and forth across her palms.

"You're cold," he said with a frown, then inclined his head toward the ice-fishing hut that still sat out on the lake. "Do you want to warm up in the hut?"

"Maybe we'd better not," she replied. "I'm afraid if we end up in there, my hands won't be the only things that get warm, and you *did* say you wanted to talk."

He nodded. "Right. I did." He drew a breath, and the mere thought that he felt the need to prepare for what he was about to tell her made Leslie's heart take a sudden dive. "I spoke to Doc last night. He'll be back on the thirtieth."

With a sick shiver of understanding, Leslie swiped her tongue across her lips. "So soon?" she managed to say. "I thought perhaps, now that Diane's had the baby, he'd want to stay out there with her a while longer."

"No. Diane's doing fine. I think he's eager to get back here where he can feel useful again."

And you're eager to feel useful again, too. Back in Chicago. Back where the life you want is waiting.

The finality of what was going to happen came rolling toward her with sudden clarity. When he left, her heart would break with the impossibility of surviving this, of somehow enduring all the long days and nights ahead for her.

She needed time to compose her thoughts. She fell silent, and Matt did the same. He rose and walked a few feet away. He stood with his back to her, his hands plunged into the pockets of his jacket. Behind him the mountains looked like bruises, a blue and purple backdrop that didn't even seem real. She stared at him a long time, thinking that every detail was precious to her now. The image of him would have to last so long.

He turned at last, walking back to her. He held out his hand, giving her an envelope he withdrew from his pocket. "I have something for you," he said. "You don't have to use any of it, of course, but I've done a little checking on the Internet, made a few contacts."

"What is it?"

"It's information I've been able to find out about your father."

"My father?"

"Your biological father—John Wentworth. I realize that, as far as you're concerned, Quentin *is* your father, and I'm not suggesting you do anything to change that relationship. I just thought you might like to have it. In case you ever wanted to find out more about your family."

She couldn't help being touched by his thoughtfulness. Maybe he was trying to give her something to hang on to while he put an end to any hope she might have of a future with him.

She had to put a good face on this. She'd known this was coming.

She gave him a small smile. "You're right. In my mind, Quentin *is* my father."

"Will you ever tell him the truth?" Matt asked.

"I don't know," she admitted. "Certainly not any time soon. He has to get his life back in order first. But no matter what I decide, I know I'd eventually like to find out more about John Wentworth. Maybe make a trip to

Pueblo. I thought I might talk to Sam eventually. Try to understand why my mother fell in love with his friend."

"Pop's memory is pretty good. He can probably fill in a lot of the blanks. He was angry at first—when he found out I'd told you—but I think he was also relieved that he no longer had to keep that secret to himself."

She lifted the envelope. "Thank you for this."

He seemed pleased. He sat back down on the log, taking both of her hands in his. "I'll do what I can to help you, Les. If you decide to go to Pueblo, I could come with you if you'd like."

"That would be nice," she told him, but all she could think was that he'd be unlikely to know when she decided to go.

How easily could he get away from the hospital in Chicago? And why should he come? For old time's sake? To help out a friend and former lover in need? It was not a telephone call she could ever imagine making.

Courage threatened to desert her. "Why don't we open our presents?" She paused to control her voice. "You first."

She watched him tear the paper off his gift, her nerves a jumbled mess. She'd given him a photograph she'd found in a gallery in Denver. But now it seemed too personal, too much like an attempt to influence him to stay.

He held it out at arm's length. "It's wonderful, Les."

"I didn't take the picture. You know how hopeless I am with a camera. Do you recognize it?"

"Of course," he said, nodding. His eyes glowed with a mischievous light. "Wolf Creek Meadow."

"I thought it might remind you of that day we pony-skied. When we…"

"Finally gave up trying to pretend?" Before she knew what he intended, he gave her a quick kiss, cool and light on the lips. "Thank you. Every time I look at it, I'll think about that day."

"I'm glad you like it."

What a fraud she was. She sounded so brave. Sensible. She wasn't either. She was terrified because she loved Matt so much. And she was losing him.

He was suddenly placing his gift on her lap. It was heavier than she expected.

"Your turn," he said.

She ripped off the paper, wishing she could find some way to avoid this. What kind of gift did you give someone who was soon to be your former lover?

She lifted the lid, then blinked. "Oh…" she said on a breathless note of surprise. The smell of new leather wafted up to her. "Ice skates."

"Yep. You don't already have a pair, do you?"

"No, because I…"

She broke off because she realized what she intended to say wouldn't sound particularly gracious. But Matt, who knew her, only laughed and finished her sentence for her. "Because you don't skate. Yes, I know. I remember that morning out here very well. You selling hot chocolate and giving Danny LeBrock the hell he deserved. You were terrific that day."

"Unfortunately, not on the ice." Remembering that day, she gave him a sideways look. "Tell me the truth. That day, did you deliberately break Danny's nose during your hockey game?"

Matt ducked his head. "I don't know. I wish I could

say I took the high road, and it just…happened. But the son of a bitch deserved it. The truth is, I never could stand to think of you taking crap from a little weasel like him."

I think that was the day I fell in love with you, she wanted to say. But of course she didn't.

He expelled a long breath and slapped his hands down on his thighs. "So. You're not a natural on ice. But I thought we could change that today. I think I can teach you to skate. In fact, why don't you try them on right now? Let's see if you can stand up out there for more than five seconds without falling down."

She shook her head. Skating was the last thing she wanted to do right now. "I'll look like an idiot."

"No, you won't," he said, and his tone was nothing but sweet, warm persuasion. He nudged the box. "Go ahead. Try them on."

Resigned, she lifted the first skate. The laces were tied together, so that when she took out a white boot the second one came with it. Matt pulled the box off her lap and tossed it aside so she could untie the laces.

She reached for the shoestrings, and something gave a little metallic clink. She thought it might be some sort of security device, but when she captured it in her hand, she discovered that tied into the laces was a ring.

A simple, beautiful band of gold with a diamond in the middle of it.

She frowned down at it stupidly a moment, then looked at Matt. "I don't understand."

He shrugged. "I figure if we're going to team up to

skate together, we ought to be willing to team up in other ways as well. Like life."

He reached out to cup her cheek. "Marry me, Les."

The words took a long time to sink into her mind. When they finally did, she had to draw in air as though she'd been suffocating. "You can't be serious."

One of Matt's eyebrows rose. "You know, in spite of the considerable number of women who've wanted to marry me, I've never proposed to a single one of them. So I assure you, I'm absolutely serious."

She stared at the ring. The diamond sparkled more brilliantly than the sun-shot ice all around them. Then she spent several long seconds studying Matt. "We can't get married."

"Why not?"

"What about Chicago?"

"Hmmm. Good point." He scraped his hand across his chin, seeming to give that serious consideration. "Do you want to live there?"

"No."

"Great! Neither do I," he said. "Well, that was easy. I suppose if you're going to insist on finding obstacles to our getting married, we ought to get them out in the open. What else is a problem?"

"What about your career?"

"I still have one, you know. You aren't going to have to support me, if that's what's worrying you."

"Matt, please don't joke about this."

He exhaled a breath, looking serious at last. "All right, Les. Here's the way I see it. The need for a microsurgeon in Broken Yoke is pretty small."

"Nonexistent."

"*However,* even if I were to go back to Chicago, that door is still closed to me right now until my hand improves. So this past week I've given it a lot of thought. I can't give up that part of my life. Not without a fight. But there are other ways to do what I love. What I do best."

"What other ways?"

"I've made a few calls. I'm not without a certain amount of presence in the medical community. There's a good possibility I can take on a teaching position at a hospital in Denver. That's only an hour away, and it would be two days a week."

"You could be happy with that?"

"I think it could give me a sense of satisfaction. After Kline sewed up that little girl's face, we had a long talk. He was incredibly complimentary about the way I walked him through it. For a while I thought he was just blowing smoke, but then I realized, I'm a pretty darn good teacher. I had the patience to teach you to drive, didn't I?"

She frowned at him, wanting to believe his words, and yet afraid to. "And what would you do with the rest of your time?"

He looked at her as if he'd expected that question. "Part two. I spoke to Doc. He likes the idea of taking me on as a part-time partner. He wants to slow down a little, and he knows we'd work well together. Besides, someone's got to make sure Polly Swinburne doesn't develop Jumping Frenchmen or Mad Cow Disease, or any number of sicknesses that she hasn't read about yet."

"She'll drive you crazy."

"Probably. But I won't be bored, and that's just as crucial to me at this point." He studied her face, and the corners of his mouth turned upward. "So what do you say? Think you'd be interested in being my nurse? I'm a terrific boss."

The thought of the two of them working side by side was thrilling. And a little unsettling. How would she ever be able to manage a strictly professional attitude being so close to Matt every day? "I think I'd prefer to keep working for Doc," she told him. "I don't want to spend all my time stroking your ego."

"It's your choice," he said with a hot, sexy grin. "But once you're my wife, I'm hoping you'll be more interested in stroking *other* things."

Wife. In the wake of that word, a sudden flowering of joy spread into her heart, filling every cell in her body.

He gave her a scowl of mock severity. "You know, I have to say that Doc seemed a lot more pleased by the idea of me staying here than you've shown yourself to be so far."

"I guess I just…can't believe it."

Tightening his grasp, he gave her a look that made her feel as though she'd been stroked by silk. "Listen to me, Les. There's only one thing you need to believe right now, and that's the fact that I love you. If I don't have you in my life—permanently—I'll be like a drowning man going down for the last time. I'm lost without you. Don't you see that yet?"

"I want you to be happy."

He ran the back of his hand tenderly down her cheek, filling her with perfect pleasure. "I can change my address. I can change my career. I can even change my future. But I can't change how I feel about you."

With the flick of his wrist he pulled on one of the laces, and the ring fell into his hand. He held it out to her. "So stop fighting this, and accept your fate. Say you love me and that you'll marry me."

"I do love you," she said, in what came out as no more than a whisper. "Yes, I'll love you forever. Yes, I'll marry you. Yes, I'll learn to ice skate."

"My sensible, practical Les," he said with a grin. He placed the ring on her finger and claimed her lips.

It was a kiss with a future in it, a ring slipped upon her soul just as surely as the one Matt had slipped onto her finger.

A long time later they pulled apart, breathing hard, both of them shaken. The skates had fallen to the ground, and Matt picked them up and put them on Leslie's lap.

"Put them on," he said. "I want to teach you to skate." He swung a glance out to the lake. "At least as far as the hut."

"I'll never make it," Leslie said. "My knees are shaking."

He lifted her hand, placing a gentle kiss against her palm. "I won't let you fall, Les. I'll always be here for you. Just as you've always been here for me."

"That's what friends are for, right?"

"That, and a few other things," Matt replied in a honey-eyed tone. He leaned closer, until their lips were no more than a breath apart. "I can think of several ways to enhance a friendship. Can't you?"

She could.

HARLEQUIN *Super*ROMANCE®

It's worth holding out for a hero....

Three brothers with different mothers. Brought together by their father's last act. The town of Heyday, Virginia, will never be the same—neither will they.

Tyler Balfour is The Stranger. It seems as if his mother was the only woman in Heyday that Anderson McClintock didn't marry—even when she'd been pregnant with Tyler. So he's as surprised as anyone when he discovers that Anderson has left him a third of everything he owned, which was pretty much all of Heyday. Tyler could be enjoying his legacy if not for the fact that more than half of Heyday despises him because they think he's responsible for ruining their town!

Look for **The Stranger,** the last book in a compelling new trilogy from Harlequin Superromance and Rita® Award finalist **Kathleen O'Brien**, in April 2005.

"If you're looking for a fabulous read, reach for a Kathleen O'Brien book. You can't go wrong."
—Catherine Anderson,
***New York Times* bestselling author**

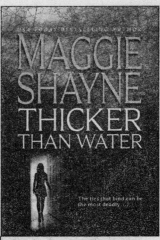

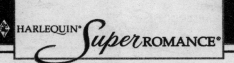

HARLEQUIN *Super*ROMANCE®

A miniseries from 2003 RITA® Award finalist

Jean Brashear

Forgiveness
(SR #1267)

Mother & Child Reunion

Ria Channing fled Austin, Texas, six years ago after committing the one sin in her years of rebellion that her loving parents and sister could not forgive. Now Ria herself is a mother, in dire straits and desperate to see that her son survives. She comes home for his sake, even though she knows she won't be welcome.

Sandor Wolfe is a man with dreams too long denied. Ria's mother took him in when he was down on his luck, and there's nothing he won't do for her. He's prepared to defend her against her bad-seed daughter.

Love and loyalty collide. Which will he choose... and what will be the price?

Look for the first story in Jean's Mother & Child Reunion two-book series, *Coming Home* (SR #1251, on-sale January 2005).

On sale starting April 2005.
Available wherever Harlequin books are sold.